THE GIFT
and
THE GIVER

THE GIFT
and
THE GIVER

A NOVEL BY

NELIA GARDNER WHITE

New York : THE VIKING PRESS : Publishers

1957

THE GIFT
and
THE GIVER

I AM A big, weather-beaten, middle-aged woman with style. That sentence pleases me. It's a good job of condensation, isn't it? But I see at once that condensation can be overdone, that the need to qualify will be the death of me as a writer. I am big-boned, but I have a flat stomach and a straight back and not an ounce of fat. "Weather-beaten" means all the hours of digging, fertilizing, spraying in the garden that have left my hands and face brown and so countlessly many small lines in my face as to make it appear smooth. The actuarial tables grow more hopeful every year, but they are not yet hopeful enough to call pushing sixty middle-aged. My mother said to me long ago, "The fact that you are a clotheshorse is no indication of virtue in you, Cornelia." How right she was! I can wear the most disreputable clothes, and often do, and still have an air of elegance. It's a gift and has nothing to do with my character, my occupation, or my bringing up. I can pull my streaked hair back into an ugly bun, or comb it carefully into an old-fashioned French roll; either way it looks right. Yes, it is a gift, and it helps me over difficult moments,

3

but it is no indication of virtue. The word "woman" I'll let stand, and not argue it.

I have two children that I can't live with and can't live without. I propose to tell their story, and my own only incidentally. Of course I will intrude—I always do. Various events have occurred that have made me pause for thought. I am not saying it will be good for my soul to put it all down. I have never taken much stock in soul. But puzzles interest me. What else but the Double-Crostic do I subscribe to the *Saturday Review* for? That's an awkward sentence and my mother would make me write it over, but my mother is no longer around and I'll let it stand. There is a pattern to all this, and it amuses me to find out what the pattern is. Perhaps a sense of humor is something a woman with an indomitable will like mine can do without, but I do find the world and the human beings in it funny. It is funny, seeing myself sitting here pecking these words out on Philip's old typewriter. Suppose I put everything in its proper order—what will have been gained? It will not change me, or the children, or anything that has happened. It is just something that my passion for puzzles makes me do. Maybe that's all writing is anyway—working out the acrostics of life.

Is that enough background? No, I've left out the house. De Maupassant, was it, who put everything necessary to know about people, places, and so on in his first paragraph? I see I've put only myself in my first paragraph, and that's funny too. I daresay that's a pretty good indication of my character. But I've never had any truck with the false notion of never putting "I" in a letter. What else are letters for except to say what "I" do and think and say? The house—well, it's the house I was born in. When I married I didn't leave this house. Walter objected. He was a chronic objector and approved of me very little. Yet he was a handsome man and I wanted very much to marry him. "You are making a great mistake, Cornelia," my mother said. "Walter is no woman's doormat." She was right again. We simply couldn't stand each other. We had the most frightful quarrels and I didn't blame him for leaving me. It's only surprising that he waited fourteen years to do it.

First, as I said, he hated the house. It's a good house as houses go—old, well taken care of, big. I like space, I must admit. You have to get away from people once in a while, and small apartments are probably the cause of many of the matrimonial troubles of the world. You can be just too close to people. Well, we had this big house, but even it wasn't big enough. My mother was houseproud and she had all this furniture, good stuff, fine linens, silver, everything polished and perfect. There's enough land about the house so that you never feel intruded upon by neighbors, and views on every side, fine enough to please anyone. We also have a huge ginkgo tree, which is unique in these parts. That is outside the dining-room window, rising up beside the terrace. The living room is paneled and there are deep window seats here and there. There's a fine garden, with great borders of perennials, an old well, no longer used, a big barn that we use for a garage, a fanlight over the front door.

That was poorly done, for the house has an air I haven't shown. It looks lived-in, fine, cared-for. Yet Walter didn't want to live here. "I can buy you a house," he said. But the truth was that he could never have bought me a house like this if he'd lived to be a hundred, which he didn't. I got my way about the house, but Walter left me after fourteen years of it.

Mother liked Walter better than she liked me. That's the

truth, whether I want to put it down or not. He was always gentle with her, and they had small jokes together. They understood each other. Well, I understood him well enough, but our temperaments clashed. He worked in McNeal and McNeal, publishers, and tried to write on the side. It was a decent job but had little future. Walter never cared about the future much. He wanted to write a book, and finally did, and that was the only future that meant anything to him. He died the year it was published.

I admit I pushed him. I wanted him to be at least vice-president of the firm, and there was no reason he couldn't have been, except that he didn't care about it. I believe in leaving your mark on the world, but Walter didn't care whether the world noticed him or not. That seemed, and still seems, foolish to me. Life's short enough, and none of us matters much, I suppose, but just as human beings we have an obligation to make ourselves count for something. Or so I think. Walter thought otherwise. I saw in the paper this morning an account of some Presidential educational committee that said, "We will not tolerate an intellectual élite in this country." Well, Walter wanted to be one of the intellectual élite. They went out with the dodo. It's the ones who *do* that get on in the world. Walter would have been shocked at that report and would have thought it indicated the end of civilization.

When the break came I wasn't surprised. We rubbed against each other's nerves always. Yet the last quarrel was about nothing more than hiring Joe Hill full time for the grounds. I can work, and do, in the yard. I have a knack for making things grow and I know when to put in bulbs, separate clumps of iris and phlox. But the flower borders had stretched; I'd put in so many bulbs and bushes that I could no longer care for them all single-handed. Joe was cheap and could do what he was told to do. A place untended might as well go back to jungle. But Walter said we couldn't hire Joe, that we couldn't afford to. I didn't ask him to pay Joe, though surely he should have been able to by then. But I have a knack with money, too. I'd got Mother to allow a mortgage put on the place and I'd gambled on the stock market with the money and increased it incredibly. In five years I'd paid back the mortgage money and had a tidy little sum in the bank. I should have been a man. I don't follow the leads of brokers, who always want you to sell when the market's low and buy when it's high. I follow my own lead, which has not failed me yet. I should have just hired Joe and let it go at that. Walter might never have known it, gone all day as he was. But I pretended that Walter had a say in things. That was my mistake—or perhaps it was not a mistake.

"We're not going to hire Joe. I can't afford it. And I am not going to do the work, either," Walter said. "I'm not cut out for running an estate."

You know, I think it tickled my pride even then, when I was so astonished and angry, that he called it an estate. But I talked back, and I suppose I was caustic. I can be, and I daresay I was. It got worse and worse, and finally he walked over by the hearth and stood there with his back turned to me, and he said, "All right, Cornelia. Stop it. That's enough. That's the end."

"End of what?" I said.

"End of our marriage. Or didn't it end before it began? I'm going to leave you, Cornelia. You can't ask a man to live with you when you despise him so."

He was quite calm, and I suppose that infuriated me. He

had one of those fine scholar's faces that appeal to women, and it appealed to me in some fashion. But that didn't blind me to the fact that he was an unambitious fool. He wanted to be the man of the house without having any of the qualifications that make a man of the house. He made no effort to keep the place up, he earned a miserably insufficient salary, he expected me to be a submissive wife without having the power to make me submit. Well, I never did submit.

"Why don't you be a man, then, and shoulder your responsibilities, if you don't want to be despised?" I said.

"My responsibility was to love you and the children and to provide for you," he said. "I can provide for you, and decently, but not with luxuries like this house, this land. It is too much. I have no extraordinary earning capacity and never will have. The love you despise also. I am through. Suddenly I am all through, Cornelia."

It was odd, certainly, that in that moment I respected him more than I had for years. He was firm as a rock. But I'd got out of the habit of reconciliations—of tenderness, maybe. And we'd gone too far in our quarrel. I have never been a woman to back down gracefully, or any way. Still, if it had been in me, I think in that moment I would have asked him not to go. It wasn't in me, and I said, "All right, you're through."

Then he turned and looked at me. He looked older than before he'd turned away. "I shall take Fanny with me," he said.

That did shock me. Fanny was only four years old then. Philip was going on ten.

"Take Fanny? Over my dead body!" I said.

He just looked at me, calm and steady. "Over your dead body, then, if necessary," he said. "I will not leave Fanny with

you. You do not love her. And surely it will be simpler for you to be alone with Philip."

That was the truth, and I have sworn to tell only the truth, so help me God. While I stood there, shocked to the bone at his suggestion, I saw at the same time a simpler life, alone with Philip.

"And I suppose you think you earn enough to support Fanny?" I said. "To hire a nurse, to take care of her schooling and clothes and all? Or were you thinking of finding her another mother?"

"I could and will support Fanny," he said. "You too, if you want it that way. But in a different place, a different house. I am tired of worshiping your ancestors."

That's amusing, for I am not an ancestor-worshiper, far from it. My ancestors are scarcely worth mentioning—poor people, farmers, carpenters, and, of course, Uncle Lorenzo. I recall going once to visit my grandmother when I was a little girl. She lived on a farm, a poor, stony, unproductive farm. I remember standing on the porch when my grandmother came out and said, "There's the fool hen out by the woodpile again." She was a worn-out, dried-up little woman. I saw what she called the fool hen, some sort of grouse, going from the woodpile toward the pine woods. That's my only memory of my grandmother. Father's mother, that was. My mother had a rich uncle, and he left her the house. She was surprised to get it, but she made the most of it. There was enough money to furnish it, or to add to the furnishings in it. She built it up to what it is today, and that's no small effort for a human being to have made. I didn't get on with Mother, but I respected her. But I don't like the house because it was hers. It's a fine house, worth caring for. I am proud of it.

There's no use evading the final fact. I let Walter go and take Fanny. I suppose it's true that in nine out of ten cases, perhaps ninety-nine out of a hundred, the father has an affinity for the daughter, the mother for the son. I was furious when Fanny came along. Philip was almost ready for school then, and I had no intention of having any more children. There is something humiliating about having children after an interval of so many years. You've got your life all set—it's an interruption. And Philip was a delicate child who needed me, and whom I understood. I did not understand Fanny, even at that age. She set herself up against me, even in babyhood. She adored Walter, but me she seemed to hate. Perhaps she did. She looked more like Walter, with fine features and nervous little hands. She would look at books a whole afternoon through. She defied me in thousands of small matters. She took the garden shears and cut great bunches of my choicest flowers. I punished her for that, and the next day she went and cut every single rose off a special bush of mine. I have a firm hand with children, but I admit I could not cope with Fanny. I kept her sitting in a chair for four straight hours. She didn't even seem to mind. After those four hours she went to the kitchen, got down the shears, which were always forbidden, crept out to the garden, and clipped heads off all along the border. So it is probably true, though it doesn't present much maternal feeling, that I felt a certain relief at the thought of not having to cope with Fanny any more, at being left with Philip, with whom I could be friends, who understood my language. At the time, however, I burst into such a storm of abuse, pretended such feelings for my daughter, that I almost moved Walter to let me keep her. Perhaps I thought I had those feelings, but now I know I did not. I let him take

her, and Philip and I settled down to our life together in this house.

If I wanted to, right now I could say that I missed Fanny incredibly after she was gone. I don't want to; it would not be the truth. She was never, at her best, an endearing child. Even at four she could look straight at you with the look of one who knew far more than you, of one who despised all judgment except her own. She wasn't saucy—that I would never have tolerated—but she went her own way. I don't know now whether she was pretty or not. She has looks now, that's sure.

To go back, I was relieved to be alone here with Philip. Perhaps I should never have married, since I have never been one who wanted to share rooms or thoughts, but we all have our weaknesses, and Walter was for a time my weakness.

The day they left was cold and frosty. Being proud, I had all Fanny's clothes in order, and I packed them carefully. I thought of court orders and went on packing. I was more angry at the thought of Walter's daring to defy me in that way than I was at the thought of his leaving me, of my living without him. Perhaps I did not believe it was a final act.

"Do you propose to let her keep house while you go to your business?" I asked Walter.

"I shall stay with my sister Mate for the present," he said.

He couldn't have said anything more likely to annoy me, I suppose. I knew his sister Mate, or I knew her slightly—no more than I could help. She was a schoolteacher, and schoolteachers I have never been able to abide. She was a plain spinster, had worked her way through school, and lived in a three-room apartment near the school where she taught in the city. Only once was I in that apartment, and once was enough. The furniture was all second-hand and ugly. There were books enough—books everywhere, up to the ceiling on shelves, and on the table and even the floor. And on one wall was a series of little sketches in pen and ink, botanical drawings of flowers. Mate had done them herself, Walter told me. I can just see her, prim and humorless, sitting making those sketches.

"I don't suppose she's given up her school to sit with Fanny," I said.

"No, of course not. She has a kind neighbor who'll come in," Walter said.

"Then you have everything arranged," I said.

"Yes," Walter said, "I think so."

I put Fanny's coat on. It was a severe little coat of dark brown. I don't like fussiness for children. Walter said, "Kiss your mother good-by, Fanny."

Well, anyone would have hated that, I think. You don't want your children told to show you affection. But Fanny was never one to be coerced into affectionate gestures. "Good-by," she said. She had a very clear voice, adult. She didn't even make a move toward kissing me. I grant this: Fanny was consistent then.

Walter took her hand and led her away. She went willingly enough. There was still frost on the grass. Philip had gone to school, and there was no one else about. Mother had been dead for six months then. Walter got the car out, drove it up beside the house. I was still standing there in the doorway—I wonder why? He stopped the car, got out, and came up to me and said, "I'm sorry, Cornelia. If you ever change your mind and want to share my life, you know where you can find me." He stood there a few seconds, as if he had some more to say, but he didn't say another word, nor did I. He turned, got in

the car, and drove away. I never saw him again till he brought
Fanny to me when he was about to die.

I have said scarcely a word about Philip, I see. I daresay
there is some psychological reason for that. If I have ever loved
anyone outside myself, I suppose it is Philip. He is now thirty-
four years old and I have had thirty-four years of loving him,
which is a long time, but not long enough. He has never, from
babyhood, been anything but beautiful. That's a word that
shouldn't be used on a boy, but I use it. He never moves but
with grace. He has my build, big-boned and straight and tall,
but his face has a sweetness mine never had. He has only to
smile and the world is his. Fanny pushed off any generosity,
but Philip received as sweetly as he gave. He was delicate
when young and didn't even start school till after he was seven.

Sometimes I think Walter would have left earlier, had it not
been for Mother. But then there would have been no Fanny.
Once Mother said to me, "Cornelia, are you trying to make
Philip despise his father?"

"I would like him to despise laziness," I said. "Walter is
lazy."

"I have never noticed it," Mother said.

Well, he was lazy. It does a man good to do a few physical
tasks after a day spent over a desk. The drive had to be
shoveled by someone. Holding Mother's balls of yarn for her
wasn't exactly strenuous or deserving to be called industrious-
ness. Of course Walter never loved this house and didn't care
how it looked or whether things were tidy in the yard or not.
You're escaping life when you come home and sit down with a
book or go to your room and fuss with writing just for your
own amusement.

Philip came home from school that day about half-past

three. He said, "Where's Fanny?" at once, and I said, "Sit down, Philip." And I told him Fanny had gone—his father too —that they would not be back.

He looked at me with such a strange look. "Not be back?" he said.

"No, never." I see no point in lying to children. But I could see Philip was upset.

"But I made her a sled," he said. "Why did she go? Are you going to be *divorced?*"

"I expect so, in time. I don't know, Philip."

He was a tall boy, even then, but he came into my arms and cried against me, and I comforted him as best I could.

"We're going to manage all right," I told him. "You and I can manage everything."

He had very blue eyes and fair hair. He still has them. His mouth is fine and his smile is very sweet.

After a while he slid from my arms and went out to the back shed, where he was working on the sled, which was to be a surprise for Fanny. He had a kindness that he extended even to Fanny, who had never appreciated it. I heard him hammering, and I went out to the kitchen and began to make cookies, though it wasn't my habit to do baking in the afternoon. After a while the pounding stopped and he came slowly into the kitchen, sat on the stool by the table, watching me cut out the cookies.

"It's lonesome," he said then.

"Nonsense," I said. "Fanny never played with you when she was here. You know that. Go wash your hands and cut out the rest of the cookies."

He brightened up and went to wash his hands. Then he began to cut cookies in funny shapes and even laughed aloud once at an elephant he'd made. He's resilient, Philip. I knew we'd manage by ourselves, and we did.

On the third day after that I went out into the back room and the sled was gone. I have never known or asked what he did with it.

I AM NOT so callous that I cannot see how shameful it was to let Fanny go away from me. She was no more than a baby, though she never looked like a baby. I was a bull-headed young woman at that time and could no more admit I was wrong than I could deny my own existence. My only defense is that she seemed to go quite willingly, that she always loved her father far more than she did me, that we both recognized this. But it was shameful, unnatural—that I do admit. Perhaps it was shameful too that Walter was willing to leave Philip with me. But they were not close as Philip and I were close. And the truth is that Philip missed Fanny more than he did his father, which is odd enough, because they were so far apart in age and had little to do with each other. But he missed her.

"Did Fanny take her pajamas with the clowns on?" he asked once.

Another time he said, "I suppose Fanny can read all right by now." He had taught her to read a little.

"I'm sure she can. She is living with a schoolteacher," I told him. I never avoided her name. I told Philip they were living

with Mate. Of course it must have been hard for him to understand the situation. I don't understand it yet myself, after all
these years.

I never got a divorce. Walter didn't ask for it, and I had no
desire to marry again. I'd had my go at matrimony and I knew
I wasn't built for it.

Philip went at that time to Miss Gray's school in the village.
It was a small progressive school with only twelve pupils. Walter wanted Philip to go to the public school, but when we had
the opportunity for a better schooling I could see no reason not
to seize it. "They are teaching him nothing, only to follow his
own sweet will," Walter said once. I know more about education now that I did then, and I believe Walter was right for
once in his life. But then I took education for granted.
I trusted teachers, whether I liked them or not, and I suppose
I thought that if you paid more you got more. Philip danced
well, he had a knack for making little animals out of clay, he
could write a poem that sounded almost adult, and I never
noticed but what he knew the ordinary things, like multiplication tables and so on. And he was very popular in the school.
He had a sweet voice and always looked like an angel at
Christmas parties and the like. Miss Gray adored him—and
who could wonder? He would pick flowers to take to her, and
he wouldn't be embarrassed presenting them. He made me
sweet little surprises with his clay. He gave away his toys if he
thought anyone wanted them. And every Christmas he made
something special to send to Fanny. Once it was a little note-
book that had a hand-painted cover. Once it was, of all
things, a rag doll that he cut out and stuffed himself, though
Fanny had never played with dolls. Once it was a small
wooden box decorated with small figures and varnished very

carefully. I never discouraged this, though I believe it made me impatient. But I daresay I never recovered from my own shame.

There's no sense in saying they were a completely easy and satisfactory time, those next months. Of course they weren't, but I do think I managed quite naturally and sensibly. There's no use, either, in denying that I felt a kind of triumph that I was managing so well, or that I found pleasure in having Philip to myself.

There were a few nonsensical things missed. Walter always drew out my chair at the table. Sometimes I laughed at him for his politeness. But I missed it. Then one night when I came to the table Philip looked up at me with some odd anxiety, then slipped from his chair, came around, and pulled out my chair for me. Nor did I laugh at him—I was touched.

And at night Walter hated to go to bed. He would sit up in our bedroom in the easy chair with the flounces and read till quite late. It annoyed me, for I am one who likes to sleep the minute I get to bed. But he always did it, and he would not stay downstairs for his reading, though I suggested it more than once. Well, you know, I missed seeing him there in the flounced chair, even though I had been bothered by the sight all those years. It didn't seem natural to be able to go to sleep immediately, and, in fact, I didn't sleep well at all those first months. But I got used to it in time. If Philip had been a little smaller I would have brought him in and let him sleep in the other bed, but I didn't think I could do that. However, I did move him into the next room, which was big and meant to be a guest room. It's been his ever since.

"Like your new room?" I asked him after the move.

"It's big," he said.

"Yes, you'll have room for all your treasures."

"It doesn't have any slant in the roof," he said.

"The safer will be your head!"

He was doing his homework. He made some little circles on the paper, then said, "Does Fanny have a room of her own or does she sleep with Aunt Mate?"

"I wouldn't know," I told him. "But she certainly has a bed, you may be sure of that."

"It would be funny to live with a schoolteacher," he said.

He kept on making circles till I wanted to tell him to stop.

"Could I go to see her someday?" he asked then.

Now I'm not saying I was right, but I said, "I don't think so, Philip. You see, they went because they weren't contented here any more. Perhaps someday you could see her, but not right now."

"Fanny was contented," he said slowly.

"No, not really. She's like that cat you used to have a story about—she likes to walk by herself. But they'll take care of her, never fear."

So he didn't say any more about her for a while. Perhaps she was a kind of idea to him, a piece of a family. And naturally it was hard for him to understand that a family isn't always a permanent thing. He made her Christmas presents after that, but he didn't talk of her much.

Jen, Jen Deemster—why haven't I put Jen in before this? She was, she is, my best friend. We're as different as night and day, except that we laugh at the same things. She was born what she is; I've made myself what I am. I went past her house one day, and she was putting some delphiniums in the front row of a border. I stopped the car and I called out to her, "Hey, you can't do that! That has to go in the back!"

She has red hair, and a husky sort of voice, like Ethel Barrymore's. She put up a hand and pushed her hair back and called out to me in that odd voice, "I'll put them where I like! Who are you?"

I got out of the car and came to her and I said, "I'm Cornelia Boone from up the hill. You won't see anything behind those delphiniums, that's all I meant. I don't like seeing gardens mishandled."

"How do you do?" she said. "Come in and have some bread and jam with me—the bread's just out of the oven."

So I came with her and we had fresh bread and jam and coffee. She has one of those faces that made you think they're beautiful, though she is not and never was beautiful. But high cheekbones and hollowed-out cheek planes and commanding eyes can deceive you.

When I left she said, "I'm glad you're my next-door neighbor—but you must never try to boss me around, Mrs. Boone."

She left those delphiniums right there in the front row. Well, I'm one to run things, but I've never bossed Jen around, and I suppose that's why we've stayed friends.

That was our beginning. There's never been an end. When she first saw the children, she looked from them to me, back at them. "Funny," she said, "I didn't expect *these* children."

The first time she came over, after Walter went, she sat downstairs on the sofa, looking more urban than countrywomen like us have a right to look. It was snowing, the first real snow we'd had. She had on a wool dress of gold color with a wide, twisted belt of leather.

"Fanny asleep?" she said.

"I wouldn't know," I told her. "Fanny doesn't live here any more."

She looked at me strangely. "Doesn't live here any more?"

"No. Walter and Fanny have taken another road. They've moved out."

"I don't believe you," she said.

"Well, you'd better. It's true. We've been what they call incompatible from the beginning. We've made a clean break."

"But—*Fanny!*" she said. She was shocked through and through, and I must admit in that moment I felt a shock too, as if it were incredible that I had allowed this to happen. But, as I've said, I was bullheaded. I've not admitted mistakes easily, even when it would be to my credit to do so.

"Look, Jen," I said, "don't go righteous on me. You know quite well I'm not good for Fanny nor is Fanny for me. We rub each other the wrong way and always have. She gets on with Walter, and he'll be good for her. They're living with his sister at the moment, and she'll look out for Fanny. It ought to have happened before this."

"She's only four years old," Jen said.

"Then the sooner she makes the break the better," I said. "I haven't cast her out into the storm or anything like that. I'm not a monster, Jen. But it's my opinion that she's better off with Walter, who loves her a good deal and is like her. I'm not at all like her, you know that. I've never been able to cope with her and never will be able to. You needn't look so shocked. It's all right. We're all better off."

"But I am shocked," she said. "You weren't forced to give her up—"

"In a way I was. Walter wouldn't go without her, and that's

the truth. I didn't put Walter out, either. He went of his own free will, because he wanted to, because he couldn't stand living with me or in this house another minute. Even you must have seen we didn't get on, Jen."

"But you didn't give up Philip," she said in a flat way unlike her. I'll say now that I was frightened in that moment. I counted on her friendship, and I had a feeling she was taking her friendship away from me.

"No. Of course not," I said.

"I see. How terrible," she said.

"It isn't terrible at all. I don't like having been a fool so long, that's all. But it's not terrible. We parted very amicably and finally. . . . Shall we have some tea?"

I have always liked having tea with Jen, who appreciates the beautiful cups Mother collected, and who always has an air with a cup in hand.

"Yes, I'd like some tea," she said.

So I went and made tea, but I was shaken. I think I would have minded losing Jen's friendship more than losing Walter —a hard saying, but true. I picked her favorite cups, brought the tray in, put it on the low table near the hearth, poured tea.

The snow was thick out there past the windows, and we seemed shut inside it. Then I said, straight out, "You've stopped liking me."

"No," she said, but she said it sadly.

"I expect to have a very good life here with Philip," I told her.

"Do you?" she asked. "I wonder if you will, Cornelia. I haven't stopped liking you. I don't give friendships up as easily as that. All the same, I do not think you will have a good life without Walter and Fanny. They're special people, not to be forgotten. Every time I look at Fanny, I think, What a special child! And I don't need to tell you Walter is special too—he always has been. He's refused to sell himself cheap. That's something nowadays, Cornelia. I feel terribly sad, that's all. And I don't understand you."

"You haven't lived with Walter," I said. "There's nothing so special about Walter. He's an ordinary man doing an ordinary job. He makes no concessions, true, but now and again you have to, to fit into this world. He's without ambition— and he doesn't like me. Fanny may be special, but have you ever lived with a child like Fanny? No, you haven't, Jen. She's intelligent, but not communicative nor friendly. She will not allow you to love her. She's completely self-sufficient, which is not normal for a child of four. Neither does she like me. But she does have a fondness for Walter, and that is where she belongs, with him. She wanted to go as much as Walter did."

"I don't believe it," Jen said. "No four-year-old *wants* to leave her mother."

When she went away she kissed me. She's done that not more than two or three times in all these years. "I'm so sorry. So terribly sorry," she said, and went out into the snow.

For a few minutes there I came close to thinking I would never see Jen again. Of course I have, often. But there was pity in her voice, and I couldn't bear that.

"Sorry for what? Don't be silly!" I said and laughed.

But she didn't answer, just walked off and down the road, with the snow falling on her.

She came over again, bringing a little pot of azaleas. She

didn't mention Walter, and everything seemed as it used to be. Our friendship has never stopped.

When Christmas came I must admit that there was a little difficulty. But we put up a tree and trimmed it, and I spent too much on presents for Philip. I got him a microscope that year, a good one, and skis too. We were invited to Jen's for dinner, and that went off all right. But of course it was not quite the same as it had been when Walter and Fanny were there. And Philip got a Christmas card from Fanny. It just said, "MERRY CHRISTMAS, FANNY," in block letters. Philip also received a book, *Treasure Island*, from Walter. I received nothing at all from either one. But Philip went out in the late afternoon and tried his skis and seemed to have fun.

When I went in to say good night to him, I sat down by the bed and said, "Has it been a good Christmas?"

"Wonderful!" he said, and smiled at me sweetly. "I'm quite good on the skis, don't you think? And the microscope's keen!"

"I liked the crèche you made, too. It was very clever of you."

When I bent to kiss him, I heard a faint rustle under his pillow.

"What are you hiding under your pillow?" I asked him.

"Oh, nothing," he said.

I didn't ask to see. But the next day, when I was putting things in his drawer, I came on the card from Fanny, crumpled, and I knew what he had had under his pillow. I didn't think this a healthy sign, but he wasn't unhappy. He had friends, lots of them. Boys came to the house quite often, and I had parties on birthdays and one at the Christmas season. I never objected to any sort of hullabaloo such as boys make. And I always fed them well.

Yes, of course there were these small difficulties, but in general life was good, very good. Philip was not one to mope, no matter what he was feeling. He liked to sing, and it was a pleasure to hear his clear voice as he took his bath, or as he worked in the garden. "Green Grow the Rushes, Ho" was one of his favorites—I can still hear his voice coming down the stairs —" 'Two, two, the lily-white boys.' " There was one spell of the one about Uncle Tom Cobley and all, and at that first Christmas it was "The Twelve Days of Christmas." He seemed to like the long ones.

He liked to have a fire going, and we burned a good deal of wood that first winter. We have a bearskin rug in front of the hearth, and Philip liked to curl on that rug and watch the fire while I read to him. He was very good at getting "just another chapter."

Though he had said those few things about Fanny, he didn't *act* lonely. He never has. He was writing little poems then. I have them still. There was one that's always stuck in my head.

> *Bird, bird, flying over the hill,*
> *Singing "Kuroo—kuroo,"*
> *Where are you going, bird?*
> *Let me come too!*

Not much of a poem, but I remember it still. Probably I remember it because it didn't seem like Philip, who clung to here and now and never wanted to leave this house, this place. We talked like grown-ups together at the table. He was never boring; he had ideas. And he never seemed bored, either. Yes, meals were better than they had been when Walter and Fanny were with us. When Mother was alive we'd done better, for she had a gentle yet interested way with her, and I suppose she flattered Walter more, asking him about publishing, all that. Mother was a little woman, but strong. And she was a worker. I got my habits of work from her. She had a blind spot about Walter, thought him more than he was, and of course he liked her for it. Who wouldn't have? She was more fond of Fanny than of Philip, too. Mother was the only one who could get Fanny into her arms. I can see them in the brown Victorian chair with the velvet cover, Fanny curled up against Mother in a way quite unlike her. But she would sit on Mother's lap in the brown chair and not try to get away. And Walter would come and sit on a stool near her, and they would talk— I hardly know what about, for I didn't listen.

"Cornelia, sometimes I think you don't know what you have," Mother said to me once.

I didn't answer her, and she didn't go on. I liked Mother, but I wouldn't let her or anyone else moralize to me. It set my back up.

When spring came on, there was the garden, and I worked like a dog out there. I did get Joe Hill for part time. I had a little break on the market right then, and I felt we'd manage, and we have. I saw Jen every few days. She never talked of Walter or Fanny. I began to get the place in shape. So much needed doing, and it began to be done. This is a beautiful place, but it's meant work to keep it so. You have to keep eternally at it. But I like gardens and know them. I like working outside.

I asked Philip if he'd like to go to camp that summer, but he said no, he would rather stay with me. There weren't so many boys up during the summer, so we were together most of the time. He even helped me with the flowers—and had a knack for it too. He was getting tall. It was toward the end of the summer that I went to the village one day and met Andy Jones.

"Hello, there, Andy," I said. "And what have you been doing all summer?"

"Why, I went to camp," he said. "I wish you'd let Philip come too. We had fun."

At supper I said, "But I thought you didn't want to go to camp, son. Andy seemed to think you thought I didn't want you to go. I asked you, didn't I?"

"But I didn't want to. I wanted to stay here," he said.

"Andy had another idea entirely," I said.

"Camp's silly," he said. "I don't like to swim very well. I like it better here."

That was all he would say. I don't know to this day whether he wanted to go or not. If he stayed it was because he thought I needed him, maybe. I don't know. Or it may have been something else altogether. It may have been that insecurity Miss Gray harped on—though I don't see how it could have been, actually. Or it may have been that other business she was talking about. Yes, perhaps it was.

It wasn't till almost two years had gone by—and they were good years, no matter what Jen or anyone thought—that I went to see Miss Gray. Philip liked being my right-hand man. We went places together, worked together. It was good. But then Miss Gray asked me to come down to the school some day soon, and I went, that very afternoon. I sat in her little office, which had three abstractions on the walls. She had always had a patter that sounded quite intelligent, but she was quiet this day—just sat there with an embarrassed look on her expressive face.

"Well, what is it? Don't tell me Philip has got into trouble!" I said.

"Philip *is* trouble," she said.

This was, as I said, almost two years after Walter went.

"I'm afraid you'll have to be clearer than that," I said. "Never mind the cryptic, Miss Gray."

"You haven't noticed, then, that—that Philip seems maladjusted?" she said.

"No, I can't say I have," I told her. "If ever a boy was adjusted, I'd say it was Philip. And don't tell me a 'divided homes' makes him feel insecure, or any of that malarkey, for no one is more secure than Philip. Isn't his work all right?"

"Philip is very intelligent," she said. "But, whether you know it or not, he *does* feel insecure. He—well, he *buys* his friends, Mrs. Boone."

"And what do you mean by that?" I asked her.

"Just what I said. He gives away everything he owns, just so others will like him."

"I call that generosity, nothing more."

"But it is more. And it's not good for the other children, either."

"Well, I will put a stop to that if you want me to," I said. "But personally, I think generosity is one of the virtues. I send him here for an education, and I'll take care of his character. You didn't say so, but I gather there is nothing wrong with his work."

She waited quite a while before she answered. Then she said, "Mrs. Boone, I believe I have been wrong in speaking to you about Philip. I believe I have been wrong about a good many things, about this very school itself. I was taught to teach a certain way, a way that is free and gives pleasure to the child. I have run this school for nine years now, and I begin to doubt my methods. The children have enjoyed themselves, up to a point, but I have come to doubt that pleasure is what school is for. I do not know whether your son is well educated or not. Everything is easy for him, perhaps too easy. But he uses his intelligence only on the things he likes. He gives the impression that he is socially adjusted, but I hate the word 'adjustment' today, though I used it to you only a moment ago. Could it not be that the educators are all wrong? If children were strong in themselves, couldn't it be that society would adjust to them?"

"I don't find Philip weak," I said.

"Parents rarely do find their children weak," she said almost tartly. "But perhaps Philip is not weak—only strange. He is complex. If you think him not too generous, let me tell you this. Yesterday he gave five dollars to Sally Erskine so that she could get a pair of rabbits she wanted. He said it was his allowance, and perhaps it was. But five dollars is still quite a bit of money for a boy to hand out. Sally Erskine's parents could buy her rabbits if they chose. They didn't want them, and they were angry."

"Perhaps you ought to talk to the Erskines about adjustment," I said. "Perhaps Sally is all full of frustrations because she isn't allowed rabbits."

"Perhaps so. But Sally had been bestowing her smiles on Andy Jones. Philip was trying to buy her preference. That is true, Mrs. Boone, whether you like it or believe it. May I ask this: was it—could it have been—his allowance?"

"He gets a dollar a week," I said. "He could have saved it, certainly."

She stood up. She looked tired.

"But you don't know," she said. "And Philip does lie. He looks so honest; his very smile is honest. But he lies, Mrs. Boone. I have loved Philip very much—he carries an enchantment in him. But I abhor lying. He wrote an essay for Sally last week and denied it. It was unmistakably his, for he has certain peculiarities of style. He is more poetic than the rest, and Sally is completely matter-of-fact and unimaginative. He looked straight at me and smiled and lied."

"But I daresay he wanted to protect her."

"I daresay. But I don't happen to call that protection. That is not the only time. If it were, I might think it only a child's idea of chivalry. I could tell you of a dozen other times, but I will tell you only one. The children had made a relief map, and the rivers were painted blue. We were to paint the names on the rivers after the first paint was dry. One morning I came in and found the rivers all named, wrongly—with made-up, rather funny names. Again, Philip is the only boy with just that kind of imagination. I found him washing red paint off his hands. No, he did it and he denied it, sweetly but completely. There are other occasions. I was taught that children go through phases of lying, but that spot should have come and gone by now. I am mostly talking for myself. I shall not teach this school another year, for I have lost my faith in it. When you come to put Philip into a preparatory school, you will find out how much he knows, if anything. I'm sorry I troubled you, for you do not look as if you were listening. Perhaps it is natural you should not. But think of what I have said."

That's the gist of what we said to each other, if not the exact words.

I'm not what you might call generous myself, but I still think generosity a virtue. It quite touched me that Philip should have saved his money to give Sally Erskine her heart's desire. But the lying? No, I have never condoned that. That's why I had a kind of respect for Walter at the end, because he told the truth about our incompatibility. So that conference about lying got under my skin. I could understand the essay business. A good many children have written compositions for other children over the years, I expect. But the paint job— well, she didn't have much proof, but she seemed sure. An odd woman, Miss Gray. She did give up her school at the end of the term and took a job in an office somewhere.

I've always been open with Philip. I've never hid things from him, or pretended something was other than it was. I called him into the living room when he got home from school and told him to sit down. He was getting a big boy then, but he had not lost that open, sweet, childish look.

"Philip," I said, "I want to know about that paint job on the rivers. Miss Gray seems to think you did it. And she seems to think you lied about it. If you did the painting, you did. It wasn't sensible, but it wasn't criminal. But I don't want any lies about it—that would be a crime. To me it would. I'm not going to punish you, but I want the truth. Did you do it?"

He looked straight at me, smiling that small half-smile of his, and said, "No, I didn't. I told her so."

"That's good enough for me," I said. "All right, go get your snack."

I FOUND out that Miss Gray hadn't taught Philip much. He tried examinations for three different schools and passed none of them. It angered me some, for Philip was brilliant. That's not just a doting mother's judgment; he was brilliant. He is. He did very well in English and history, but he did nothing at all in mathematics.

"It's ridiculous," I said to him. "What have you been doing all this time? You can't multiply or divide or even add."

"Well, I don't like figures much," he said, not humiliated at all.

"You'd better like them a little!"

"I could go to the high school in town," he said.

"Nonsense! You're going to have a decent schooling if I have to go ragged. I'm going up to Endley tomorrow and see what's what. You're coming with me."

"I'd just as soon stay here. I don't care whether I go away to school or not. You'd be all alone here," he said.

"I know that. Don't think I wouldn't miss you, but you're going to have an education, and not in our local schools, either. There'll be holidays."

"I don't think I'd like it," he said. "Why do I have to be educated? I don't want to be anything special."

"Fiddlesticks!"

We went up to Endley and we talked to the headmaster there. He wasn't very encouraging.

"Why doesn't he spend another year in grammar school?" he suggested. "He's young yet. It's not a good idea to enter a school when you're not prepared. However, I will give him an examination if you like."

Afterward this Mr. Buckley asked me to come and see him.

"We will take Philip on one condition, Mrs. Boone," he said, "that he be tutored in arithmetic this summer. It is obvious that he is an imaginative, clever boy, but I doubt whether he has applied himself to anything. In Endley he will have to apply himself. This is a progressive school, but we prepare for college."

"I hope so," I said to him. "And Philip is clever and imaginative. He can apply himself if he chooses."

"That's just it—he will have no choice at Endley, Mrs. Boone."

I got Maggie Elliot to tutor him. She lives on our road and I knew she often substituted in the schools and was considered good. She came to our house five days a week all summer. She liked Philip—how could she help it?—but once she said to me, "He doesn't listen, Mrs. Boone. I think I'll give it up."

"I think not," I said. "I'll see that he does listen, Mrs. Elliot."

So I took him in hand. "Philip, this is what I want for you," I said. "I don't look forward to having you away from home, but I want you to do well in school, to make me proud of you. I am proud of you now, but we don't just sit still in this life.

We have to go on learning more and more. There's no reason on earth that you can't get this arithmetic, if you want to. You learn other things you want to—why not arithmetic?"

"It seems silly," he said. "And honestly, I don't care about going away to school. I'd just as soon go in town."

"You'd have mathematics in town too. No, Philip, I want you to work on this. When you're finished I'll take you on a jaunt to New York. Would you like that?"

I suppose that was bribery—sounds so, putting it down. I also got permission from Endley for him to come home week ends. But that was conditional on his marks.

Then one night we built a little fire. It had turned unexpectedly chill for August. We sat there by the fire, and all of a sudden Philip said, "I guess you don't want me with you—like Fanny."

My heart turned right over. That's a saying, but it felt like that.

"Don't *want* you, son?" I said. "You're all I want in the whole world. But I want you to grow up educated and useful. I don't want you wasted, Philip. You're not going away from me, you're just going so you can come back to me, wiser and better. And that was an unkind remark about Fanny. Fanny wasn't happy here. It hurt terribly to let her go, but I was thinking about her happiness, son."

But was I? I cringed a little, putting that down. I don't believe I was thinking of Fanny's happiness at all. Oh, I suppose I justified myself then by believing so, but it isn't true. I could hardly bear it that Philip should think I wanted him gone. If I could have been sure, I think I would have found a tutor and kept him at home. He loved our home, as I did, and he couldn't bear to leave it, and me. I stuck to my guns, though.

I took him to New York and we did everything you do in New York, and he seemed to enjoy it too. And when September came he went to Endley.

But before that, Andy Jones came up to play, and Jen was here that afternoon. It was warm, and we sat out on the terrace near the ginkgo tree. The boys had been out practicing archery, but after a bit we heard them in the living room.

"Oh, I want to go," Philip said. "Nothing to do here."

"Well, I sort of want to. But they're very strict at Exeter," Andy said.

"My mother can't stand it to have me go," Philip said. "She mopes around all over the place. She wants me to go to school in town, but not me!"

"Well, I have to go where Dad went," Andy said. "Did your dad go to Endley?"

"No."

Then there was a silence, after which Philip said, "That was a lie—my mother's really glad to get rid of me. She can't stand it having me underfoot."

"Oh, your mother's all right. She doesn't nag at you every minute like my mother does."

"That's what you think. She wants me to be something special, a great doctor or a great artist or something. Well, I won't be. I'm not going to be anything at all. She'll see!"

"I think I'll be a lawyer," Andy said.

"I won't. I won't be *anything*."

Their voices drifted away. They went back to their archery. Jen said, "He's just lonesome."

"How could he say a thing like that?"

"I told you—he's just lonesome, scared about going away to school."

"If he doesn't know I love him, he doesn't know anything."

"Boys like to be dramatic. They like feeling unloved."

"But how could he feel unloved? He's all I do love. But I can't let him grow up ignorant."

"He won't. He'll be all right. Or I hope so, Cornelia. He's a troubling boy, complex and troubling. But he adores you, as you know. And why shouldn't he?"

"He didn't sound so, Jen. I've certainly tried to give him a good life."

"Maybe you've tried too hard. Maybe you've made everything too easy for him—though I know you respect work, all that."

"Of course I respect work, and I don't think Philip is lazy. He doesn't like concentrating on things he doesn't like, that's all. That's why I've had to spend all this money on a tutor this summer. But he can work forever on something he likes. He's worked like a man in the garden. He knows as much about it as I do. He'll find himself in time. But that conversation got under my skin, Jen, I admit."

"It shouldn't. He was just being dramatic, as I said."

I didn't tell her what he'd already said about Fanny.

He was so sweet at supper that night. He noticed that I had cooked his favorite dishes. He made a centerpiece of phlox himself. He was very loving and beautiful.

"Will you write to me every day?" he asked.

"I'll try—a small letter, anyway. But you'll be home for week ends if you tend to your knitting."

"Oh, I will. I promise! I wouldn't go if I couldn't come home every week!" he said. "You won't touch anything in my room, will you?"

"Not a thing."

I couldn't tell him I'd overheard him and Andy. He was so *loving*. After dessert he came around behind me, put his arms around me, and kissed me.

I took him up to Endley next day, and when I saw him walk away from me I felt as if I'd died a little. I suppose I had, in a way. But I have a lot of life in me still, in spite of the chunks taken out of me. He walked away and into the building without looking back. He'd said he'd rather go in by himself, and I let him, knowing how boys feel with other boys. But he didn't look back once.

I came back here and the house was so empty, I felt as if I couldn't bear it. I went out and worked in the garden. I got myself some lunch and then couldn't eat it. I was still hurt at what he had said to Andy, but I remembered all his loving ways. I told myself Jen was right, that he was just trying to sound like a story-book character. But the hurt went in like a barb, all the same. I don't suppose it has ever come out.

Walter sent me a check once a month—two hundred dollars. It must have left him short, but I took it and used it. I needed it. There was never a note, just the check. It's cost a good deal to keep this house up, far more than Walter sent, but, as I said, I was lucky in the stock market and I managed. I suppose people gossiped about us, but I have never been one to dwell on what people think of me or what the public thinks of me. Jen has stuck by me, and that's enough.

I hate even now remembering that first week Philip was gone. I even thought of Walter and Fanny and wondered if I'd done wrong. One night I even contemplated writing to Walter and saying, "Let's let bygones be bygones," but I didn't write. When morning came I felt more sensible and I thought of the week end and Philip's coming and his telling me all his experiences at school. I began to plan what I'd cook, what we could do to make the week end gay.

Then he didn't come. He called me up, collect, and said they wouldn't let him come the first week end. But he thought he could come the next one.

"Is everything all right?" I asked him.

"Oh, yes, it's fine," he said. "Are you all right, Mother?"

"Of course. Well, I'll count on next week, son."

I find it hard to put down what Philip looked like, except to say he was beautiful, which says nothing. He was always tall for his age, slender, and he had the clearest blue eyes ever, and that mop of fair curly hair that wouldn't stay down flat, and all his gestures were full of grace. He never went through that stage where he was all pimples and awkwardness. His skin stayed clear and smooth and he had the solid teeth all my family has. At school he wore the school jacket, blue, piped with red, and slacks. He was never grubby, always immaculately clean.

He did come home the next week end, and he had changed a little already. He was sweet, but he was quiet.

"You really do like it at Endley?" I asked him.

"Yes, it's all right," he said. "Algebra's hard, but I can do it."

"Of course you can! The food's all right?"

"Well, not like yours, but it's all right. I see the chrysanthemums are blossoming."

"Yes. Tell me about the masters. Are they good?"

"They'll do. They aren't like Miss Gray, if that's what you mean."

"I should hope not! She didn't know what she wanted, Miss Gray. I never quite forgave her for not trusting you, I'm afraid."

He gave me his best smile, loving and teasing a little, and he said, "Mother, I did paint the rivers. It just seemed like a jolly thing to do."

I even laughed, heaven forgive me. "Well, confession is good for the soul, they say," I said. "But no more nonsense of that sort, Philip. You're a big boy now." Then I came to myself a bit and I said, "Then you lied to me too, Philip."

"I didn't want you disappointed in me," he said.

What should I have done? I was disappointed, that is sure, and yet I told myself that that had been a phase. Hadn't Miss Gray herself said that boys did go through a phase of lying? I gave him a credit mark for telling me now.

Then he didn't come home for three weeks. He called me up every time and told me he was sorry, but his marks just weren't good enough. He'd try awfully hard the next week. The fourth week he did come.

"See, I told you!" he said. "I made it!"

He seemed so glad to be home, I didn't scold him much.

Then—it was near Thanksgiving—I got a letter from Mate. I thought she must be writing me about Fanny, but she wasn't, or not altogether.

"My dear Cornelia," she wrote, "This is a difficult letter to write for I do not hold with tale-bearing. Perhaps it will not be that. Perhaps you already know what I have to say. If so, forgive my seeming interference. In itself, this does not seem wrong . . ."

I remember saying, "Get to the point!" She got to the point.

". . . but I wonder if it is wise. This makes four times Philip has come on a Saturday to see Fanny. He is a nice boy and it is plain that he is very fond of his sister, but if they are to have separate homes, does it seem wise to let them become too fond of each other? Something that Philip said gave me the impression that you do not know of these visits. He has merely taken Fanny for walks, once took her to the museum, once to the zoo. He is very polite, very mannerly. I like him. But I have wondered whether you knew or approved. He is welcome, but there is a psychological problem involved, as you must see. If he comes with your permission, ignore this. Sincerely, Mate Boone."

Easy enough after the event to say what you should have done. But what should I have done? I felt sick. I sat there a long time, just looking at the letter. I'd been putting in a few last bulbs and I had on slacks and the old red sweater. After a half-hour or so I put on a leather jacket and walked down the hill to Jen's. Jen had a husband, whom, I see, I haven't even mentioned. Odd—I hardly think of Jen as anyone's wife, just as my friend. Yet she had a husband, John Deemster, who was a top-notch lawyer, older than Jen, set in his ways. I found Jen dusting John's study, which is a cozy room, lined with law books, and with a globe on the wide window sill. There was a fire burning there, and everything was quiet and shining.

Jen said, "Why, hello, Cornelia," and I came and sat in the red leather chair that was John's.

I should have kept it to myself. I can keep secrets.

Jen sat on the corner of the desk, dustcloth in hand. "What's on your mind?" she asked. "You look upset."

"I am," I told her. "Philip's been going to see Fanny week ends. I am upset."

Jen frowned a little. "That's not so bad, is it?" she asked.

"Yes, it's bad. Because he didn't tell me. He pretended his marks were so low he couldn't get home. That's what's bad."

"Oh. Yes, I'd say that was bad enough. But perhaps he feels compelled to go. He knows you wouldn't let him. Perhaps you ought to just make it easy for him to go. After all, she is his sister, Cornelia."

"Look, Jen, she's a baby beside him. They can't possibly have anything in common. They're as unlike, as far apart, as the poles. It's as you said—he likes to dramatize things."

Jen got off the desk and went and stood in front of the fire. She still held on to the dustcloth.

"Did you ever think—he might just love her?" she asked then.

"No, I never did. She's too young to interest him. She's not his kind at all. She will no doubt grow up to be a prim spinster of a schoolteacher like Mate—and certainly, whatever Philip becomes, it will be nothing like that. No, he's putting on an act. But I must say I don't know what to do about it."

"I can't tell you," Jen said. "Unless you'd consider bringing Fanny home where she belongs."

"Well, that is out. The thing is done, Jen—over and done. I don't believe in hanging on to something that there's no juice in any more. So don't get romantic ideas."

"That's my only solution. I can't help you," Jen said.

I was sorry already that I'd told her. I am a strong woman and I don't beg other people to help me out of my difficulties. Yet, I admit, it was comforting to be there with her.

"Well, no need to bother you with it," I said. "I'll work something out."

"Did you ever think, Cornelia, that it might seem truly horrible to Philip that you don't even miss Fanny?"

"Oh, I miss her," I said. "But the thing's *done*."

"Children never think things are that final," Jen said. Then she said slowly, "And Walter? Didn't he see Walter too?"

"I don't know," I said. "Mate didn't mention Walter. I suppose he was there."

She asked me to stay to lunch, but I couldn't. I went home, up the hill and into the empty house. She hadn't helped me much, except by just being Jen. I read the letter over again, and then I went to the phone and called the headmaster and asked him how Philip was doing.

"He's doing very well indeed. I have been pleasantly surprised at his application," he said.

"Will he be able to come home this week end?" I asked.

"Yes. Certainly. He hasn't missed a week yet, has he?"

"Tell him I'll call for him Saturday noon," I said, and hung up.

So then I had to put in the time till Saturday noon.

His face was radiant when he came out to the car. "Hi, Mother!" he said, threw his bag into the back of the car, jumped in beside me. "We've started bookbinding," he said. "It's fun! Could I have a boy home for Thanksgiving? Jerry Baker's his name. He doesn't have any place to go and I thought maybe you'd let me ask him."

"Of course," I said.

"Thanks! You'll like him."

He chattered on as if he didn't have a care in the world. I didn't say much, not being able to find words for what must be said. We reached home. I had a dish in the oven, so we had lunch. Then I couldn't wait any longer. We sat there at the table, with the sunlight streaming in—a cold sort of sunlight, pre-winter.

"I had a letter from Aunt Mate," I said.

"You did? How come?" he said, looking at me guilelessly.

"I think you know how come. Philip, have I ever denied you anything that was sensible? Couldn't you have asked me if you could go to see Fanny? Was it necessary to go through all that rigmarole about bad marks? I understand that your marks are very good—as there is no reason they should not be. I don't like this, Philip. I don't like it at all."

For just an instant his glance slid away from mine, then came back, with no cloud in it, no guilt.

"Oh, I just thought Fanny might be lonesome," he said easily, as if that were all there was to it.

"That's not quite the point, is it? Did you need to lie? Isn't it true that it would have been better just to ask me if you might go?"

"But you wouldn't have let me," he said. "I did ask you once and you said no."

"That was when you were younger. I don't think it a good idea, however. If you have a life, you don't want it cluttered up with an old life. It makes for confusion. That applies to Fanny and you. Fanny has made a life at Aunt Mate's. Your life is here. They don't go together, Philip."

"Maybe not for you," Philip said, "but I don't see why not for me. Look, Mother, she's just a nice little kid. I don't think she has much fun. I don't see what's wrong in trying to give her a little fun, do you?"

"Well, Philip, Fanny was never the kind to know what fun is. She was born serious."

"I can make her laugh," he said. "She was very funny at the zoo. She's clever, too."

"I don't doubt you. Again, you're evading the point. You deceived me, Philip, and it makes me sad. There was no reason to do so."

"But you wouldn't have let me go otherwise," he said.

"Perhaps not. At least you would have had to give me better reasons than you have so far. And I want it stopped, as of now. Nothing good can come of it."

No, I see now I shouldn't have said that. I should, as Jen suggested, have made it easy for him to see Fanny. Then he wouldn't have cared whether he did or not. But I was suddenly angry, and anxious too. I couldn't have deception of that sort, or we wouldn't have a good life together at all any more.

"When you're older, of course you may do as you like," I said.

"How much older?" he asked.

"Twenty-one," I said.

"She won't understand why I don't come," he said.

"I'll write to Mate and tell her why. And you needn't think Mate doesn't agree with me. She does. No good can come of it. You must believe me, son. I'm sure your father would agree too. I am quite sure he didn't urge you to come—did he?"

"He wasn't there," Philip said.

"Wasn't there? Where was he?"

"I don't know. He has a Saturday job somewhere. Not at the office. I didn't see him."

Odd, he didn't make any more objections. He didn't even seem angry at me, or hurt. He let it go. He had Andy up for Sunday dinner, and in the late afternoon I took him back to school. I remember thinking that I didn't really know a thing about his life at school. I remember resolving to ask him more questions about the boys and the teachers and his classes.

I wrote a stiff sort of note to Mate and told her Philip would not be coming again. Then I began to prepare for Thanksgiving. And then it was Thanksgiving and Philip was home with Jerry Baker.

Jerry Baker. I'll have to wait till tomorrow to tell about Jerry Baker. "It's nice of you to have me, Mrs. Boone," he said. It wasn't nice at all. *Jerry Baker.*

I PICKED them up Wednesday night after classes. They were watching for me, and I didn't have to go into the school. I saw them coming quickly down the front path under the bare elms, two tall boys, but so different. *Black*, I called him. I don't mean anything to do with skin. He was tall and dark and handsome enough, with a sallow skin, dark, wide-set, but small eyes—very expressive eyes, though. But when I saw him coming I had the feeling there was something sinister and *dark* about him. He looked older than Philip and was, by more than a year. Beside Philip's guileless face, his looked ancient.

Philip raised a hand and called out, "Hi, Mother!" and then Jerry was saying, "It's nice of you to have me, Mrs. Boone," and the boys were together in the back seat and we were driving homeward. They talked back there, mostly about the masters.

"Well, I've been to his house," Jerry said. "He lives with his mother and she's a queer old bird, got a voice like a croaking raven. She looks at you as if she was looking through one of those old glasses—lorgnettes or whatever you call them—and she always starts out the same way: 'Well, young man, and what do you imagine your destiny in life?' "

Philip laughed. "And what do you say?" he asked.

"I say, 'The fates will decide that, Mrs. Morley.' And then she forgets me. A very queer old girl. She'd be surprised if I told her what I really imagined my destiny was. They have good cake there, and cucumber sandwiches."

Philip laughed again, and I didn't like it. I didn't like anything about this friendship. Philip's laugh was too much like a chorus. I didn't hear any laughter from Jerry. In fact, he was an extraordinarily serious boy.

That was a very queer holiday. Jerry Baker walked into our lives and has never gone out. He seemed quite at home in our house, almost the host instead of the guest. He was never embarrassed by anything, but, on the contrary, almost apologetic *for* us at times. By and large, he has been a great trouble to us. He could play the piano and did—quite well, too. But he liked the violent kind of music, and sometimes you got the feeling that the very house was being shaken off its foundations. Then he liked Philip's microscope and spent quite a few hours playing with it. I tried to ask him questions about his family.

"My father's abroad right now," he said. He never said anything about his mother at all. When I asked him where he lived he said, "New York, mostly." Very evasive, he was. Yet he talked.

"Are you boys in the same classes?" I asked, and Philip said quickly, "Oh, no, Jerry's ahead of me."

"I'm very bright, Mrs. Boone," Jerry said.

The day after Thanksgiving, Jen came up. Jerry was at the piano, and Jen raised her brows questioningly toward him.

"This is Jerry Baker," I said. "Mrs. Deemster, Jerry." And he looked around, took Jen all in, and said, "How d'y'do," very briefly and went on playing.

Jen came out into the kitchen with me and we had tea out there at the kitchen table.

"Now that's a very strange boy," Jen said.

"You can say that again. I don't like him," I told her.

"Isn't he too old for Philip?"

"Yes, he's old. I can't make him out at all. He seems to be conferring a great favor on us by being here."

"He can play, at any rate. That's good playing for a boy— for anyone, I'd say."

"I wish he would go in for something more gentle," I said.

"Well, he doesn't look exactly gentle."

"No, he doesn't. He isn't. He looks like something out of the Dark Ages to me. I shall nip that friendship in the bud, you may be sure."

Jen didn't answer. She sat there looking down at her tea.

"I can't stand him," I said.

"I know. But it might wear out. Driving a friendship underground isn't always so good either, is it?"

She was quite right. She generally is. But I really felt this boy was a bad influence. I'd stopped the going to see Fanny and I thought I could stop this. It was something about Jerry's attitude toward Philip I didn't like. He patronized him, even while he seemed reasonably fond of him. "Oh, come now, Philip, that's not poetry!" I heard him say once. And once he said to me, "Philip's a bit confused, Mrs. Boone. But I'll look after him."

"Confused?" I said. "I don't think so, Jerry. Philip's got a good head and he uses it."

"Oh, he uses it. But for what?" Jerry said. "He's really mixed up, you know. He's so pretty, the masters just swoon over him."

That made me angry. "*Pretty?*" I said. "That's a word you don't use for boys Jerry."

"I know. It's a handicap. I'm ugly, and that's better. Really it is."

He wasn't ugly, just in character, that's all.

"I think Philip'll make out," I said.

He just looked at me from those odd, small, expressive eyes of his. "Oh?" he said doubtfully.

"Yes, he will. He's done very well so far."

"Oh?" he said again.

"Yes, Mr. Buckley has assured me that he has. But frankly, Jerry, I think he's too young for you to befriend."

"Yes, I've always been grown up," he said. "But give him time, Mrs. Boone. I'll look after him."

"Please don't," I said. "I'd rather he took more time."

"But he needs somebody, Mrs. Boone. He's very mixed up."

I tried to talk with Philip about him, but Philip wouldn't hear a word against his friend. "He's all right," he said. "He's my best friend. I like him. Well, for goodness' sake, he came home with me, didn't he? And he's in the next to top form. Everybody wants him, but he wanted to come with me."

"That was certainly kind of him," I said.

"Well, it was. He could have gone with anybody. He's my *best* friend."

So I had to let it go, or completely spoil the holiday. Philip was so pleased at Jerry's condescension, as I suppose any boy would have been at an older boy's taking him on. But I didn't like it at all. And then another thing happened. Andy came up on Saturday. The boys went up to Philip's room, and I could hear them talking up there, but not what they said. After only a half-hour Andy came down, looking distressed.

"You aren't going already?" I asked him. "Why don't you stay for dinner?"

"Thanks, I've got to go home, Mrs. Boone," he said. "I have to go."

And he went off.

"You weren't rude to Andy, were you?" I asked when they came down to dinner.

"Why, of course not," Philip said.

"He looked as if you hadn't made him welcome."

"Well, I guess he was bored. We were reading poetry," Philip said. "He thinks poetry's silly."

"I more or less agree with him," I said. "And if he was bored, couldn't you have done something else?"

"No, not just then," Philip said. "He didn't have to go."

"He's the football type," Jerry said.

"What if he is? He's a nice boy and a friend. You don't stop being friends just because you go to different schools."

"But you do outgrow people," Jerry said. "This boy wasn't Philip's kind at all."

"Maybe *you* outgrow people," I said to him, "but maybe you don't have any real friends. Andy's been to school with Philip, and I don't like this, not at all."

"I don't see why you can't outgrow friends just as well as you can outgrow families," Jerry said.

That was hitting below the belt. I just looked at him, though I wanted to strike him. "Yes, you are too old for Philip," I said, and went into the other room.

When they went back to school they had an extra bag. "What's that?" I asked.

"Oh, I thought I'd take my microscope back with me," Philip said.

The microscope never came back. He gave it to Jerry, though I didn't know that for sure for several years. It just never came back. And maybe Jerry had been promised it before he came. I don't know. Maybe he'd been told of the good piano, the good meals, the microscope. But what did a boy that age know about outgrowing families? Well, perhaps he did know, for his parents were separated, I found out later. Perhaps he really did. But he had no right to attack me in that way. And I must say I worried a little about what sort of picture Philip had given him of our life. He had dramatized himself before, and perhaps he had done it again. I didn't ask Jerry to come back any time, as I would have most boys. But he did come again, many times. I have never understood this friendship and I daresay I never will, though that's why I am putting this all down, in an effort to sort the puzzle out. I even had the evil thought once that it stemmed from the fact that Philip was "pretty," as Jerry had called it. But I do not believe now that I was right to have ever entertained such a thought. That was just something I dreamed up to justify my dislike of Jerry.

So Christmas came along again. Jerry wasn't here that Christmas, though he has been at others. It was during those holidays that Philip asked if he couldn't spend a day with a school friend in the city. I asked all about the boy, and Philip was very open about him; said his name was Mark Jeffers, that they were going to have a skating party in the park, and that he could take the bus in in the morning and be back at night. I said I'd take him, but he teased to go on the bus and I let him. He said Mark would meet the bus.

He came back on the bus as promised, and I asked him if he'd had fun and he said, "Sure! Of course! The skating was keen!" He even elaborated on the fun they'd had, and talked about Mark Jeffers. I thought he sounded like a sounder character than Jerry Baker. But then Philip said, "We had hamburgers—with huge dill pickles." Now that had been the favorite treat of Fanny's, and suddenly I knew he was lying. He had been with Fanny again.

"Philip, you disappoint me," I said. "You haven't been with Mark at all."

"What do you mean? Of course I have! Haven't I just been telling you?"

"You've been with Fanny," I said. "You disappoint me. Didn't you promise me?"

"But I was with Mark. I don't know what you mean," he said. "Don't I always keep my promises?"

"I wish I could say yes, son. But I think you've been with Fanny. That was her favorite treat, hamburgers with dill pickles."

"Well, can't I like them too? You know I do. You know that little house in the park where they sell hot dogs and things— that's where we got them."

And he did not admit it. But I knew. I went in to help him pack, but he had his suitcase all filled, though it lay open on the bed. He was in the bathroom, and I went and looked at the suitcase, lifted piles to see if he had missed anything. And I came on a scarf that he had surely never worn. It was red and knitted, very clumsily, as if by a young child. I left it there and said nothing. When Philip came back he closed the cover of his suitcase, though not secretively. He looked around carefully to see if he'd left anything, finally stuck a book in, closed and snapped the lid down.

Suddenly I thought, I haven't trusted him enough. I said, "Maybe you ought to stick at school till midyears. You don't do much studying when you come home."

He gave me a quick, appealing, reproachful look. "Gee, you can't do that to me!" he said. "I couldn't stand it if I didn't have week ends!"

I didn't remind him of how many he'd spent somewhere else. "Well, we'll see how you make out," I said. "But I don't want any nonsense about passing your courses. You can do it. See that you do!"

He lifted his suitcase off the bed. "Could I have Jerry for midterm vacation?" he asked.

"Jerry? Jerry Baker?"

"Yes, Jerry Baker. You don't like him," he finished flatly, as if I'd sinned against him somehow.

"To be frank, no," I said. "I don't like him."

"He's very lonesome," he said. He walked over to the window and looked out across the valley to the white hills. For some reason I remembered that little poem about the bird he'd written once. He had the look of one seeing a bird going away and away, where he couldn't follow.

"That doesn't seem the word to describe Jerry Baker," I said. "He seems very self-sufficient to me."

"Yeah—like Fanny. Like the cat who walked by himself," he said. "Well, he's not like that at all, any more than Fanny is. He's lonely and he likes to come here—and he likes me. I want him," he said.

"I didn't say you couldn't have him," I said. "You know this house is always open to your friends. But I would like more care in your choosing of friends."

"What's wrong with Jerry?" He was stubborn, and he comes by that honestly, I admit.

"Well, for one thing, he's much too old for you—not only in years, but in experience."

"Oh," Philip said. "Then I should think he'd be good for me. You have to get experience somewhere, don't you, Mother?"

"Yes. But he's evasive. He keeps things to himself. He's inclined to be rude. He plays music too advanced for my taste—not that that's against him, son, but it means he lives in a more adult, sophisticated world. He's not grateful for a visit here; he takes it as his right."

"Well, maybe it doesn't seem special to him—he's been all over the world. But he wasn't rude. He wasn't ever rude. And I like to find out about music; you can't just go on doing scales forever, can you? He's the nicest boy in the whole school and he's my friend."

"What about this Mark Jeffers?" I asked him. "He could come out for a few days, couldn't he?"

"Oh, Mark's got a home of his own and a family and everything," he said. "He's got a gang in town. Jerry doesn't have anybody."

"Where's his mother?"

"Oh, divorced, I guess. She doesn't live with Jerry. She's an alcoholic."

"All right. Have him if you like," I said. "Only you must remember that this is your friendship, not mine, son."

He came to me, threw his arms around me, and kissed me,

first on one cheek, then on the other. Then we were off for the school once more.

I knew Jerry was too old for him, I felt him as a sinister influence, unwholesome, and yet I let him come. Why? Because I felt it good that Philip stuck by him; because I felt it sad and appealing that he had said Jerry was lonesome. Because perhaps I thought of a boy with a mother who was an alcoholic and pitied him a little. And it may be true that I wanted Philip to come home at any price.

That seems to be the truth, that I wanted Philip with me at any price. I knew he had lied to me about Fanny. I didn't know but what he had lied to me about a good many things. But I felt like a whole human being only when Philip was home. I had resolved not to hang on to him in the way of possessive mothers. I had sent him away to school, hadn't I? I knew he wasn't perfect, and I knew too that somehow I had failed a little with him. There should have been no reason for him to lie to me, for he was my light and my life. He was doing good work in school, in spite of his bad start, and I thought he'd come out all right in the end. How could he help it, with my love and protection behind him? But I was troubled because of the day in town, the scarf, the insistence on having Jerry for a friend.

I got to thinking about Fanny those days, wondered what she was turning into, what she looked like. But I could not imagine her any different from the way she had been at four, with those disturbing straight looks of hers, that stiff, unresponsive manner. I remembered how Philip had said she laughed at the zoo, how he'd said she was clever. "Clever" never seemed the word for Fanny—she was too stubborn and set for cleverness.

I didn't wonder much about Walter. Odd, but I didn't. I knew he would go on in his dull job, his dull habits, as always. He had his sister Mate to look after him. I don't know that I would have thought of Fanny either, except that she made this trouble between Philip and me. I did wonder sometimes about Philip's seeing his father. I wondered what they thought of each other. But Philip had never mentioned Walter, and I couldn't. I didn't exactly *miss* either Walter or Fanny. No, I was born to be single, to have the say about my house, my life. I don't work in harness with anyone.

One day before Mother died I was sitting in her room, beside her bed. She was very low, and she seemed to be shrinking away to a shadow. But she was proud and always wanted her hair combed and a good bed-jacket on. Her hair was still black and smooth, but it was thin. She wore the plum-colored bed-jacket with the lace on. It was becoming to her.

"Is Walter home yet?" she asked me.

"No. He should be soon, though. Do you want to see him?"

"Yes—when he comes. And the children, too."

"Fanny's here somewhere."

"I'll wait," she said.

The doctor had said it wouldn't be long. I was frightened. We'd had a hospital bed brought in, and she was sitting up part way. "Is the head too high for you?" I asked her.

"No, it's fine," she said. Then she said, "Cornelia, it would be better for you not to be so hard."

"You have to be a little hard, Mother," I said. "It's a tough world."

"Not that tough," she said. Then she said in a far-off way, "I should never have taken the house."

"Never taken it?" I said. "Why, why ever not? It's a good house and I intend to live in it the rest of my life."

"It's too big. Too much has gone into keeping it," she said. "It seemed important—I can't think why."

"Well, it is important," I told her.

"No, it isn't important at all. Walter and the children, they're important. When I die—I am dying, Cornelia, there's no use denying it—when I die, sell the house."

"I couldn't promise that, Mother. I love this house. It's all my life here," I said.

"That's what I mean, child. It shouldn't be," she said.

She called me "child," though I was in my thirties.

Walter came then, and I called him up, and the children, but I didn't stay. I couldn't. I went to my room and even wept a little. Mother had always disapproved of me in many ways. She kept a little tartness in her voice just for me. Otherwise she was gentle enough. Funny—remarks of hers come to me every now and then—always tart. "You remind me of Uncle Lorenzo sometimes," she said once. He was the one who had left her the house. "He thought owning something made it special." True, I've always felt like that. My house was a special place, my furniture was special, my silver, my—well, how can I say my children? I'll skip that. But I see nothing wrong in that approach. If you didn't feel that way, you'd take care of nothing, care about nothing. You make them good because they are special to you, and your own. But I remember her saying it. And once I said something about Walter's reading at night, how I hadn't got to sleep till all hours. Mother was fixing flowers for the table. She said, "If he read to you, I should think it might be quite pleasant, when the house is quiet and all." The truth is that he would have read to me, but I don't like being read to. I loathe it, actually. I believe in letting everybody be himself—I stood Walter's reading, and there's no reason he couldn't have stood my not listening to reading. Oh, I'm not illiterate. I read enough. I astonished Philip once by trying to read *Finnegans Wake*. But I'm not one to fill every wall with books, like Mate. Looks stuffy to me, as if you never got out into the world at all, just lived on what other people said. Makes me impatient not to see people *live*.

I said something like that to Walter once and he said, "But you live on what's in your head and heart." Only part true. You've got a body that has to be active or die. You can forget that easily enough, and just sit with a book, or writing papers that nobody really cares about, and shrivel away to nothing. I've got a good strong body, and it has served me well, far better than what I've learned out of books.

Take that Joyce now—what was he, when it comes right down to it? A clever man who knew a lot of languages and thought it was smart to show off his knowledge. He doesn't even make sense, not unless you know all the languages he did. There was just one spot that I thought made sense—when she dies at the end and everything goes through her mind. That seemed quite grand and beautiful to me, and made me think of Mother dying. For Mother went through a lot, by and large, too, what with Father drinking the way he did, and getting such cruel spells and making Mother out a fool for liking the house and getting, as he said, "too big for her breeches." Of course he came out of that awful little farm I visited once, where the fool hen was out by the woodpile. He didn't have much to build on, and he didn't like building at all. So Mother had it hard, but she hung on. . . . Well, when Anna Livia died, whoever she was, I thought of Mother, and how she must have lain there thinking of all the years and what had gone into them, and I thought that part was good. But I don't like that kind of show-off writing. There's no reason not to say straight out what you mean.

How did I get off on that track? I swore to myself I'd go straight forward and not wander the way some writers do.

THE NEXT thing I remember is the midterm vacation. I thought I would have a party for the boys, with all Philip's old friends from the village. I had it, too, but it wasn't a success. Jerry Baker was bored with it, and I think the rest were shy with him, for he seemed so much older. They didn't even eat as much as usual, and they went home quite early.

"Well, that wasn't much of a party," I said to the boys.

"It was all right," Philip said.

"No, it was a flop. No one had a good time."

Jerry was sitting on the stool near the fire, smiling to himself in an irritating way. Then he said, "But you see, Mrs. Boone, you *do* outgrow people."

"But they're nice kids—all the ones Philip went to school with. I daresay you'll outgrow Philip any day now, too."

"Could be," he said. That was cruel. I saw a look go over Philip's face—lost and frightened. But Philip laughed and said, "Or it might be the other way around."

He went and put some records on the player I'd given him for Christmas. It wasn't music I liked, but the boys seemed to.

And then Jerry said, "Oh, I forgot!" And he went upstairs and brought down some records he'd brought with him. Philip must have been sure about getting the player.

"This is Stravinsky," he said. "Not bad, either."

But when it was finished he said, "Not good, either," and put on one by Sibelius. He must have played that Sibelius record a dozen times while he was there, and I got so I hated it. He would sit there engrossed and expect Philip to hear every note.

I tried to get them to go skiing, but Jerry never wanted to. "Oh, we get enough sports at school, Mrs. Boone," he said. "Do you like that phrase? I could hear that a thousand times! It's perfect, isn't it?"

But I have never had much ear for music. Then one afternoon Jerry said, to my surprise, "Let's take the player down to Mrs. Deemster's, shall we?"

So they went off, carrying the player and an armful of records, and didn't get back till dinnertime. Jerry hadn't even seemed to notice Jen much when he'd met her, or I'd thought not.

"Well, did Jen appreciate her treat?" I asked.

"Oh, yes, she liked it," Philip said.

"Did she indeed? Well, she is always polite, at least."

"She has a very critical ear," Jerry said. "I knew she would have."

"I don't know how you could know anything about Mrs. Deemster," I said. "Not possibly, from one brief glance."

"I'm clever that way," Jerry said. "Just a look—I know all about people. Really, that's true."

"You just imagine you do. Most people aren't that transparent."

"Most people are that transparent. But you know, Mrs. Boone, I keep looking for someone who isn't, who has a secret that doesn't show. I keep looking."

The truth is that I fancy myself as a quick and accurate judge of people. I suppose it irritated me in my vanity that this boy should profess to be able to judge in the same way.

"You'll live to learn how mistaken you've been," I said.

"I hope so," he said. "It's no fun to know people so soon."

What kind of talk was that for a boy in his teens? Oh, he was old, *old*. Yet sometimes I saw Philip give him a look that made him seem old too, as if, after all, he understood Jerry better than I did or could.

Jerry walked to the piano then and began to play. Philip was sitting on the sofa, his knees hugged up against him. He appeared to be listening, but presently he got up and wandered off upstairs. When he came down he was lugging a big lump of Plasticine or some sort of synthetic clay I'd got for him years back. He put it down on the coffee table and began to fuss with it, looking up now and then at Jerry. Philip's hands always amaze me. You might think he'd be the one to play the piano, but he's liked mostly to listen to it. His hands look intelligent, as if his brain resided in them. I sat and watched Jerry's long head appear out of the clay, bent a little, as it was before the keyboard—the same shock of hair, the odd mouth, the look of age, the thing that made Jerry different and strange. Jerry never looked his way, just went on playing for almost an hour.

I had things to do, but I remember sitting there as if I couldn't move, watching the two boys. I suppose I was interested in anything Philip did, and I was proud of his clever hands. Then, too, there was something about the relationship between the boys that interested me. I didn't understand it, but I was interested.

At last Jerry stopped, letting his arms drop in a queer way, tired and finished. He sat that way for a minute; then he got up and came over to Philip. He stood there, looking down at the head; then he knelt beside the coffee table, looking at Philip's work all around.

"You never told me you could do that," he said at last.

"There are lots of things I don't tell you," Philip said.

Jerry had an excited look. I hadn't seen him as human and interested before. "It's not bad—it's not bad at all," he said. "Come on out for a walk!"

"It's dark."

"Oh, the snow makes it light! Come on!"

So they went off in the snow in the dark. I don't know what I thought then. Now I think that Philip was the one he was looking for, the one who didn't tell him everything at first acquaintance. I think he was excited because he realized this —he was grateful that Philip hadn't told him of this talent of his. It made Philip really important to him—though he had come twice now, and perhaps he had felt it before. I don't know. But does being secretive mean you are deep? They went back to school, taking the player with them but not the clay. Philip was strong enough to make the talent unimportant to himself—to make himself seem strong, at any rate.

I went down to see Jen, and John was home with a cold. Jen was fussing over him and didn't pay much attention to me at first.

But at last she came down and sat with me. "I worry when

John has a cold. It always hits his lungs," she said. "He has a pretty big case coming up next week, and I have to get him on his feet."

"Men always think they're dying if they get the sniffles," I said. "Women keep going, but men give up."

"Don't be such a feminist, Cornelia," she said. "John isn't like that at all."

"Well, Walter was."

"Oh? I never thought so. I remember that time Philip had the flu. Walter got it too, but he kept going, he was so worried about Philip."

"Oh, he didn't really have the flu."

I knew she didn't like it when I spoke that way of Walter, and usually I kept my opinions to myself.

"John's had pneumonia three times," she said. "I worry. Have the boys gone back to school?"

"Yes, they've gone."

"I've changed my mind about Jerry," she said. "I like him. I like him very much. He has a real *passion* for music."

"He has that, but I don't think that has much to do with his character."

"Oh, it must have!"

"No, it doesn't. Not a thing. He professed to know you very well—he judged you at first sight and knew you appreciated music, so he said."

"Did he? Well, he was right; I do love music. I was very pleased that he should think I would."

"Well, I haven't changed my mind about him, Jen. But Philip thinks he's wonderful—because he's older and notices him, I expect."

"Philip's old too. That's why they stick together, maybe.

But I don't think you need to worry about Jerry—he's all right."

"Oh? Well, I'll probably pay as much attention to that remark as you paid to mine about worrying over John."

John coughed, and Jen was on her feet and moving toward the stairs in a breath. After she'd been gone quite a while I went to the stairs and called to her that I had to go. She said, "All right—see you!" but as if she couldn't care less whether she did or not. Funny marriage, John and Jen—he was so stiff, so much the big-lawyer type, more like a judge, which he did get to be two years later. I don't see how you could love or marry a man like John. Jen is so fine, and she has a gay streak in her that I'm sure John has never appreciated. I wish just once the right people could marry each other; they never seem to.

A very unsatisfactory call, that was. I didn't like it that Jen should change her opinion of Jerry. It made me feel edgy, and I did sound edgy, talking to her. And I didn't like, either, that remark about Walter. I had been really scared about Philip. I hadn't had my clothes off for two nights. I went into the bathroom and Walter was sitting on the edge of the tub, taking his temperature. It made me angry, I admit, that he could be thinking of himself at such a time.

"Ninety-nine?" I said.

"A hundred and three," he said. "But you needn't worry. I'll be all right."

I didn't worry; I thought he was just trying to get some of my attention away from Philip. I didn't believe in the hundred and three. When the doctor came he looked at Walter and said, "Good heavens, Mr. Boone! You get to bed!"

"I can't," Walter said. "There's too much to do."

"Well, there will be if you don't get to bed."

"I'm all right," Walter said.

Trying to give the appearance of nobility! I thought. Well, maybe he was sick, but I still think you have to ignore your own feelings when a child is sick. And I didn't like it that Jen felt sorry for Walter. Walter did get along all right; he didn't even go to bed, and if he'd been as sick as Philip he'd have had to. He just wasn't. He went around looking very limp after that for quite a while, though. One day I asked him to burn some leaves and he said, "I can't. I'm too tired. I don't know why, but I seem to feel terribly tired all the time these days. Get Joe Hill to do it." As if everyone didn't feel tired sometimes! Well, to tell the truth, maybe I don't know what tiredness is.

"I'll do it myself, if you're too weak," I said.

He did go out and burn the leaves. I went to the window once and I saw him lean over to pick up the rake. He was a long time in doing it; then when he got the rake up he stood there leaning on it, as if he didn't have the strength to stand up by himself. But, as I said, all I felt was exasperation. It's always seemed to me, when people were sick, that they were retreating from life, trying to get attention or something like that—not children, but grown people. Oh, you can break a bone, but these vague diseases of the nerves, headaches, such things—even arthritis, they say—they seem to come from a desire to be noticed, or a laziness about living. A man can be a man if he wants to. With Walter, he had to get away from active living into his little world where he wanted to write books, so he imagined he was sick.

One night Walter said, "Come out on the terrace, Cornelia —or Maud, or whoever you are."

I didn't know what he was talking about. Something literary, I expect. I came out and sat in the wicker chair beside him, I don't know why. I never liked much just sitting, but Walter was a born sitter.

I saw that the grass down toward the flowers was high and I said, "The grass needs cutting."

"Well, not now," Walter said. "Couldn't we just sit and look at our world a little while and not do anything to it?"

"Somebody has to do something or it wouldn't be a world you'd want to look at," I told him.

"How purple the hills look!" he said. "I wonder who planted the ginkgo tree. Surely not Uncle Lorenzo!"

"Why not Uncle Lorenzo?"

"I don't know. It doesn't seem in character. It's a tree Fanny would plant." Fanny was only three or so.

"Well, she didn't. Uncle Lorenzo must have."

"I love the leaves of the ginkgo tree—and the trunk too. It's so strong and so strange. I shall put it in a book someday."

"You'll never write a book," I said. "You'd rather just sit and look at the world."

"Oh, but the looking comes first, of course," he said. "I'll write it, I promise you."

"Well, you don't need to promise me," I said. "I'd rather you got up at sunrise tomorrow and cut the grass."

"Oh, Cornelia!" he said. It was sad, the way he said it. I notice men often get sentimental and melancholy in the early evening.

"And what do you mean by that—'Oh, Cornelia!'?" I said.

"I was just thinking of how it might have been if you'd loved me," he said.

"Well, I never thought love consisted of sitting and mooning over the sunset," I said.

"Did I say it did? But there ought to be time for that, even, hadn't there? There ought to be time for everything. I wonder why you married me, Cornelia. I do wonder. Why did you?" He reached over and put a hand over mine on the arm of the chair.

I don't know why, but I drew my hand away. "If you don't know why, I can't tell you," I said. "I suppose I wanted to, that's all."

"But why? Why did you want to? I wasn't any different then."

"Maybe I thought you'd change," I said. I suppose I was tart. I often was.

"Oh, you thought I was malleable clay, you thought I was something you could work on. Well, I haven't been so malleable, have I? I'm sorry to have disappointed you, but you can't really change me much. It's a pity, isn't it?"

"Well, you could do with a little changing," I said. "And what's this all about, anyway? Are you trying to stir up a quarrel?"

"Heaven forbid! I'm just trying for something—I want something honest said between us for once in a way. I'm not just something to push a lawnmower."

"Who said you were? Oh, stop it, Walter. I don't like this kind of talk. It's childish."

"Oh?" he said, and then he didn't say another word. After a while I got up and went inside.

Now, why did I remember that right now? It was a foolish conversation. It was Walter who didn't know what marriage was and should be. It means two people working together toward the same end—which we never did. Or did he think I should have been willing to spend all my time looking at sunsets and coddling him over his writing? How could I, that not being my nature? Did he ever make a move toward working toward my desires? No, he never did. It might have been half and half, I suppose, but not two people always going different ways. It never was half and half. It was Walter looking at purple hills and me keeping the place going. We were incompatible if two people ever were.

Once I heard him talking to Philip, who was lying on the rug, looking at the fire.

"That's right, son, learn to be lazy," he said. He sat down near Philip on the stool and said, "Do you know *The King of the Golden River*? That begins with a fire."

"No. Tell it to me," Philip said. He had a book on his shelves with that name.

Walter told it to him in his slow, lazy voice. I liked that voice when I first heard it, but it got so that it was too much *Walter*, if you know what I mean. It was pleasant and cultured—and lazy.

Once Walter said to Mother, "What was Mr. Ventray like?"

Mother was surprised and embarrassed. "Well, I knew him too well to say, Walter," she said. "I doubt if any woman can describe her husband."

Walter smiled at her in that intimate way that he never used on me. "I was just wondering about him—you never talk of him, and there's no portrait over the mantel," he said. "I think he was big and competent and a little tyrannical. Am I right?"

I laughed out loud—I couldn't stop laughing. Then I saw that Mother looked upset and I stopped, but I said, "You're wrong on every count. Father was weak as water, and no one in the world was less competent. He was thin, not very tall, and he wanted always to have his own way and no one to trouble him about troubles."

"Odd," Walter said.

"Cornelia's wrong, Walter," Mother said. She could look very stern sometimes and she looked stern then. "I'm afraid Cornelia never troubled to know her father. He was not weak."

"That's just Mother's pride speaking," I said. "And Walter's part of the family now. He might as well know the truth, Mother."

"All right, Cornelia, I know now," Walter said. "I was just thinking about inheritance, such things."

Mother got up and left the table. I said, "You didn't need to bring up the ghost of Father, Walter. Though Father wouldn't have a very lively ghost, I can tell you. But there's no need to upset Mother. She had enough of him, living."

"All right. Let's leave it," he said. He went in and asked Mother to walk around the garden with him. He was exasperating, Walter. He thought I didn't see my own father clearly, but I lived with Father.

Well, I never stopped anyone from liking Walter who wanted to. Jen always liked him, it's hard to see just why. Of course, if you just heard his pleasant voice once in a while, perhaps it was easier. I remember Jen, walking up and down the living room, looking like a tiger, her red hair every which way, waiting for Walter to come home. John had been taken sick in town and she wanted to get to him quickly. Walter came in, and Jen stopped pacing, went to him, and put her hands on his arms and said, "You're so tired—but will you take me to town? John's sick. I have to go, Walter."

"Of course, Jen. Right away. Come along."

John was in the hospital, being taken care of. It wasn't so urgent as all that. But when someone responds to your urgency like that I suppose you like him. She'd never believe Walter didn't respond to my urgencies in the same way. And it was a kind of flattery, noticing that he was tired when she was so upset herself.

This isn't reminiscing just for the sake of reminiscing. I'm trying to see what we were like then, all of us. Odd—I feel exactly the same person now as I was then. By and large, I don't believe people change much—inside, that is. You get gray hair and false teeth—neither of which I have, thank God, except for a bit of streakiness in the hair, and the general impression is still darkness—but age doesn't seem to change your character, it just makes it more so. I said a while back that Philip had changed, and certainly Fanny doesn't look at all as I remember that little girl, but they're the same people after all. Didn't Jen say way back then that Philip was complex? He was and is, and just because I can see into his character a little more now doesn't mean that it's changed, does it? We make plans to change but we never get around to it.

Jen and I didn't agree on Jerry Baker, way back then. I don't believe we've agreed on many things. Then why are we friends? I don't know. I have a neighbor up the road, Lucia Adams, who's a lot more like me. She's houseproud, ambitious, successful. But we're not friends and never have been. I'm not Jen's kind at all. Actually, she's more like Walter, except that she's more dramatic. Then why? I haven't figured that one out yet.

It's snowing, a soft, heavy snow. It's quiet here in Philip's room. Yesterday I typed along like a streak, but today I type in jerks. Why didn't I carry the typewriter into my room? I haven't liked this room much, though it is beautiful, I suppose. Philip has furnished it in his own way, which is not my way. For a man I like heavier furniture—a leather chair, maybe, a heavy desk, hunting prints on the wall. But on the wall is the Chinese print of the horse in the moonlight with its gold mat and gold frame touched with black, and there is a sketch of Jerry Baker, charcoal, in a narrow black frame— Jerry sitting at the piano. The curtains are striped, gold and black and rose, though dimmed down. Around the corner are the bookshelves, white, lined with a faded rose like the rose in the curtains. There are all the big art books there, some piles of music, poetry. . . .

This table is just a card table strong enough to hold a portable typewriter. Philip used to have a maple bed, with stubby, strong posts, suitable for a growing boy. Now there is just the daybed, with the plain homespun blue cover. Yet the blue goes with the gold of the Chinese picture. Philip has a color sense.

You can see the row of pines along the field, loaded down with snow, and the hills are quite dimmed out with the snow. Philip used to put sunflower seeds on little shelves in the pine trees—for the grosbeaks. "I was a grosbeak in some other life," he said once.

"They have cruel beaks," Jerry said.

"Well," Philip said, "suppose they do?"

Jerry sat right here near the window, but in the chair with the carved back and the tapestry with the blue vine against tan. He looked down at the flock of grosbeaks. "Yes, I see the likeness," he said.

Actually, Jerry is more like the grosbeaks. He is startling, as the grosbeaks are against snow. And he has his cruel side, that's sure. Philip has a radiance, but not so sharp and brilliant as the birds'. If he is cruel, and he is sometimes, it doesn't show —not on the outside. There seem to be no birds at all about today, but there are no seeds in the pines now. . . .

There's another picture that I haven't mentioned. It hangs over the bookshelves. I have never liked it. It is modern and says nothing. Well, there seems to be some sort of city, though you can't say that this and that are buildings, and it seems far off behind a mist.

"I'll get you a picture," I told Philip. "That is nothing."

"Thanks, I'll get my own pictures, Mother. But you're quite right—it is nothingness. That's not quite the same thing as nothing, though, is it?"

"You're more like your father than I ever thought," I told him. "That's just what he liked to do, sit and contemplate nothingness."

He had a record on, and it annoyed me when I was trying to talk. I went over and turned off the machine. He didn't fly out at me, but went and stood by the window there, looking down at the pines. He was very tall and thin. He never said a word, and the room was still, with the music gone. Well, I must admit that was nothing new. Philip has always been able to turn off a conversation, make you feel it should never have been started. You want to start again, but you can't. Or I couldn't. I went away and left him alone.

Yet no one can talk more gaily than Philip when he wants to. No one.

PHILIP cut himself off from the village children after that. They just weren't his friends any more and he didn't pretend they were. Maybe that is admirable, I don't know, but it always upset me. Even little Sally, whom he'd bought the rabbits for—after a while he didn't like her. She'd come to his parties always, and she was a pretty child, fair and delicate, elflike. Once her mother phoned and asked Philip down for a Sunday afternoon, but Philip wouldn't go.

"Oh, Mother, tell her I'm sick, tell her I'm dead," Philip said. "I don't have much time at home—I don't want to waste it down there."

I made some excuse for him—I don't know what now. "That wasn't very polite," I told Philip. I think I was half glad that he'd rather be at home with me.

"Only the silly people are always polite," Philip said.

"Well, you aren't going," I told him. "Let it go at that, son. You don't have to try to justify rudeness, for you can't, not to me."

"Oh, you know you'd rather have me stay home," he said, smiling at me in his teasing way. "You *know* you would,

74

Mother. Let's plan what we'll do next summer, shall we? Could we go to the seashore?"

"And let this place go to pot?"

"Couldn't Joe Hill take care of it? For once? I've never been to the seashore—except when we took the ferry in New York last summer. And that isn't the shore, is it?"

"You said you didn't like swimming."

"No, I don't, not much. But you don't have to swim, do you? I just want to be where there's sand and sea birds, all that. Do you like Bach, Mother?"

"I wouldn't know," I said.

"You would if you'd heard Mr. Abingdon play. He goes to the chapel afternoons and plays Bach. Sometimes I go in and listen to him. I wish I could ask him here sometime."

I shouldn't have said it, but I said, "Oh, you mean Jerry is out of favor? That you've outgrown him already?"

"Of course not. Jerry could come too," Philip said.

"I doubt very much whether the masters spend their holidays visiting the students," I said.

"I think he would come. I think he likes me. And we've got a good piano. Jerry says it's a very good one—he thinks it's funny, when we don't play much, that we have a good piano."

"I daresay Jerry thinks we're a funny pair anyway, every way," I said. "He likes to laugh at people, especially when he's taking their hospitality, I fancy."

"That's not true," Philip said. "He doesn't laugh at *us*, he just sees that a lot of things are funny, and they are. It *is* queer, about the piano. You know I can't play very well, and you don't even like listening to music. Why did you get it?"

"I didn't. Your grandmother did. She got it at an auction in Granby. She paid only a hundred dollars for it. People don't

like grand pianos any more, but your grandmother knew it was
a good instrument and she knew it was a bargain. She had an
eye for bargains."

He gave a bright, amused smile. "Oh. It was just a bargain,"
he said. "That's funny, isn't it? Isn't *that* funny, Mother?"

"Not particularly. Certain things belong in a home, and a
piano is one of them. You've had pleasure out of it, haven't
you? Or Jerry has, at any rate. It's served its purpose, hasn't
it?"

"Is everything here just a bargain?" he asked, looking around
as if he'd never even seen the things in our house. I suppose
you do take your own house for granted.

"Probably," I said. "Some things were here when your
grandmother inherited the house. The corner cupboard in the
dining room was here. That's a very fine piece. And most of
the bureaus and beds—that tip table. Uncle Lorenzo bought
those. Most of the rest your grandmother bought, a piece at a
time. There are lots of auctions around here, good things sold
off. Your grandmother had an eye for what was good. These
rugs came from the McAllisters' place. They used to have a
place on the hill—New York people. Well, these are rugs that
will last a lifetime and more."

They are good rugs. I went to that auction with Mother
when I was quite small. She sat in the back, looking stiff and
small in her black suit, and I sat beside her, listening to Mr.
Grubbs singsonging his way through the auction. When the
rugs came up for bidding, Mother got stiffer and paler, and her
hands were tight on her handbag. She was still pale, but limp,
when we went home with the rugs. "Cornelia," she said, "don't
ever want anything so much as I wanted those rugs." But
when the rugs were on the floor she cried with pleasure,

though she wasn't one to cry, not ever. The floor is big down there; the two rugs don't even cover the room. They are mostly a gold color, but they have a little blue in them, a light turquoise; one has some white with the gold. They are like sunshine, actually, and have remained so all these years. Yes, Mother knew, I don't know how, what was good.

"What a lovely house!" Jen said the first time she was here. "What a lovely, lovely house!" But for just a minute there, when Philip made that remark, I had a queer feeling, as if I didn't have any right to my own possessions, as if I'd stolen them or something, which I certainly did not. You have to collect your house furnishings from somewhere, don't you?

Mr. Abingdon came for Easter. Oh, yes, I invited him. I don't know what I expected, but certainly not Mr. Abingdon as he was. He wasn't one of these wildly melancholy young musicians at all, but a surly, gruff man past forty. Jerry came too. Jerry was more polite to Mr. Abingdon than I'd ever seen him. He carried Mr. Abingdon's bag upstairs.

"They tell me you're a musician," I said.

"I play some," he said. "Actually, I am a teacher of physics." I must say that's more what he looked like.

"Oh, I was under the impression that Philip studied under you, but he doesn't have physics this year, does he?"

"No, Philip is not in my classes," Mr. Abingdon said. "Next year, I expect. Baker is a student of mine."

"But he *is* a musician, Mrs. Boone," Jerry said.

After dinner Mr. Abingdon played for us. I must say it was more restful to listen to him than to Jerry. I suppose it was Bach he played—a little monotonous, I thought, but restful. He looked ugly sitting there at the piano, a middle-aged, thick-set, ugly man. But Philip, watching him, listening, looked beautiful. Jerry sat on the stool, frowning in an anxious way, listening with his whole body, you might say. When Mr. Abingdon finished he came away from the piano, sat on the sofa beside Philip.

Jerry jumped up and said, "Come on, Philip, let's take a walk!" He seemed too excited, his dark face all lit up and almost twitching. He didn't thank Mr. Abingdon at all, though Philip gave him a smile of thanks before he went.

"Why did you invite me here, Mrs. Boone?" Mr. Abingdon said suddenly.

"Philip wanted you. Didn't you want to come?" I asked.

He gave me an odd look, a look as from an enemy. "Not particularly," he said. "I do not think it a good policy to visit at the students' homes. Do you?"

"Why not?" I asked him. "If you're friends?"

"I am not a friend," he said. "I choose my friends from among my contemporaries. I am nothing but Baker's teacher. I scarcely know your son at all."

"He goes to the chapel to hear you play," I told him.

"Does he indeed? I didn't know that. Does he play?"

"Not well. But he appreciates music."

"Baker has talent," he said. "I believe your son asked me for Baker's sake—a bribe to Baker, you might call it. I didn't realize that till we were nearly here."

"That's an ugly word, Mr. Abingdon," I said. "Is it so wrong to want to please your friends?"

He looked at me from under bushy brows, not liking me. Well, I didn't like him much either.

"I believe Baker's coming was conditional on my coming, Mrs. Boone," he said.

"I doubt that very much. Jerry has been here often. He's my son's best friend."

"Is he? But is it not natural to choose your friends among those of your own age, Mrs. Boone? Your son seems precocious, but not as precocious as Baker, who is, I might say, as old as time. Your son has winning ways; he wheedled me into coming against my better judgment. He said his mother had said he could ask his favorite master, and, though he wasn't in my classes, I was, he said, still his favorite master, and would I come?"

"Perhaps you are. I told you he listened to your playing."

"Yes. So you did. And perhaps he was telling the truth. It seemed so as he coaxed me, Mrs. Boone. But I doubt it. I think Baker insisted on his asking me—for what purpose I don't know, unless he was interested in Bach. I am interested in Bach, and I enjoyed playing your piano, but I must say I do not fancy being used by boys, Mrs. Boone."

"You're free to go," I said.

"Then, if you don't mind, and can take me to the nearest bus or train, I believe I will go in the morning. I am not trying to be rude, Mrs. Boone, but I think it would be better if I left."

"As you please, Mr. Abingdon. I do not force my hospitality on anyone."

"Do not sound as if I'd insulted you," he said. "I appreciate your hospitality, but do you not think yourself that it is odd my being here at all?"

Now I did think it odd. And I wanted him out of my house. And I didn't like what he had said about the reasons for his being here. But I thought of how disappointed Philip would be, no matter how he had wangled the visit. It even came to me that perhaps Jerry would go too and that Philip would be hurt. I laughed and said, "Why don't you just forget your suspicions and take it for granted that you're welcome here, and let it go at that? You are welcome, you know. And you ought to be pleased that two boys like so much to hear you play."

"That's not quite the point, is it?" he said. It wasn't, of course.

When Jerry and Philip came in, Jerry began at once to talk about Bach, using technical terms that I didn't understand. He sounded very eager and intelligent, and I saw Mr. Abingdon softening up, deciding to stay. He did stay. There was a good deal of music.

I didn't like that. I was right not to like it. I remembered what Miss Gray had said about Philip's buying his friends. Yet he couldn't have wanted those friends as much as she said, for he had certainly cast them off easily enough. If he was fickle, why had he wanted to go and see his sister the way he had? Or had that just been a piece of dramatics? He seemed to have forgotten her, anyway—or so I thought.

"Where have you been?" Jen said.

"Oh, one of the masters at Philip's school came for the week end. I've been busy. I ought to have asked you up, for Bach is coming out of my ears. You'd have appreciated it more than I did."

"Well, why didn't you ask me? I'd have loved it."

"I don't rightly know. I didn't like the man much. But the boys like him, I can't imagine why. He's on the rude side, and certainly no beauty. But he plays Bach, Bach, Bach. I'm glad they've gone."

"You *are* a barbarian," Jen said.

"I suppose so. But I don't see why you can't be civilized without liking Bach. I might as well call you a barbarian for not knowing one flower from another."

"Oh, I know a few," she said. "Not by their Latin names, but I know a few, Cornelia. I'm learning. And I've got a green thumb. I can grow them. Jerry Baker was there too?"

"Naturally."

She pushed her hair back in a way she has. "It's too bad Walter couldn't have known Jerry," she said.

"Yes, I'm sure he's just Walter's cup of tea," I said. "He'll never be mine, that's sure."

"You're wrong about Jerry," she said. "Quite wrong. He's all right."

"No. He's sly and rude and altogether too precocious, as even Mr. Abingdon admitted. He *uses* Philip."

"Well, what are friends for?" Jen said. "It may be Philip likes being used."

"He ought not to like it. Don't be silly, Jen."

She has a little mocking grin she uses sometimes, and she used it then. "*Who's* silly?" she said, and changed the subject.

Well, I've thought about that, about what friends are for, and I still don't know for sure. But how could it be right to force Philip to ask Mr. Abingdon to his home just to please yourself in some way? No, that was wrong, no matter what Jen said. I didn't like anything about that friendship. I never have.

I don't like going away from this place in the summertime, but I went to the Cape that summer with Philip. He didn't ask to have Jerry go along. He wanted to go just with me, and I admit I liked it that he did. Who wouldn't have? We went

to Wellfleet, which is just a little unimportant town with nothing there at all. I'm not so fond of sand and sea birds as Philip
is, but I stuck it out and Philip was happy and loving. He went
clamming with some people across from us, and sometimes he
went out in a boat with a fisherman he scraped up an acquaintance with. But he liked just to lie on the sand and look at the
sky. He could lie without moving for an hour at a time. He
collected some shells and made drawings of birds, those stiff-
legged birds along the shore—sandpipers, I guess—and gulls.
He didn't seem to want anyone at all except me. It was, in
some ways, one of the best summers I have ever had. We
stayed in a plain little boarding house, had good food, but
little else except being together, and that has always been
enough for me.

I didn't know why he was content that summer, anxious
about nothing, begging for nothing. "What a handsome boy!"
I heard a woman say one day when Philip walked along the
shore. And the fisherman loved him and was so gentle and
kind with him. Everyone loved him. One day we went across
the bay in a boat, and he climbed up to the top of a dune
and stood there with the stiff grasses blowing up against him.
His fair hair was blowing in the wind too. He had on a blue
shirt and white slacks. I looked up at him and had a strange
feeling that he would take off, like a gull, swoop over the sea
and away. It frightened me, that feeling.

"Come up!" he called. I didn't want to climb that steep
dune, but I did, and stood there by him, looking out over the
bay. I know the frightened feeling went away as I stood there
in the wind beside him. If he flew, I would fly with him.

"I wish we lived here," he said.

"You wouldn't like it in the winter," I said.

"Why not? I would. I'd like it awfully."

"And leave home?" I said.

He turned and smiled at me, shoving his hands in his pockets. "Oh, no, never leave *home*," he said. "But summers—we could come here summers, couldn't we?"

"That I can't promise. We'll see," I said.

"Can't you have two homes?" he said. "This feels like home too. It does, really."

It didn't feel like home to me. I wasn't used to having nothing to do. I think I was even a little homesick at times. Yet I was happy too. It is good to have someone you love want to be with you, and he did want me that summer at Wellfleet. He didn't so much as mention Jerry Baker all summer.

Oh, it wasn't as perfect as I thought at the time, I know that now. Still, he did want me with him; he really tried to make it a good and a happy summer.

In our second week there he asked me if he could rent a bicycle, and I let him. He'd go off for rides along the Cape, but he always got back when he said he would.

"Why don't you rent a bicycle too, Mother?" he said.

I laughed at the thought, though when I'd been young I'd had a bicycle. "Thanks, no," I said. "I'm past the stage."

He even teased me to try, but I didn't. He didn't go often. Most of the time we were together. It wasn't till years afterward that I knew that Fanny had been ill and that Mate had brought her to the Cape that summer. There wasn't a word to show Philip wasn't quite alone that time, except for me, that he had a care in the world—not a word. But I didn't know about Fanny's being there and I only felt the barb long afterward. Yes, I've had some hurts in my day, and that's one of them.

Still, I remember the summer as happy, and it was. Only the other day I came across the drawings of the birds and the whole summer came back, clear as crystal. We never went back.

7

M R. BUCKLEY'S office was nothing like Miss Gray's. It was dim, untidy, with books piled everywhere. There was a silver inkwell on the desk, and on the wall past Mr. Buckley I could see an old engraving of a winter landscape, very gloomy, with moonlight only adding to the gloom. Mr. Buckley was a thin man with a big, bulging forehead, a small mustache, and nervous hands. He had a way of looking down, then looking up at you suddenly as if surprising you at something.

"This is difficult, Mrs. Boone," he said, "but I am not doing it on impulse. I would like to have you remove Philip from this school."

"Remove Philip from this school?" I said. "Why?"

"I do not believe this is the place for him. Nor that he is good for the school."

"You'll have to do better than that, Mr. Buckley," I said. "He's done good work here. I see nothing wrong with his report cards."

"Yes, he's a clever boy, and he can do the work without much effort."

85

"I'm afraid I don't understand you," I said.

He looked down, then up and straight at me. "He is incorrigibly dishonest," he said sternly. "Surely you know that, Mrs. Boone. He is a bad influence. I am proud of this school and I do not want it corrupted. Philip has what is known as charm, so that whatever he does takes on charm too. But dishonesty is not charming to me, Mrs. Boone."

"Did you ever think that perhaps the school had corrupted Philip?" I asked him.

"No, I never did, Mrs. Boone. And while we are always conscious of the necessity for building character, we are not a reform school. Would you like some specific instances?"

"I most certainly would," I said.

"There are too many, actually, to tell all. In sports, for instance, your son has no interest. We are not a school that goes in heavily for sports. We do not raise money because we have a fine football team, anything like that. But some sports are included in the curriculum. Philip has evaded almost every appearance in gymnasium or on the track. He has a sore throat, or he has presented a note from his doctor saying running is out for him because of a heart murmur. His doctor was one John Wade. We find no such doctor listed in your section, Mrs. Boone. He does not like swimming, so he induces a rash from some allergy—pork, I think—and so finds he cannot go into the pool. Skating he likes, and that is the only thing he likes. He never has a sore throat in the skating season. We have a very good printing press, and the letterhead on the note from John Wade was printed on that press—very cleverly, too.

"You have sent him a good many boxes, Mrs. Boone. We have good food here, but we have never objected to boxes of cake and cookies sent by the parents. Philip *sells* his supplies,

Mrs. Boone—oh, not for money, but for help in mathematics. So many problems for a slice of cake, and so on. He is quite capable of doing his own problems. Then he does essays for the other boys, for what recompense I do not know. He is clever at that, too. At first his work was unmistakable, but he has now become able to write essays that seem to come from the boys supposed to have written them. Literarily, that takes some doing. For instance, if a boy has some special interest, such as dramatics, he will twist the subject around till he can bring in something from the boy's own interest. Very authentic, these works seem, some even with misspelling such as certain boys would have, while Philip spells perfectly. But we happen to know the authenticity is false.

"You must see that this is something that creeps into the whole life of the school and is evil. I can have no more of it, though one cannot help liking Philip. That is the trouble: he is liked and admired by so many, and he should not be. I would like to help him, but I have never been able to reach him. He seems so open, but he is unreachable. I am sorry, Mrs. Boone."

I was angry through and through. Oh, I didn't doubt what he said. It was too familiar to doubt. I was angry at the school, at Mr. Buckley, at Philip, who had had everything given him, every chance, and who was trying to throw all away. I hate stupidity, and I hated it in Philip, though at the same time I loved him so dearly.

"You must realize that it will be difficult to get Philip into another school at this time of year, Mr. Buckley," I said.

"Oh, I didn't mean he must leave at this moment," Mr. Buckley said. "Of course he must finish out the year. But I felt you must be informed as to our intent."

"You make it quite clear," I said. "Philip is delicate and has been from babyhood. He has never liked violent exercise and I daresay he was frightened at being compelled to take track, football, such things. I do not excuse such evasions, but you must realize that boys cannot bear being different from their kind and might feel driven to have excuses other boys would accept. As to the essays, I do not take that as seriously as you seem to. I think perhaps Philip has literary ability—he likes to exercise it, that is all. I am not excusing him, but I understand him."

"That is more than I do, I admit," Mr. Buckley said.

"Did you ever look into the character of Jerry Baker?" I said. "Philip sees a good deal of Jerry Baker, and Jerry has visited in our house several times. If anyone has an influence on Philip, it is Jerry. I do not believe it a good influence."

There was a paperweight of amber glass close to Mr. Buckley's hand, and he picked it up and put it down with a thud.

"Jerry Baker, Mrs. Boone," he said, "is one of the finest and brightest boys in this school. Far from being a bad influence on Philip, he is the only one who has a good influence on him. He has protected him on several occasions, but Jerry knows quite well the difference between wrong and right. There is nothing amoral about Jerry, Mrs. Boone. You need have no fear that he will corrupt your son. I only pray it will not be the other way about."

"Perhaps I know the boy better than you," I said.

He looked as if he might say something sharp, but he said quite softly, "I'm sorry, Mrs. Boone. I'm truly sorry."

I stood up, proud as proud, and I nodded to him and walked out, straight as a ramrod. I only hoped I would not see Philip or Jerry. I went out of the building and almost ran into Mr. Abingdon. He looked like a frowzy bear, and he scowled at me, then smiled briefly and said, "How do you do, Mrs. Boone. And what are you doing at Endley?"

"I was called in by Mr. Buckley," I said.

"I see," he said, and he turned and began to walk with me toward my car. "Is anything wrong?"

"Depends on what you mean by wrong," I said. "I daresay it's a blessing, even if disguised at the moment. They are going to let Philip out of Endley at the end of term—sooner, if I can find a place for him."

"What a pity!" he said. "I've come to be very fond of Philip. I *am* sorry. But I understand his marks are very good."

"Yes, they are quite satisfactory. You weren't so fond of Philip when you visited us, Mr. Abingdon."

"No, that's true. I hardly knew him. I know him better now. He comes very often to the chapel to hear me play, and we discuss music. He is very knowledgeable about music—other things too. We have good discussions. I will speak to Mr. Buckley if you like. I don't know what the trouble is, but I will be glad to speak for Philip."

"I have no intention of leaving Philip in a school where he is unwanted," I said. "But thank you all the same."

We had come to the car now. I shook hands with him. I hadn't liked him much, but I must say he seemed like a friend that day.

"It is hard to be young," he said. "Terribly hard."

I said, "You have something there, I expect," got into the car, and drove off. I was shaken and couldn't say another word, and was sorry I had said anything to Mr. Abingdon. Yet he was kind. But I didn't feel he was right about youth—about

Philip's youth, at any rate. There was no reason on earth for
Philip to find life hard at this age. He had brains, looks, manners. People liked him—which was not always the case with
me in my girlhood, for I was too outspoken. He had no reason
to resort to tricks, to falsehoods.

That was a bad week. I didn't tell Jen this time of our trouble. That was the week John Deemster was made a judge.
Jen was very pleased and proud. It was then she told me about
her past. Odd—I'd met her sister, who was very much the society woman, with red hair, lighter than Jen's, and not half
her niceness. . . . Well, the day she told me about John she
said, "I've always been afraid it would hold him back—I
would, I mean."

"Good heavens, why?" I said. "Don't know how John could
have found a better wife. He doesn't deserve you."

She smiled at me, but in a sad way, unlike her. "My friend!"
she said, mocking a little.

"Well, I mean it."

"That's what I meant. But judges don't marry girls off the
stage, not often. It's held against them."

"Off the stage?" I said.

"Yes. I don't talk of it. I was as stagestruck as anyone ever
was. I was in *The Cherry Orchard* in a little theater, and then
I was caught. But I was in a chorus on Broadway. I had good
legs then." She was sitting by the hearth, and she suddenly
stretched her legs out straight in front of her and looked at
them with a small grin. "Not bad now," she said.

I was surprised, I admit. I could see her in *The Cherry
Orchard*, but not in the chorus. I laughed and said, "Well,
you've done a mighty good job of acting as the judge's wife,
I'll give you that!"

"But that's not acting," she said. "That's real."

I've never understood it, but it's true—her marriage was real to her. Pompous, stern man, John Deemster. He's always called me Mrs. Boone, though Jen's called me Cornelia from the beginning. Passionless as a stick, you'd say, to look at him. If you'd lived the life of the theater it doesn't make sense that you could be satisfied with a life with John Deemster. But now it made sense, the way she walked and talked, the dramatic way she'd come into a room.

"I call it mean you've never told me," I said.

"Yes, it was," she said. "But if I ever hurt John, I'd die."

So it wasn't the time to tell her about Philip—and anyway, I didn't want to.

Sometimes I went to school on Friday to fetch Philip, but sometimes he came on the bus, which stopped in the village. That week he came on the bus, and I drove down to the village to get him. I was early and sat there in the car for fifteen minutes. I was confused and didn't know what I was going to say to him. Then, when he got off the bus, Jerry was with him. Jerry was close to six feet tall now, Philip not quite so tall.

Philip always asked if he could have a guest, and I was angry. "I got Jerry to come!" he said quickly. "Isn't that good?"

It wasn't good at all, but there he was.

I don't remember all the boys did that week end. I know I didn't talk with Philip about school. But I remember the talk I had with Jerry. I was in my room, upstairs here, and there came a knock at the door.

"Yes?" I said, and the door opened and Jerry came in.

I was going over bills at the desk. Jerry came over and sat down in the window seat. He looked like a man now, not like a boy at all. He looked out of the window toward the woods across the road. Things were just starting to stir into spring—faint reds and greens everywhere. I like that view.

Then he turned around and said, "I don't want to interfere, Mrs. Boone, but I wanted to tell you you needn't worry about Philip—he's going to stay at Endley."

"That's where you're mistaken," I said. "He is not going to stay at Endley. But I must say I don't know how you knew anything about it."

"Well, I do know," he said. "But it will be much better if Philip sticks it out there. Mr. Buckley will give him another chance."

"I am not asking any favors of Mr. Buckley," I told him.

"No, of course not. But I'm sure you don't want to hurt Philip," he said.

"Naturally not. But it will hurt Philip to be at Endley on sufferance, won't it?"

"Not if he doesn't know it. Listen, Mrs. Boone, I see a lot of Philip. I told you I'd take care of him."

"And a good job you've done of it!" I said.

"Not a very good job. But I do try. It's harder for Philip than for some. I have music for a goal; Philip doesn't have any goal. He could do anything if he wanted to. He can write, he can act, he can sculp. But he doesn't do anything with a purpose. . . . But he ought to stay put, Mrs. Boone. You don't get a goal, wandering around from one school to another. You have to see things through. You see, it's different with me, because I got away from my folks. I really got away—inside, you know. Philip hangs on to you and his sister and his father. It would be better if he didn't come home week ends, Mrs. Boone."

"You think it's good to throw away your loyalties?" I said to him. "Yes, I might have known you would."

"But so have you," he said.

"Don't be impertinent!" I said.

"I'm not. I just like looking right at the truth. My mother drinks, Mrs. Boone. She's a confirmed alcoholic and is in a sanitarium right now. I see her occasionally, and I pity her too. But I can't spend my life with her—nor with my father, either. I'm going to be a composer, Mrs. Boone. I've known that for some time. You can't change your parents."

"Well, Philip has never attempted to change me," I said. "But of course I'm not an alcoholic."

He gave me a quick, cruel look. "No," he said. "But you're something of a vampire, Mrs. Boone."

I wanted to strike him. "You certainly are a good one to turn Philip over to!" I said. "You'd better leave, Jerry. I don't like this talk."

"Sorry," he said, but not as if he were sorry. "That was an ugly word. I just meant that you live on Philip and it's bad for him."

"Nonsense!" I said. "If that were true I wouldn't have sent him off to school, would I? If ever anyone was free, it's Philip."

"You don't know how strong you are," Jerry said. "I guess it was a mistake to talk with you. But I like Philip. I like him very much. I think—in the end—he'll come out all right, if you just let him go. You see, inside, he's *desperate*. He does things that aren't right because he's *desperate* inside."

"Desperate about *what?*" I asked.

"Oh, just everything. He isn't as strong as you, you know. He wants you to think he's special, and he *isn't* special yet. I told you before, he's mixed up. But Endley's a good school, and if he could hang on till he finished there, I think he'd be all right."

"*You* think he'd be all right! Do you know how like poppycock everything you say sounds? Desperate? If anything, Philip takes life too lightheartedly. If you're so fond of the truth, isn't it the truth that you aren't good for Philip? That he looks up to you because you're older, and that he gets some of his ideas from you?"

"I've just tried to look after him," he said.

"But I thought he ought to be left on his own. Wasn't that what you said? Isn't it just as bad for you to hang on to him as for me?"

"I don't hang on in the same way," he said. "I'm just his friend, that's all."

"I suppose you think I'm not his friend?"

He got off the window seat and stood there against the light, looking very dark and tall. I hated him.

"It's useless, isn't it?" he said. "But no, I don't think you're his friend. Only—please think of it, and don't let him leave Endley. It would finish him."

He walked out of the room without another word. I was so angry I tingled all over. I know I was more determined than ever that Philip should not stay at Endley, letting this dreadful boy who had cast off his own parents befriend him, look after him.

ALL THE NEXT two weeks I spent running around from this school to that, asking about chances of transferring Philip. I am afraid I spoke against Endley more than I should have. I had Philip's marks to present, and they made an impression, but there seemed to be some sort of brotherhood that stood firm about taking a boy from a different school. They all seemed to feel it was wrong to transfer a boy unless there was a very good reason. "Endley has not been a good influence on Philip," I said more than once. But they all looked skeptical, knowing that Endley had a fine reputation.

One man, a Mr. Masterson, said, "Mrs. Boone, are you sure Endley doesn't want your son to leave?"

"Certainly not!" I said. "Philip doesn't even know I am here, nor does anyone at Endley. I just don't like his surroundings, his friends, and I intend to see that he finds another school."

I had no real assurance from anyone. They would have to have a personal interview, perhaps an examination. No one just said, "We'll be glad to have your son."

I wanted to take Philip out of Endley at once, but I couldn't take him without a new school to go to, and so two weeks went by and the situation hadn't changed. Philip hadn't been home during that time. Then he was home, alone.

Spring was really coming on now. Leaves were more than a pale green or red haze. The grass was getting green, the red nubs of the peonies were showing, and the daffodils were coming out. Spring is the time I like best, with everything to do, new plants to set out, the first flowers showing, and the woods coming alive.

Someone gave Philip a ride home, so he got there sooner than I expected. He came down the drive and found me out at the tiny greenhouse I had fixed against the barn wall. I was taking out a flat of asters.

Philip bent and picked a daffodil and waved it to me. "It's spring!" he called out.

He had on his school jacket, and I said, "I thought you weren't supposed to wear that jacket off grounds."

He laughed, broke off part of the daffodil stem, and stuck the flower in my hair. "I got a chance to ride and couldn't take time to change," he said. "It doesn't matter."

"All rules matter," I said. "You go take it off. I can do with some help out here."

He took the jacket off, but made no move to change his clothes. "What is to be done?" he asked. "Where are you putting the asters?"

So he helped me till it was time to go in and get supper.

At the table I said, "How would you like to change schools, Philip? You aren't so fond of Endley, are you?"

"Why, of course I'm fond of Endley," he said. Then: "What school?"

"I'm not sure yet. A good one. I've been a little disappointed in Endley for several reasons."

"Oh, I guess it's as good as any," Philip said. An odd little frown went across his forehead, disappeared. He gave me that frank, loving smile, and said, "You don't like Jerry. But he won't be there next year, you know. He'll be going to college."

"I thought he was only a year ahead of you."

"No, he'll be through in June. So you don't have to worry about Jerry any more. I don't believe I'd like to change. Endley's all right."

"Nevertheless, I think you will change—if I can find the right school, that is. You shouldn't have any trouble getting in anywhere, with the marks you've had."

I got out the catalogues I'd collected and put them down on the table beside Philip. "Look them over and see if one appeals to you," I said.

He looked at them all, but when he was through he said, "Endley's all right. Really it is, Mother."

It made me angry to have him so blind to his own interests, not to know how near disaster he was. I had intended never to say a word about Mr. Buckley, just get him settled somewhere else, but I saw he was going to be stubborn and so I burst out with it.

"They don't *want* you at Endley, Philip. They *want* you transferred. You've done some very stupid things at school, and Mr. Buckley doesn't want you there any more. I don't know why you've been so stupid as to lie about your doctor, write essays for other boys, and all that, but it seems you have. Mr. Buckley doesn't like it. So don't keep saying Endley's all right. It isn't all right for you."

I wished at once I hadn't told him, for he seemed to go

limp and pale all of a sudden, and he looked at me with such pleading that I could have cried. Then he stood up, replaced his chair very carefully.

"I know," he said. "But it's all fixed up. I'd rather stay."

"Nonsense! They'll all hate you and discriminate against you. I don't see why you should even want to stay, and I certainly don't want you to."

"But I want to," he said. "I don't know what makes me do silly things—I can't seem to help it. But they won't discriminate against me. It's all fixed up."

"How could it be? And how do I know you won't do the same sort of things all over again?"

"Would it be any better if I did them in some other school?" he asked me.

Well, I admit now that he showed more courage than I did. But I couldn't bear it that he accepted their judgment of him, that he was willing to be humiliated for two more years in that school. I kept saying I wouldn't have it. I knew he'd done wrong but I thought he'd be better off to get a new start somewhere else. But I suppose he knew better than I did that you don't get fresh starts that easily. Yes, I think now he was right, but I didn't think so then.

Then he laughed out loud and said, "You ought to have seen my note from the doctor! It was really *good*, you know! And I do hate track. If it hadn't been me that did it, they wouldn't have gone snooping around like Scotland Yard, hunting for clues!"

"And if you go back I suppose you'll do track work like a lamb?"

"Oh, I suppose so," he said.

I saw what Mr. Buckley meant—he was *unreachable*. He

wasn't ashamed of what he'd done, and if he could have got away with it he would have. He had been unlucky, that was all. And he accepted their judgment and would obey if he had to. That wasn't normal. He wanted to stay where all the masters would eye him with suspicion and examine all his work to see whether he'd done it himself. I must admit I couldn't possibly have wanted that.

"Mr. Abingdon is going to let me play the organ," he said suddenly.

"*Is* he?" I said sharply. "Philip, you haven't heard a word I've said."

"Oh, yes, I have. You think I ought to leave Endley just because they caught me cheating. Buckley was really quite decent about it. He told me he'd asked you to take me away but he said he'd changed his mind. Well, that was decent, don't you think? It doesn't do you any good to get kicked out of schools. I'd rather not go to school at all, but, if I have to, Endley's as good as any."

"I suppose Jerry talked you into this attitude. It sounds about like him."

He gave me an odd look, more secret than usual with him, and just walked away. No, I couldn't understand him. I have an unholy pride, I suppose. Pride would have made me walk out of Endley and never look back. He made me think of Walter for a minute there.

I did try a few more schools, but without having assurances given me. I might have wangled it somewhere, but I didn't. I let him go back to Endley. Jerry wouldn't be there, and that would be good, I thought. Mr. Abingdon liked him and would look after him, I thought. I don't suppose anyone in the world has really been successful in looking after Philip. "Unreachable" is the word. I think I was quite firm that time, and yet I did find it funny that he had printed the note from the doctor on the school's press. Seems so, even now.

Jerry didn't come again that year, and I was relieved when June came and he'd graduated. I thought that that was the end of Jerry Baker and I was glad. That he had called me a vampire stuck in my head. I let Philip go, didn't I? I didn't keep him by my side. I'd have sent him to camp summers if he'd wanted to go. I didn't insist that he go to the Cape—he suggested it and wanted it. You'd have thought from Jerry that I was one of those possessive mothers that I hate as much as anyone. I believe in freedom and I tried to see that Philip was free as a bird. But I couldn't help wondering whether Philip himself had given a false picture of me just to make an impression on Jerry—whether he hadn't tried to match the picture of the alcoholic mother. Yes, that did enter my mind, but there was little I could do about it. Jerry was gone, and I breathed a sigh of relief.

As events have turned out, it was a false relief, but I didn't know it then.

A couple of things happened that summer. We stayed home. After all Philip had said about wanting to go back to the Cape, he never mentioned it. He took to helping Joe Hill, and Joe liked him in his sour fashion. "Gettin' useful, the kid," he said. But something interrupted his usefulness.

We aren't chummy with our neighbors, except for Jen. I've always been one to keep to myself, and I never get bored with my own company. I mentioned Lucia Adams a while back. She was a social creature, always having people out from town, giving cocktail parties, and so on. At one time she used to ask me, but I went once and that was enough. There was too much drinking, nothing sensible said. So I never went again. She had two daughters, one almost grown-up, one in her early teens. The older one, Susan, was just like her mother, but the young one was strange, not belonging in that family at all. She was homely; her hair looked stringy. She wore jeans and dirty old sweaters and sneakers—a very unprepossessing child with a sullen look. I took a dislike to her the first time I saw her, and as a matter of fact I believe her mother disliked her too and tried to keep her in the background. Susan was in a junior college somewhere—Bradford, I think—and the young one, Amelia, went to the Fairchild Day School for Girls. It was hard to imagine her in a fashionable school, I must say, but perhaps she wasn't quite so slovenly when she was away from home.

Philip rode his bicycle quite a good deal that summer. This is hilly country, not good for bicycles, but he went off just the same, pushing his bike when he had to, I suppose. Well, one day I saw two bicycles on the grass outside. Then I saw Philip sitting under the big maple, and this Amelia Adams was sitting cross-legged beside him, her head bent and her hair flopping forward untidily. Philip looked very grown-up beside her, very much a young man of the world. She was the last girl on earth to attract Philip.

After a while Philip came lazily into the house and out to the kitchen, where he made two big sandwiches and got out a couple of bottles of ginger ale, and then he wandered back to the maple tree. I could see him passing the sandwiches to Amelia, and they sat there eating and drinking, and I suppose talking, for a long time. Then she jumped up, got her bicycle, and rode away up the road. Philip lay there on the grass some time before he came in.

"And where did you pick up that ragged little orphan?" I asked him.

"Oh, she's not an orphan," Philip said. "That's Amelia Adams."

"Well, I know who she is. But she looks like an orphan. I've never seen a child quite so grubby looking."

"That's just because she's not a beauty like Susan. She's all right. She's quite interesting, really."

"It wouldn't make her any less interesting to wash her neck, would it?"

Philip laughed and said, "Oh, she's clean enough—it's just her sweater that's dirty."

"I must say I can't see how you'd stomach that. At least you've always kept yourself clean."

"It tells about that in Freud," Philip said. "What it means to be forever washing yourself, I mean."

"It means you're a civilized human being, I hope."

"No, it means something else, not so pleasant. But I like Amelia. She's interesting. Funny—right next door, and I've never known her."

I stopped right there, not wanting to set his stubbornness up, as I knew you could do if you went too far. I thought I'd bound him all the tighter to Jerry by criticizing Jerry, and I didn't want to make that mistake again.

I suppose he pitied the child, as he'd pitied Fanny before. He certainly couldn't have been attracted by her face. The next morning he announced, going out the door, "I'm going for a ride with Amelia."

"You haven't finished the weeding," I said.

"Well, maybe Amelia'll help me."

And not long after I saw them out kneeling by the flower-bed, weeding. She had on a plaid cotton shirt and had her hair pulled back with a ribbon, but she didn't look any neater or prettier. I decided I'd better do something about it, so presently I called out the window to them, "How about a snack?"

They came up to the house, and I got out sandwiches and milk on the kitchen table and I said, "How are you, Amelia? Are you going to let this lazy boy make a slave out of you? The weeding's his job."

"I don't mind," she said. She had a clearer, more intelligent voice than I'd expected.

"Well, you ought to. Don't let him impose on you."

"Nobody's imposed on me, Mrs. Boone. I *like* weeding."

"Do you, indeed? You're the first young person I ever heard say so."

"Come on, swig your milk down," Philip said. "And let's get back to the galleys. Don't mind Mother—she's got a sharp tongue but a heart of gold."

Amelia put her glass down and smiled at me, not so shyly as you'd have expected from her, said, "Thanks, Mrs. Boone," and they were off to the garden again. Well, I saw she wasn't quite so helpless and shy as I'd believed. But she certainly was untidy and ugly. They worked for an hour and then went off somewhere together.

In fact that got to be the pattern of that summer, what was left of it. Philip was with that girl most of the time. Sometimes they took books out under the maple and read to each other. A couple of times they played records, but mostly they were outside.

"I do pity that child," I said once. "It must be tough on her, having Susan for a sister. Susan is a real beauty, though selfish, I've always thought. But she's clever and she's lovely to look at, whereas this poor child couldn't be homelier. It's so kind of you to see she has a little fun, son."

"Don't run her down, Mother. I like her," Philip said. "She isn't so homely when you know her."

"I'm not running her down. But the fact remains that she's the kind who never has much fun in life. She'll have to take to books or art or something like that or she won't have any life at all. Lucia Adams could at least see that she looked respectable. I do pity her—but pity's not what you want to feel for anybody."

"I don't pity her," Philip said.

What upset me was that Philip saw that girl instead of Sally Erskine or one of his more attractive friends in town that summer, when he was just the age to notice girls. Philip has a streak of kindness in him that makes him like the most unprepossessing people. I'd certainly had samples of that. And he was kind to Amelia Adams, who truly was a pitiful child, with nothing to her credit at all so far as I could see. If he wanted to read poetry to a girl, it ought not to have been to that girl. Of course she worshiped him for his kindness—how could she have helped it, being what she was?

The other thing that happened was that I got a letter from Walter, a pretty cool letter, saying he was finding it impossible to meet his monthly payments and asking if he couldn't cut them in half for the present. Now I suppose I could have managed. I have done very well for myself, and yet everything cost so much, with Philip's schooling and all, and the house to keep up. . . . I said I didn't see how I could manage with less, that this arrangement of keeping up two establishments was his idea. He didn't answer, just sent the two hundred the next month as usual. I wondered if he were interested in some other woman and wanted a divorce, but he never said so. He didn't so much as ask how I was, or how Philip was—or mention Fanny.

Jen said one day late in the summer, "John saw Walter in town today. He had lunch with him."

"Oh?" I said. "Well, that was nice for them both."

"He's thin, John says, awfully thin."

"He always was thin. He's been whining about his monthly payments. But he's got a job, and he can pay as long as he has. I suppose he thinks it's easy for me to keep things going here."

"Don't be like that, Cornelia," Jen said. "Maybe you couldn't live with Walter—I don't know—but don't be vindictive. If you don't want him here—and you say you don't— why make him suffer so? He has Fanny to look after too."

"Actually he has it pretty easy, living with his sister," I said. "She dotes on having him and Fanny there, I don't doubt, never having been able to get a man and a family for herself. I'm not vindictive, but it's justice that he pay his share here, and I see no reason to let him off from paying. He's the one who wanted to leave, you know. I didn't ask him to."

"But John said he looked *ill*."

"He didn't say he was. He always had a fading-away look, you know he did. He liked looking delicate."

Jen got up, said she had to go.

"You think I'm too hard on Walter," I said.

"Yes, Cornelia, I do," she said. "But it's none of my business, is it?"

"No, it isn't. But I don't like you thinking hard thoughts of me."

Funny—I didn't. It was just that Walter pay his share, and

I wanted Jen to see that it was. I could see well enough she didn't, and it hurt me some.

She stood there at the door. She had on a yellow skirt and white blouse and looked very young. She said, "I'm afraid my thoughts are my own, Cornelia, just as yours are yours. But I like Walter; I always have. I won't talk about him any more to you, though, I promise you."

And she went off, not saying good-by. It upset me. But she kept her promise, or she did for a long time. She didn't stop being my friend. And maybe it's part of friendship that you are allowed to keep some of your thoughts to yourself. Yes, I expect it is. I know there are things about me Jen doesn't like, but she's hung on.

The day before Philip went back to school he asked for a picnic.

"I'd rather eat at a table," I told him.

He grinned at me and said he hadn't invited me, he just wanted food. He was going to hike along the creek with Amelia.

I didn't refuse the food, but I did say, "Well, I suppose it's too much to expect that you spend an hour or so with me before you go. And what on earth do you talk about? She doesn't look as if she had an idea in her head."

"Oh, she's got lots of ideas. She knows a lot about science. She's trying to explain Einstein to me."

He didn't answer my first remark, but when I gave him the basket he kissed me and said, "I would ask you too, but you'd be bored!"—and went off.

9

THERE'S a wind today, and the snow is lifting in gusts, swirling about, hitting against the window. Though spring's my time, I like winter too. I just like weather, I guess. On a day like this my house is snug, safe. The wind can do its worst, but it can't reach inside, because this house has solid foundations and can last forever. Whatever I may have lost, I still have my house. Mother was wrong to want me to sell it. Where would I go, what would I be, without it? This is where I take my stand against the world; this *is* my stand against the world. A room in some boarding house, an old folks' home, even if genteel enough, is not for me. I would die in such places. I have room to turn around, and good views to look at, and solid, fine chairs to sit in, and the best of china to eat from.

Things went well the next two years—or must have, because I remember them so little. I remember Jen coming in with a little straw-yellow sailor hat on. She pulled the hat off and sent it spinning down the room and said, "I loathe hats!" I remember Mr. Abingdon stopping for tea one day, just in passing. He said, "Philip has a fine, critical mind, Mrs. Boone," and he said, "Philip is fortunate in having you for a mother, Mrs. Boone. It was very far-seeing of you, if you don't mind my saying so, to insist that Philip finish at Endley." He thanked me in a polite, somewhat old-fashioned way for giving him tea, and took his departure. I didn't tell him that it had not been I who insisted.

I got a new suit for Philip's graduation from Endley. It was black linen, and I had a good black hat to go with it and an expensive blouse. Philip stood out in that class. There was no one so handsome, so appealing—no one. I had the feeling that I had insisted he stay there, that I was responsible for the way he walked forward across the platform to get his diploma. I was proud as Lucifer. He had honors in English and in Latin, of all things.

There was a reception after the exercises, and I met all the masters and their wives. Mr. Buckley shook hands with me, looked at me gravely, and said, "Shall we congratulate each other, Mrs. Boone?" He went on almost at once, before I had time to answer him.

The boys were all very polite, passing plates of sandwiches, tea, and so on. They did look well brought up, I must admit, though mostly I saw only Philip—so tall, smiling at this one and that, remembering Mrs. Buckley, who had a forsaken look.

Then he put a tray down, came straight to me, and said, "Come on. I have a surprise for you!"

And we walked down the room between the groups and the chatter, and there was Jerry Baker standing by a window. It seemed for an instant that it was that last time I had seen him, also standing against a window.

"Look who came!" Philip said.

Jerry put out a hand, said, "How do you do, Mrs. Boone? I thought I'd come to see if Philip actually got his diploma."

"Why wouldn't he?" I asked.

"I told you I would," Philip said. "Let's get out of here, shall we? Haven't we been polite long enough?"

We went out and walked around the school grounds, the three of us. Jerry was a man now—but then, he'd seemed that before he left Endley. He wasn't as antagonistic as he'd been the last time I'd seen him. He talked quietly about this and that. Then he said, "Have you decided on college?"

And Philip said, "Princeton."

"Oh? Good!" Jerry said.

Philip had applications in at several colleges, but he'd never said he preferred Princeton. "Princeton?" I said. "That's too bookish. I thought you wanted Yale."

Jerry laughed. He did so seldom, and it surprised me. "Well, Mrs. Boone," he said, "what is a college but books and professors?"

"It's a little more than that, isn't it? You have to get along in the world. Books don't teach you that."

"They don't? They help you get along with yourself. The rest follows, doesn't it?"

"I haven't any patience with introverts," I told him. Nor have I. "I lived with one for fourteen years, and I know what I'm talking about. It's just another word for bone selfishness."

"You're going to be awfully disappointed in me, then, Mother," Philip said. "I'm never going to be a doer, you know."

I remembered when I'd heard him talking to Andy that time, saying he was never going to be anything.

"Nonsense! You certainly are going to be a doer. Otherwise you'll waste your life, and there aren't going to be any wasters in our family."

"You think thinking is a waste?" Jerry said.

"Too much of it, unseasoned by work, is," I said.

Philip said, "Come home with us for overnight."

"I can't. I'm getting a bus in half an hour for New York. I still have three days of school. I just wanted to see it with my own eyes, that's all. You made it, kid!"

Philip gave him a strange look—not smiling, just a straight look that said a lot, but what the lot was I didn't know.

"Yes, I made it," he said. "Thanks for coming, Jerry."

Jerry went striding off away from us toward the bus stop. He turned and lifted a hand once, and then was gone. It hadn't pleased me to see him. In fact, it had made the day somehow less, not so shining and important as it had been.

"Let's go home," Philip said.

On the way he said, "I thought Mrs. Deemster was coming."

"Well, she was. She sent her congratulations. But the Judge forgot his medicine, and she went way into town with it. He could have sent out for more medicine if he really needed it, couldn't he? I don't like that kind of coddling. But she was disappointed. She's very fond of you."

"Oh, it's all right. I just wondered."

"I don't much like the idea of Princeton," I said. "There are good colleges nearer than Princeton. Even Harvard's nearer. But Yale—you could get home in an hour and a half from Yale."

"No one's taken me yet," Philip said. "Don't fuss. But Princeton's what I want, if I can get in."

"Why?"

"Oh—you'll like this—they don't coddle you. They make you work things out for yourself. Nothing's easy there."

"I thought you didn't want to be a worker."

"Oh, in school I don't mind. I don't want school *easy*."

"You contradict yourself with every sentence," I said.

"I know. I guess I do. I just mean I don't want to be a doctor or a lawyer or a chemist, anything like that. I want to know everything—then I'll see if I want to *do* anything with it."

"I've yet to meet anyone who knew everything," I said to him. "Learn one thing well and apply it, that's my motto."

"It's not mine," he said. "No, I'm going to know everything."

Now, that's a big order, to know everything. I laughed at him. It's stupid to turn yourself into an encyclopedia. Besides, he wasn't the type. "As you say, you haven't got in anywhere yet," I said.

We saw Jen's car in her driveway. Philip said, "Let me out. I want to say hello to Mrs. Deemster."

Philip was always considerate that way. He never forgot Jen. Afterward Jen said to me, "Philip was so sweet yesterday. Really sweet. He didn't hold it against me at all that I didn't come to see him graduate. He knew John was more important. Not many boys would, Cornelia. He does have great sweetness."

Graduations are milestones to boys. I don't think Jen should have disappointed Philip. But Philip was sweet—too forgiving, maybe.

I see I've left Amelia Adams out of those two years. I shouldn't have. Philip saw her often, but hardly ever at her house or his. They went off on their bicycles or on hikes, or in the winter they went up to Miller's Pond and skated. It was a

great annoyance to me, but I couldn't stop it. After a while I
didn't try to, knowing that Philip would cast her off as soon as
he got to college. One day I saw her dressed for school, and
she did look more respectable, even if far from pretty. She had
washed her hair and had on a decent suit, plaid, and a little
plaid cap. She even looked faintly interesting. But when holidays came she was as grubby as ever. Once I even saw her
walking barefoot in the road.

"I saw Sally in town. She asked after you," I said one day.

"Did she? I couldn't care less," he said.

"She's a lovely girl," I said. "Beautiful, you could call her."

"You could? She's stupid," Philip said. "Vain and stupid."

"Well, I must say she was a relief to look at after Amelia," I
said. I had tried not to say such things, but I couldn't resist it
that time.

"Mother, you wouldn't like it if I took cracks at Mrs.
Deemster every other minute, would you? Leave Amelia alone,
why don't you? She's *my* friend."

"Yes, I know. Your friend. You have picked some queer
ones, son—some very queer ones."

"They aren't queer to me. I like people to be *interesting*."

"Well, who doesn't?"

"You don't, do you? You want my friends beautiful. I *like*
Amelia. Her mother does the same thing—always puts her up
against Susan for comparison. She's worth ten Susans, you
know. She thinks. Oh, I forgot—you don't like thinkers, do
you?"

He didn't often speak to me that way, so he must have been
really upset.

"Well, I like time out from thinking to put on clean
clothes," I said. "I haven't stopped your having any friends

you like, have I? Not even Amelia. But you can't make me like her; I just don't."

"And when you just don't, you never do, do you? You can't see it's quite wonderful that she's as she is, out of that dreadful house. It's a horrible house, Mother, all full of social things, no one caring anything about anything except how to put on more dog than other people. You ought to like her, you know. She's like me in lots of ways."

"Heaven forbid!" I said. "That's just it—she isn't remotely like you. You always choose your friends out of pity, and pity is a sin."

"I don't pity Amelia. Why should I?" he said. "Oh, skip it, Mother. Just skip it."

Then one day that summer—well, first Philip was accepted at Princeton. He was pleased, though it was too far away to get home easily, and he did love his home. I suppose I should have realized why he was so pleased, but I didn't, not at first. And maybe what he'd said about the university was partly true. I don't quite know even yet.

This day came. I went into my room and Philip was sitting at my desk, looking through my papers, the bank book, and so on.

"What's this?" I said. "Those are my papers."

"Well, aren't we partners?" he said, just smiling at me.

"Of course. But I still handle the money, son. What are you looking for?"

"Just looking," he said. "Does Father send you two hundred dollars every month?"

"Yes, he does. Is there any reason why he shouldn't?"

"Couldn't we manage without it? You seem to have a lot in the bank."

"There's no reason why we should manage without it. He still has a responsibility, even if he shirks most of it. I've asked nothing else of him."

"I wish you didn't ask that," Philip said. "Would we starve without it?"

"Of course not. I'm a businesswoman, Philip. I could manage all right, but I don't intend to. We have a good many expenses, and you'll be going to college in the fall and will need a good deal, as you'll find out."

"It's half of what he earns, isn't it? Look, Mother, I'd rather not be obligated to him. Not at all. I'd rather not go to college than be obligated. I should think you'd rather not be, either, if you don't like him."

"I'm not obligated. It's my right. Do you think he ought to just go scot free?"

"But you said you didn't get along. You don't want him here, do you?"

"Certainly not. But a man must support his family. Not that he supports us, but it's right that he should try."

"I don't like it," Philip said. "I think we ought to be free from him, if we can afford it. And it looks as if we could. I just don't like the *feeling* of taking his money."

"Well, when you can support us we'll consider it," I said. "You don't need to feel sorry for your father. He's doing exactly what he wants to do."

"I don't feel sorry for him, not at all. I just think we'd be happier if we swung it all ourselves—if we could, that is."

I suppose he was flattering me in my capacity as a moneymaker. He made it seem that we were two against the world and that we didn't need to ask favors of anyone, least of all Walter. I did something I was at once sorry for. I wrote Walter that he needn't send any more money, that I could take care of us from now on. I even felt proud writing it, and I think now that was Philip's doing. I don't quite know how he did it, but he made it seem that he loved me more, that I loved him more, by giving up that two hundred a month.

Walter simply wrote, "Dear Cornelia, Thank you. Walter." That was absolutely all.

"All right, Philip. We're on our own from now on. I trust you're pleased," I told him.

He came over, bent down, and kissed me. "That's better," he said.

I missed those monthly checks. That's all they were—checks. But I had a queer feeling after they stopped coming. I'd certainly been grown-up a long time, but I had that feeling as of at last being grown-up. I felt older even a little frightened of not being able to pull it off, though I'd done all right so far. I don't seem to want to put that down, but I'm sworn to honesty and I want to remember everything. But I remember walking through the house, just walking all around downstairs, then coming up here, going into every room, just looking— feeling it was now all mine, with no strings attached. I was proud and yet I had a half-frightened feeling too. But I made out. Of course I did. And I had this extra sense of closeness to Philip, of our being bound together in our complete independence. That wasn't, I see now, so good.

I didn't take Philip to Princeton as I had to Endley. I just took him to the train at Cornwall Bridge. It was worse, that parting, because he wouldn't be coming home week ends any more. Thanksgiving was the first I could hope for. I saw him through the window, tall and fair, walking down the aisle. I saw him fling his suitcases up on the rack, and then he looked through the window at me, smiling like a boy, but looking so grown-up.

Jen was at the house when I got back, and I was glad to see her. "Well, he's off," I said.

"Yes, he's off. Really off," she said. "There'll be just a few holidays, then he'll be gone for the rest of his life. It's tough— but I'd go through it, to have a son of my own."

"I must say you're cheerful," I said. "You're not a crystal-gazer, though. I have a feeling Philip will never marry, that we'll have a good many years together in this house yet."

"Of course he'll marry."

"Most do, but Philip doesn't run true to form. He's the kind girls want, but he's very choosy."

"That's so, but he'll choose somebody, and you might as well get used to the idea. I should hope you wouldn't want it any other way."

"I want him happy, but whether it'll be with some girl, I doubt."

"Don't doubt. You might make it come out that way. These men who stick to their mothers aren't much good—really they aren't, Cornelia."

"Oh, I'm not stopping him from anything he wants to do. But what he will do remains to be seen. He says 'nothing'— but he's too smart for that."

"Nothing? What does he mean by that?"

"I wouldn't know. You ask him sometime. That's my worry —that he might not be useful. I've had my share of looking after the unambitious. But I shall see that he does something; you have my word on that."

I'M NOT MAKING it clear how close Philip and I were, in spite of those small deceptions of his. We did everything together when he was at home. We worked side by side in the garden. We sometimes took long walks. I have good long legs, and we used to swing along like two men. We didn't talk much then, just walked. He liked the furniture kept nice and didn't mind polishing the piano or the dining-room table, and sometimes he arranged flowers in odd but interesting ways.

When I wrote that about polishing, I remembered how when Philip was little he would say, "May I shine the teapot for you, Mother?"—and how carefully and anxiously he would rub away at the teapot. And I remembered too how he would say, "May I brush your hair, Mother?" And I would let him brush my hair and I'd see his face in the mirror beside me, so lovely and fair and loving. He always wanted to do things *for* me.

He and Joe Hill got on well, though Joe is a crude man, often profane, and I don't believe he's ever liked me much. He generally does what he's told to do, but he shows very plainly that he'd rather do it without supervision, and now and then

he breaks out and just doesn't do something at all. But by and
large he's been helpful, and I couldn't have got on without
him. He always brought manure, good horse manure, for the
garden and he saw there weren't any bare places on the lawn,
and every spring he made the flowerbeds as neat as a pin.

When he talked with me it was generally in grunts, but I've
often heard him going on in a steady stream to Philip. "Yeah,
now you take my ma, she hangs on like a bull pup, my ma
does. She don't think nobody's good enough for us boys—and
now we ain't boys any more, and who's going to look at us
now? Ain't nobody. But my ma ain't going to last forever, and
then where'll we be, Bill and me? Where'll we be, I ask you?
Got a crick in my knee, and I ain't going to be able to weed
forever. . . ." That's the way he went on, complaining about
his mother, about this and that. And Philip used to listen as
if he found Joe interesting, which he was not.

Once Joe thought he'd quit, but I talked him out of it.
That's when I heard him say to Philip, "Well, I get my pay
every week. I guess I'd be a fool at that. Might be worse. Better'n that Mis' Busby I worked for with her parakeet and all
—parakeet'd get out when she cleaned the cage, musta done
it ten times while I was there. Had to stop everything and
chase that damned bird. When Busby had his stroke—well,
now, that was one of the times the bird got away, and she had
me chasing the bird before I got the doctor in. Women! I guess
I been lucky, you might say. Anyways, this is better'n Busby
and that damned bird. Dogs is all right, but *birds!*"

Philip liked to talk over the books we read, though I've
never much liked chewing the bones of things. Read it and let
it go, I always say. But I'd talk with him, all the same. He liked
to talk about Darwin, how things got started, all that. "But I

read about Lamarck, and he said the same thing," he said. "I wonder why they listened to Darwin and not to him? Is that what they mean by being ahead of your time?" And after that he had a spell of fussing with flowers, seeing if he could breed a new species.

He brought home a book about Linnaeus, and it seems this Linnaeus did the same kind of experiments. "He must have got a shock!" Philip said. "After all he'd said about things never changing, being all put on the earth by God in just the same way they were today. That must have been a shock!"

But I say, "Here we are—let's go on from here." It seems a little silly to dig up those old theories. We can't do anything about it now, heaven knows. . . . Funny. I just had to stop and laugh at myself. Because isn't that just what I'm doing this minute—digging up the past to see what sense it makes? But I don't care whether we came from fish or birds or apes; I just have a curiosity about character. Philip tried to explain Einstein's theories to me—diluted by Amelia, I expect—but they seemed nonsense to me, I must say. My own time and space are real enough to me and for all practical purposes will do me to the end. I'm here in this chair at this table, typing away—no use telling me I'm not. Well, you might say my mind wanders into the past, but I don't believe that's what Philip meant about time. Odd, though, when you come to think of it, that I get to feeling I'm back there. I do forget I'm here in this chair—but that doesn't mean I'm not here.

Still, I liked to hear Philip talk, no matter what it was about. I'd even draw him out, just so he'd keep on talking.

Philip didn't even get home that first Thanksgiving, though I'd ordered a turkey and had the house as shining as a new silver dollar. He said he had some lab work to make up and he didn't think he'd better come. "The work's certainly tough enough," he wrote. "But I can do it, I think. You have to get through the first semester, though, and I don't want to fall down on anything. I know you want me to do you proud, Mother. I have a couple of good instructors, one who's a stinker, very distant, but clever. Actually, I like the stinker best. It's silly of teachers in college to be just mother-substitutes, don't you think? I've got a mother. I don't need to have someone else coddle me. You do coddle me, you know. But I like it. Still, this cold creature is good at his job. He ignores us, except in class, and then he's very scornful of us. But he knows his stuff, I'll give him that. He expects us to make up our own minds about the material. . . . I miss you. I'll be glad when Christmas comes. . . ."

I didn't like that remark about mother-substitutes. I suppose a lot of the teachers in the lower schools are just that, though. I canceled the order for the turkey and waited for Christmas. Philip wrote me every few days. He wrote good letters, telling a lot about his work, showing he missed me. I've always liked his letters, but of course it is true that they never showed what went on inside him, not at all. He has the mind of a writer, and he's able to make a letter say anything he likes. He tried to make them pleasing to me, and they were. Then he asked if he could bring Jerry home for Christmas. I said yes, not because I wanted him, and goodness knows how he could have had the face to come after what he'd said to me, but I did want Philip to have a happy Christmas, and I suppose I thought, too, that Philip wouldn't bother with Amelia Adams if he had someone as grown up as Jerry on hand. But I did think it queer that Jerry would bother with Philip any more. Philip must have seemed quite young to him.

"Hello, Mrs. Boone. Nice of you to have me," Jerry said—the very same thing he said to me the first time. But of course I hadn't asked him for his own sake, just for Philip's.

He held out his hand, and I took it, though I must say I didn't want to, and then he said, "Friend or enemy?"

I laughed and said, "Just behave yourself, that's all I ask." But it wasn't all I asked. I was his enemy. I wanted him somewhere else, not in my house.

He looked around and said, "It doesn't change. It's a beautiful house, Mrs. Boone. I like to be in it."

Now that was certainly more friendly than anything he had ever said to me, and I remember feeling soft toward him for a minute. He'd never seemed to notice the house, just took it for granted.

He walked over to the piano, ran a finger along the keys, said, "In tune," which was more like him.

He played different music that visit, queer music that I didn't like but remember still. I don't know who wrote it—maybe Jerry himself. The boys got the tree, but not from our woods. I never like cutting down my own trees. They trimmed it Christmas Eve, and Jerry said, "These ornaments look very old—and very German. Are they?"

"Yes, they're old and German," I told him. "My mother—"

Then Philip laughed and said, "Grandma got them at a bargain at some auction or other."

"She did not. They were her mother's," I said.

"Then we must treat them with great respect," Philip said. "I like this bird of paradise." They were very gay that night.

But on Christmas Day, Amelia came over. Philip phoned her and asked her to come.

"I doubt if Jerry will be entertained by Amelia," I said.

When she came I was out in the kitchen. I came in later, and Jerry was sitting on the stool, looking at her on the sofa with interest. "No," she was saying, "I'm going to MIT next year."

"Good heavens!" Jerry said.

She had taken off her coat but had her cap still on, that same plaid cap she'd used to wear to school. She had on a plaid skirt full of pleats and a white blouse and looked clean for a change. She'd grown some and looked a little different, not quite so hopelessly plain, though she's never been pretty. She has a narrow face, flat at the sides, and a wide mouth. But her skin is good, and her eyes too, I must admit. She has a clear voice that surprises you because in general she looks so shy.

"Will you play for me?" she asked suddenly. "Philip says you play like an angel. You couldn't play as well as Philip says you do."

"Oh, couldn't I?" Jerry said, and went to the piano and played.

When he finished, Amelia sat there with her hands pinching at her plaid skirt as if she had to hang on to something. He smiled at her with that not quite pleasant smile of his, always mocking a little, and she said, "You're better than he said." She got up quickly and put on her coat. "I have to go, so as not to spoil it," she said.

"Wait. We'll walk you home," Philip said.

"I don't want you to," she said firmly, and went to the door. The boys followed her, went out onto the side porch with her, leaving the door open.

"But I don't want you to come," I heard her say. "See you!"

"Wait. You're not polite," Jerry said. "You see, I know you

better than you think I do. Philip told me all about you in Philadelphia."

She didn't answer, and presently Philip laughed and said, "Well, go home, then!" And the boys came back into the house. Philip didn't even look at me.

"A very special girl," Jerry said. "You mustn't let her get away from you. She's the kind that will get clear away if you don't look out."

"And what's special about Amelia?" I asked. "I'm afraid I can't see it." I was trembling, though I'm not shaken easily.

"Well, she goes to the heart of things. That's rare, Mrs. Boone."

"You mean, she liked your playing."

"No, I mean she heard it," he said.

Well, no one could have helped hearing it. What did he mean by that? I wanted to say something about Philadelphia, but I didn't. I see the same pattern repeats itself over and over. The only difference this time was that I said nothing. I just felt a little older and was more conscious of this hurt.

One night they went to the city to a ballet performance. They took Amelia. "I think I'm going to invite that girl to come with us to the ballet you were telling about," Jerry said. "Would that be fun? You, too, of course, Mrs. Boone."

"Thanks, but I don't much like ballet," I said.

"Oh, come on, Mother. It'll be fun!" Philip said. "You know we wouldn't go off and leave you alone!"

"You would if it suited you to," I said. "Go, of course. It's your holiday. But leave me out of it. You may be sure I won't be lonesome."

They went, and without me, though afterward I wondered why I'd been stubborn about it.

They came in late, looking handsome and excited.

"Well, Miss Self-sufficiency!" Philip said. "Have you enjoyed your own company? You'd really have liked it, Mother." He came and kissed me and rumpled up my hair and asked if there wasn't something to eat.

While we sat eating Jerry said, "It was the first ballet Amelia had ever seen. That was what made it fun, Mrs. Boone. It makes you feel it's a brand-new world—instead of the old and tired one that it is."

I thought Philip had been watching the mail, though he pretended indifference, and then one day, the day before they went back, he did get a letter. He had gone out in the snow to meet the postman, and I saw him shove this letter in his pocket before he came in. I didn't let him get away with that, though.

"Who was your letter from?" I asked him. "I saw you put one in your pocket."

"Why, Mother, I don't have to pass around my own mail, do I?"

I'm not one to snoop. I think mail should be private. But I was curious—especially since he was evasive. "I just wondered," I said.

Then, right before my eyes, he took the letter out, opened and read it, never saying a word. He put it back in his pocket then, and said he had to finish his great creative effort and went up to his room. His creative effort turned out to be a little statue of some sort, I won't attempt to say what, for I don't know. It could have been meant to be a bird just taking off, or it could have been a rocket. He said it was a ballet dancer, but it wasn't.

"It has a real lift to it," Jerry said. "How would you like to have it cast?"

"Don't be silly," I told them. "It's nothing but a piece of clay."

"I'd like it," Jerry said. "An early Boone. Could I have it?"

He spent more time packing that piece of clay. You'd have thought it was a Rodin or something. And when they went he carried the box in his arms and made Philip manage the bags.

11

I DON'T SEEM to want to write of those college years, and
perhaps I don't need to. I remember them, but they run
together in a queer way. I don't let myself give in to loneliness, and I didn't then, except now and then when the day's
work was done and I had a chance to sit still and think. Then
the house would seem empty and I would have the fear that
Jen had been right, that Philip had really left forever. But I
didn't give in to that nonsense often. I kept busy. And of
course I did have Jen.

In that first year, toward spring, though, I got Bessie James
to come and help in the house. I could manage the house all
right, but I persuaded myself that I couldn't, and that I could
afford Bessie. I suppose I just didn't want to be here alone any
more. Not that I admitted that then, or ever. Bessie was in
her forties but looked hard as a rock—like a piece of wood,
rather, brown and solid, not an ounce of fat on her. She had
been "doing" for a lot of people, housecleaning, special washing, things like that, since she'd been in her teens. She knew
all the gossip of our neighborhood but didn't give much of it
out. She didn't much want to come steady, but I persuaded

her. She wasn't what you'd call the servant type, though she did work for others always—but she was proud, and that I liked in her.

"Well, Mrs. Boone, I thank you for the offer," she said, "but I don't think I'd like being in one place all the time. I'm used to taking a week off when I want to. I don't like being bound to anyone. No offense meant."

"You wouldn't be bound," I said. "You could have a week when you wanted it. But this is a big house and I don't feel up to taking care of it alone any more. I want it kept right, and you're the only one I could think of that I'd trust with my things."

That flattered her, and I saw her looking around at the furniture, respecting it, wanting a hand in keeping everything as it should be.

"I could try it, I expect," she said. "When I get Mrs. Lawson's spring cleaning done, that is. I promised her, and I wouldn't disappoint her."

She had the back bedroom, and I put a bath in back there for her, which ran to quite a bit of money. I didn't have to tell her what to do—she knew, having been in fine homes all her life. She had a good strong arm for rubbing furniture and she cleaned the silver once a week. She respected good china and never so much as broke a cup. Sometimes I almost wished she weren't so competent. There didn't seem much for me to do after Bessie came. Only in the fields of cooking and gardening was I better than she.

When I told Jen I'd hired her, Jen looked at me as if she were sorry for me, but she said, "That's the smartest thing you've done in ages." She had a housekeeper, too, a temperamental girl called Anna, who thought Jen would go to pieces without her.

"I'll turn out your son's bedroom today, Mrs. Boone," Bessie said. "So long as he'll be home in a week."

She didn't ask me; she just said she was going to do it. That was her way. I never did get her to ask me anything. I liked having her here, though I suppose I didn't like that characteristic in her that kept her always in charge, but her presence gave some purpose to all we had to do. And it was someone in the house, someone for whom I didn't have to be responsible, to whom I didn't have to talk unless I wanted to. She went to church on Sundays, but aside from that she went nowhere. She didn't seem to have any feelings for anyone, just feelings for pieces of furniture, china, and so on. That suited me fine, for I didn't want to be friends with her.

Then Philip was there. I hadn't told him about Bessie, and he was surprised but pleased enough.

"Am I supposed to call you 'Bessie' or 'Miss James'?" Philip said.

"It doesn't matter," Bessie said. "No one's called me Miss James in a month of Sundays and I don't know as I'd come to it. No, I guess Bessie is more practical, Mr. Boone."

"Well, then, I'll think of you as Miss James, but I'll call you Bessie," Philip said.

He said to me, "You've surprised me. I didn't think you'd ever let anyone touch your treasures. But it's fine. We can be lazy all summer, you and me, lazy as cats. That's what I'd like, not to do anything all summer, not even to think anything. I'm worn to the bone."

But he looked radiant with health.

"Bessie doesn't do the garden nor much of the cooking," I

said. "I haven't stopped working. When I do, you can be sure I'm dead."

"I like her," he said. "She's never been tired in her life. But I meant it about being lazy, Mother. I'm tired, and I'll just let Bessie wait on me all summer."

"You look it!" I said. "You look as if you'd never lifted a finger all year!"

"Oh, but you're wrong. I've worked like a dog. I've even earned a little pin money typing papers."

"Or writing them?" I asked. I shouldn't have said that.

He just laughed. "You misjudge me, Mother," he said. "Though I must admit I could hardly resist putting in a sentence or two as I typed. I could have done them better. You know, I don't remember learning much, but somewhere I must have learned how to spell and punctuate. Or maybe I was born knowing how."

"And what do you need pin money for?" I asked him. "I thought I gave you a generous allowance."

"Oh, for my dissipations. I can't expect you to pay for them, can I?" he said.

"You don't look as if you'd taken to drink," I said.

"Dissipations are private!" he said. "Do you think Bessie would throw me out if I got a glass of milk?"

I heard him laughing out in the kitchen, talking nonsense to Bessie. Then, to my amazement, I heard her give a dry cackle of a laugh. She was a stern, serious woman, no nonsense in her.

So he conquered her, as he did everyone.

"I hope Jerry didn't waste money getting that silly statue of yours cast," I said at supper.

"Why, yes, I believe he did," Philip said. "But it's his money. He's rich, you know."

"Jerry?"

"His father is a Croesus. No fooling. Didn't you know that?"

"No, I didn't. He seems like a tramp, loose on the world."

"Jerry? Is that the way he looks to you? But he's had a hard time, all the same. His father has no respect for music—he works at it all the time, trying to get him away from music. But Jerry's strong—only it's a strain."

"Well, I agree with Jerry's father, I'm afraid. Unless you're big, you don't get anywhere. And Jerry's not that big."

"Oh, he's big enough."

"There are hundreds of little musicians, thousands, but how many have you ever heard of? Just a handful."

"I've heard of quite a few, actually. You'll hear of Jerry in time, you may be sure. Stop disliking him, Mother—he's my friend."

"Yes, I've heard you say that before—Jerry and Amelia and Mr. Abingdon. I think you might have done better, Philip."

"Oh, they'll do. I'm like you, Mother, I don't like many people. You don't begrudge me three, do you?"

"I don't begrudge you anything. But you're too good for those three—don't bother to defend them, I know exactly what they're like. One's a lump of a teacher of physics, not very bright, not very polite; certainly you can't call him successful. One's a plain, untidy girl who wants to be a scientist, of all things. She's not only homely, she's sexless. And Jerry— well, his being rich doesn't change him; it only makes him out a greater fool than I thought him, and that was great enough."

He looked at me as if he were studying me, and it made me nervous. Then he said, "But darling, suppose *I* wanted to write a book or something—you wouldn't call me a fool too, would you?"

"It's certainly not what I'd want for you. I'd never call you a fool, for you aren't one. But I do think writing is foolish. Your father had an urge to write a book. In consequence he's never done anything you could call important. He's stuck to a minor job because his mind is always elsewhere—or was. How do I know where his mind is now?"

"On the book," he said quietly. "Do you know, you've never mentioned that book to me before? Why haven't you?"

"Why should I have? He hasn't written it, only dreamed about it. Life's not for dreaming. The first thing you know, you're dead and have nothing but the dreams."

"You're not as tough as you sound, Mother," he said. "And I'm a dreamer too, you know."

"Not that kind, I hope. And didn't you say you'd been working like a dog?"

"Oh, I have. I have. But didn't you ever think that maybe it's the dreams that keep us going? You must have had a dream or two yourself."

"No, I never went in for that sort of thing. I do the day's job, and that's it. If I'd been mooning around all these years, do you think you'd even be in college?"

"Maybe not. Was that your dream, sending me to college?"

He annoyed me and maybe confused me a little too. I'm just not a dreamer. I hadn't hoped for college for him, I'd just seen that he got the chance, that's all. I had taken it for granted that he would get a good education. Maybe I'd longed for this house as my own—I don't know. Maybe I'd wanted friendship and companionship with Philip. But I wouldn't say they were dreams; they were just things I worked at year in and year out. And it bothered me to have Philip ask if I'd think him a fool if he wrote a book. It does make a difference, I admit, who has the dreams. I suppose I would have been proud of anything Philip chose to do, only I did want him to *do*, not dream about it. I always wanted that for him. I didn't want him to be *nothing*, as he'd said, when a child, he was going to be. I didn't quite like it that he thought I would forgive him anything, coddle him whatever he did. That's what he thought, though, that was plain. And I didn't like the look he gave me when I said that about Walter—as if I'd cheated him somehow, by not telling him Walter wanted to write. What difference did it make?

Amelia came home a couple of days after that.

I was annoyed with Bessie that summer because of the way she waited on Philip. She seemed to look on him as one in a decline, which he certainly was not. She'd bring him cold drinks, his sweater, the mail, as if he didn't have two feet of his own. "You are my angel of delight, Bessie," he said to her once. She even waited on Amelia too.

The only thing Philip did all summer was drive the car and pick huckleberries when they were in season. A couple of times he was gone all day in the car—both times he had Amelia with him.

"Look here," I said to Bessie, "you're coddling Philip too much. He's perfectly able to look after himself. Don't wait on him."

"He's overdone, Mrs. Boone. He's studied too hard, I expect. He's still a growing boy, you might say. I don't mind doing things for him."

"A growing boy! I should hope not. He's got his growth, Bessie. And you can be sure he hasn't weakened his constitution by overstudy. He just likes being lazy and having someone fuss over him. I never found it a good idea to encourage laziness. So no more of it, please."

She acted as if she hadn't heard me. She went on doing just

as she pleased. His marks that year weren't so impressive. He passed, and that was about all you could say. He'd shown what he could do at Endley, if he wanted to, so I couldn't take those marks as evidence of hard work.

Now I didn't have confidences with Bessie, and it startled me to have her say one day when I was in the kitchen with her, "What's ever become of your little girl, Mrs. Boone? Or am I speaking out of turn? I've always felt right sorry for you, his taking her off that way."

"She's in good hands," I said, as cold as could be, and walked out of the kitchen.

The next time I saw her she said, "I *did* speak out of turn, Mrs. Boone. I'm real sorry. I don't know what got into me, not being one to pry, Mrs. Boone."

"That's all right. Forget it," I said.

But I didn't forget it right away. It probably helped me in a way, thinking folks felt that way about Walter's departure. They must have thought he ran off, really stole Fanny. They felt sorry for me.

But it didn't end there. Bessie was just upset because she thought she'd upset me—rubbed salt in the wound, you might say. She went to Philip and must have told him all over again about not meaning to pry, about feeling she'd hurt me, and she ought to have kept out of it and all, and Philip came in to me as I was sitting in the living room doing the needlework cover for the piano bench.

He touched the colored part of the cover, said, "That's nice. But it doesn't seem in character for you to sit doing it."

"I like to do everything, at least once," I said. "I've made one bedspread, one hooked rug, and now I'm doing one piece of needlepoint."

He sat on the stool facing me. "And what have you been telling Bessie?" he asked. "About Fanny?"

"Nothing at all. I said she was in good hands. That's absolutely all. And I don't like people prying into my family affairs."

"But she thinks you're sitting here like Niobe or somebody, mourning your daughter. Or not sitting, but working yourself to the bone so you won't have time to mourn. Which doesn't happen to be the case, does it?"

"I don't like prying from you any more than from anyone else," I said.

"I thought we were partners," he said in that appealing way that always softens you.

"Well, I daresay I tell you as much as you tell me. And what I do tell you can count on," I said.

"And what do you mean by that, darling? Look, Mother, don't get that look on—I don't like it, it makes you someone else. But I don't think you can count on what you say about Fanny. Bessie's got the wrong idea from somewhere, that's sure. For you never have mourned over Fanny, have you?"

"No more than natural. Of course I've been hurt, but I don't hug my hurts. And Fanny is certainly happier where she is than she would be with me. I cancel my losses, which you should be grateful for."

"Oh. Then it was a loss?"

"I don't like inquisitions, son."

"Just answer this one thing, Mother—how do you know she's happier where she is?"

"She's with people of her own kind. We rubbed each other the wrong way, even when she was tiny."

"I see. Yes, I thought so. Then it wasn't a loss."

"I didn't say that."

"No, you didn't, did you? I don't suppose you ever will. Did you ever think it might be a loss to me? But no, you never did, did you?"

"Oh, don't go dramatic, Philip," I said. "The truth is that she was a baby when she went, and you were a big boy. If you hadn't deceived me and gone to see her, you wouldn't even have remembered what she looked like."

He stood up. It made me nervous, having him standing there so close, looming over me. Then he laughed, said, "Anyway, you're consistent, darling," and went away.

Now this is what I can't understand: if he felt that way about Fanny, why has he seemed to love me and want to stay with me all these years? That's what's not consistent. Has he thought I'd give him more, or what? Now he hasn't seemed to be greedy, and what I've given, I've given freely. But of course he wouldn't have had so much if he'd been with Walter. And maybe Walter wouldn't have forgiven him so easily for all the mistakes he's made—I don't know. No, he isn't greedy, that is sure. He's given things away all his life, more than he should have—though of course a lot of the things were what were bought with my money. But he's been generous. It's a puzzle, especially the way things have turned out. I'd swear he has loved me, in his way. He's so tender when he wants to be, so loving in sweet ways. Some mornings he used to bring a breakfast tray up to me, though I'm not one to dawdle in bed. He'd have a little vase of flowers on the tray, sometimes a little poem. No, it doesn't come clear, the reason for anything. I ought to be able to think it out.

12

Yes, I can see I wasn't firm enough in those years. I have been firm about everything all my life, except Philip. I suppose that's what happens to you if you love anyone enough. I should have broken up the friendship with Amelia by hook or crook. I should never have allowed Jerry Baker in the house. I should never have allowed Philip to get away with his lies. I don't know how often he went to Philadelphia, where Jerry was studying music. He never said he went at all. Perhaps the money he earned typing was for those trips—perhaps he felt it wouldn't be honest to use my money for deceiving me. I don't know.

One day I saw something that really disturbed me. Philip and Amelia were out on the terrace reading poetry. Amelia wasn't the sort of girl you would think would like poetry. Well, I guess that's wrong. She certainly liked music and the ballet, or she seemed to. Maybe it was just an act to make the boys accept her. Anyway, they were out there, and I went through the dining room and saw them through the window. I saw Philip lean over and just run his finger along Amelia's cheek, like an artist learning a curve. It upset me. There was something too intimate about it. After all, Amelia was still a child, not even in college yet. Of course she would be flattered to have a boy like Philip notice her. But I gave her a thought, then—for herself, I mean. There wasn't any doubt at all in my mind that Philip would discard her when the right time came, and I thought, He's going to hurt that girl. He's going to hurt her bad. I saw her as if she were a woman, like myself. I suppose I pitied her.

Then the summer was over and Philip was gone.

Not all my thought was with Philip, though I see it begins to seem that that was the case. I thought a good deal of Jen that year too. Something strange happened to Jen that fall, though at first it seemed more a joke than anything else. In October, it was, when the leaves were falling fast, that Jen came up the hill one afternoon and into the house without knocking. I looked up, and there she was, standing by the door. She had on a corduroy jacket of very dark brown and a brown skirt. Her red hair was blown about. She held a letter in her hand and she laughed and said, "I'm so excited! I'm being *blackmailed!*"

She came over and dropped the letter in my lap. It said: "Would you like the Judge to know about the winter you spent on Peach Street? If you wouldn't, send a line to Box 128 and perhaps we can arrange something."

"That's so funny—so awfully funny," she said. "That was one of the most innocent winters of my whole life. . . . Did you ever get a *blackmail* letter?"

"I never did," I told her. "And you'd better slap this blackmailer down fast. Have you told John?"

"It just came. No, and I wouldn't tell John. It's the kind of thing he'd worry about. . . . The funny part is that it's about *Peach Street*. I was so poor that year—I didn't have a job yet—

and this girl Pansy said I could bunk in with her. Well, there was Jean, he lived with us, too, in a way. He slept on a couch in the living room. Probably, to an outsider, it might have seemed odd, but, oh, we were so proper, so *innocent!*"

"Well, don't answer it. Tell John and forget it."

"I don't think I can just forget it. I don't want anyone going to John with some lurid, even if imaginary, account of that winter. Nor do I want John worried about it—no, I'll take care of it somehow."

"Don't you dare pay him anything! That would really be the finish of you!" I told her.

"I haven't anything to pay with. John's incredibly generous, but I don't have much money. I may come to you for a loan, if worst comes to worst." But she said it jokingly.

"You'd better not!" I said. "I wouldn't give you a loan for that purpose. You're silly not to show it to John—he knows you were on the stage and poor and consorted with strange characters."

"Look, Cornelia, John's a busy and an important man—and he's got a bad heart. I am *not* going to tell John. . . . You know, it begins to seem not a joke. I was so startled, and it seemed like something out of a cheap novel—I laughed all the way up the hill. It begins not to seem funny. . . . Oh, well, don't give it a thought!"

She stuffed the letter in her pocket and went off, still grinning, down the hill.

After a while I called her up and said, "Look, Jen—let me take care of that letter. I'll put the fear of God into whoever it is!"

"Oh, I'll manage!" she said. "Forget it."

I thought once that maybe I ought to have been freer with

offering her a loan, even though I thought there should be no need for one, that maybe I ought to have said I'd give her anything I had, but she had been so amused that I hadn't at first taken it too seriously. And the more I thought of it, the more I thought that it was stupid to protect John to that extent. John's heart wasn't as bad as all that. I considered going to John myself, but I knew he wouldn't take it kindly, coming from me. He's always called me "Mrs. Boone" in a distant sort of way, and even when they have proper dinner parties, with John's important, stuffy friends from town there, they never ask me. Odd, Jen's and my friendship seems quite apart from John. She asks Philip and me there sometimes, but not with other people.

I didn't think Jen could possibly be fool enough to let herself be blackmailed, she's so far from being a fool about anything else. But when I mentioned the matter later she just made a little face and said, "Skip it! Everything's under control."

"Then you answered him?" I said.

"Yes, I answered. But it's all right—I don't want to talk about it."

So I didn't pry any more. But she had a look the next couple weeks as of not finding anything so funny as once. Then she was unnaturally gay for a week.

The very day Philip was coming from school for Thanksgiving, with Jerry, she came up. I was making mince pies and she came out to the kitchen and sat by the table.

"I'm frightened," she said suddenly.

"Frightened? About what?" I said.

"I'm really in a mess now. I must have been out of my mind. . . . I'm really sensible ordinarily, wouldn't you say? I gave him my diamond brooch."

I put the pies in, and sat down at the other end of the table.

"Yes, you must have been out of your mind," I said. "And of course you've kept it all from John."

"That was the whole point," she said. "He gave me a paper, saying that was the end of it. He signed his name—Anthony Besten. Phony name, wouldn't you say? But still, he signed it. I thought I could just say I had no money, that his efforts were useless. But of course he knew that John wasn't poor. And I made the mistake of wearing the brooch. Oh, I *was* a fool—but I put on that brooch automatically with my suit. . . . He even gave me tea and cakes. Very smooth, very polite, he was. Like a modern stage villain. I feel as if I'm in a nightmare, Cornelia. It simply can't be true."

"You have to tell John, and at once."

"I can't. You must see that if I could have once, I can't now. Why did I give him the brooch unless I had something to hide? Wouldn't you think that? . . . But you see, it can't go on, because I haven't anything to give him. My pearls aren't real— he couldn't get much for anything I own. . . . I know you think I'm coddling John, but John's my whole life, Cornelia. I cannot, *cannot* have John hurt."

"You could go to the police."

"It would get in the papers. No, I'll have to stop it some other way. In the movies, I'd shoot him. . . . Did I say I was innocent back there on Peach Street? Well, it looks as if I were still innocent, doesn't it? I can't seem to get it through my head that such a thing could actually happen to a person like me. I was haughty enough, brave enough, when I went to see him—but now this new letter has come, I'm frightened."

"We'll fix it, somehow. We have to."

"You can fix almost anything," Jen said, "but somehow I don't think you can fix this."

The boys came as she walked down the path to the drive. I saw them pause, shake hands with her.

"What's the matter with Jen?" Philip asked at once.

"*Jen?*" I said. "Aren't you getting familiar?"

"I'm grown-up now," Philip said. "I feel like her contemporary. But what's the matter with her?"

"Nothing. How are you, Jerry?"

Then Philip took Jerry off to meet Bessie. But when we were at the table Jerry said, "But what *was* troubling Mrs. Deemster?"

"Isn't that her business?" I said.

"Ours too," Philip said. "She looked right through us."

"She has other things on her mind than you boys, perhaps," I said. "We have our small dramas, even on this back road. Jen's being blackmailed."

"I don't believe you," Philip said. "Jen?"

"Blackmailed for what?" Jerry said.

So I told them the whole thing, as much as I knew of it. Fantastic, Philip said it was.

"She must love the judge very much," Jerry said.

"Yes, goodness knows why," I said. "He's not a lovable man."

"Some people are like that. They love till death do them part," Philip said.

I told them I'd made up my mind to see the judge myself, but Jerry said he wouldn't do that, that there must be some more subtle way to handle it. "Leave it to us. We'll do something about it," he said. But I told them the judge wasn't as vulnerable as Jen thought, that he'd been preserved in vinegar and would last till he was a hundred.

"Still," Jerry said, "if she loves him that much, nothing must happen to her love. Nothing."

"I never thought you were sentimental, Jerry," I said.

"Do you have to be sentimental to believe there's such a thing as love?" he said. "I grant it's rare."

Then Philip lifted his cup, put it down and said, "I ought not to have called it fantastic—Jen's always seemed like someone in the middle of a drama to me. Everything she does stands out somehow. I remember the time she gave me the Toby jug. It was a very *special* jug. And that yellow dress she gave Fanny once. It had a bow in the back, very crisp. Remember that, Mother? And those picnics she took us on—she made them into *events*, if you know what I mean. I remember thinking once when I was first at Endley, 'Why, she's in love with Father!' I don't know why I thought it exactly, because of course she wasn't. She liked to talk about books with him, that's all. She's always been faithful to the judge, that's sure. Still, she *did* seem the kind of person things happen to."

Funny, I suddenly saw Fanny in the yellow dress. She wasn't more than three. It was yellow organdy, and it made a stiff little flare, and Fanny was pleased with it. It was one of the fanciest dresses she ever had, for I didn't think she was made for fussiness and always dressed her plainly. I thought it incongruous on her, for she had those serious gray eyes and straight hair, but I can see her sitting on the stool with her knees showing and the yellow skirt sticking straight out. . . . I can see Jen too, sitting talking with Walter. Not that she was ever in love with him—*that's* fantastic—but she did talk books with him, and Walter would look animated and would talk a lot, more than he ever did with me. He would have a book in his hands, keeping the place with a finger. He had long,

scholar's hands, fine but useless. I remember once Jen came
in with sunglasses on. Walter started talking with her and suddenly he said, "Take those glasses off. I'm talking to a ghost—
your life comes through your eyes, Jen." That was a bit personal, wasn't it? And a few times he walked down the hill with
her, but just in a neighborly way. . . . It was like Philip to
have said that, trying to make me uncomfortable. He knew
very well it wasn't true, but he knew I'd think about it. I remember it even now.

Right after breakfast Friday morning Jerry piled up some
records, picked up the player, and said, "We're off to begin our
campaign. Ready, Phil?"

"We're good at conspiracies. Don't worry, Mother!"

I felt guilty and didn't want them to go. I didn't want Jen
to think I told all about her affairs. Jen must trust me. They
didn't trouble to tell me the plan of their campaign. They
spent that afternoon and all day Saturday in town. To make it
short, they found Jen's brooch in some second-hand shop and
Jerry bought it back for her. Nor was that all. But first Amelia,
of whom they'd not said a word and, I hoped, had forgotten.

They hadn't forgotten her. Amelia had had a touch of flu.
Sunday Jerry said, "Well, Amelia must be over her bug by now,
don't you think?"

"I thought you had come to your senses and had picked
someone your own age," I said.

"Oh, Amelia is as old as I!" Philip said.

"She's seventeen or eighteen, that's what she is," I said.
"And as plain a girl as I've ever laid eyes on."

"Plain? Amelia?" Jerry said. "She's going to be another Nefertiti."

"Whatever—whoever—that is," I said.

"Don't pretend to be such a lowbrow," Jerry said.

Philip ran upstairs and came down with a book, hunted through it, and brought it over to me. "There she is— Nefertiti," he said.

Now Amelia didn't look remotely like this statue of a woman. Well, she had a long face, flat on the sides like that, and maybe a longish neck. That was all. This woman was a queen, it seems, and looked like a queen. I always thought of Amelia sitting out there under the tree, with her hair so stringy, flopping over her face, her sneakers and sweater dirty—or in blue jeans, streaking off on her bicycle.

"Yes," Jerry said, "that's our Amelia."

"Fiddlesticks!" I said, and shut the book.

They went off to Amelia and I went out to talk with Bessie.

"That's a nice friend of Philip's," Bessie said, "but I feel kind of sorry for him."

"Well, you needn't," I told her. "Jerry Baker does exactly as he pleases. He's got money and talent, or thinks he has. There's no need to pity him."

"It's just something about the way he looks," Bessie said. "As if he'd had a hard life."

The boys were supposed to go back that day but they stayed over Monday. They said they had "unfinished business." The truth is, they saw this Anthony Besten, as he called himself. They were at the age to like conspiracies but they didn't seem too pleased with themselves after they'd seen Besten. They didn't even want to talk about it. "We're smart cookies," Philip said. "But we're just not slippery enough."

Jerry frowned and said, "We were suave and tough, as in the best European spy drama—but he was more suave, tougher. He quoted *Voltaire*. We think we frightened him, a little. How

much, we can't say. He promised to lay off, but promises come
easy to him."

I hadn't seen Jen since the day before Thanksgiving, but
after the boys went Tuesday morning, I walked down the hill.

"Well, I hear the boys have been playing cops and robbers,"
I said.

"No, they were quite serious about it, bless them," Jen said.
"Only now I have to pay Jerry back for the brooch. It's going to
take some doing."

"Forget it—he's rich."

"I couldn't do that. I'm terribly glad to have it, anyway. . . .
Cornelia, I don't think they succeeded. . . . I don't quite see
the end of this nightmare. You know how I live—in an orderly,
sane fashion. I can't see how I ever got into this disorderly,
insane business. It seems real only in the way dreams seem real.
I sit here and look around this room and know I am awake, and
that that is all just something that happened in the night.
What seems strangest of all is the way I *laughed* when that first
letter came. It seemed so *funny*. Now I find myself just waiting,
all the time waiting for the next thing to happen."

Then she grinned at me and said, "Stay to lunch, will you?"
I stayed and Jen told funny stories all through lunch and we
laughed as if we were schoolgirls and never mentioned Anthony Besten again that day.

13

LAST NIGHT I wrote late and when I turned out the light the moonlight was making the snow bright as day. The pines stood out black, except for the snow on the branches, and all the maples seemed limned with moonlight. I am not a poetic woman, but I have moments of feeling almost poetic about this land, this house. Last night was one of them. It washed all over me, through me, this feeling. There's a stone in the wall along the road that says 1829. It makes me feel good that that wall has endured so long. I want this house to endure forever. I felt, watching the moonlight, that I too would endure forever. In the daylight I know that was silly. Twenty years more, if I'm lucky—probably ten or twelve. The truth is that I think it has aged me, writing all this down. I want to do it, and yet I get this notion that this is the final summing up. I'm strong, strong as an ox. I don't even have twinges of arthritis, and my heart goes along steady as a watch. There's no sign of hardening of my arteries. No, it's nonsense, this feeling of age as I write.

There is a shadow over the next years. I would skip those

years if it were not that it seems important to tell of the shadows.

The business of the blackmailer wasn't over yet, but I didn't know it for some time. Jen never talked about him and the whole thing began to seem a fantastic interlude in our outwardly quiet lives. Jen got thinner that year, and I did notice that. I was worried about Philip right then, or perhaps I would have noticed Jen's thinness more. He didn't pass his mathematics course in June. He asked me whether it wouldn't be possible to send him to summer school for a make-up course. He said he was sorry, he'd tried, but he didn't like math.

"To tell the truth, Mother, I got off to a bad start at Miss Gray's," he said. "And I never caught up at Endley."

"Nonsense, I had you tutored before you went to Endley," I said.

"Yes, I know. But you have to be automatic about multiplication, all that. I scraped along at Endley, by hook or crook— crook, largely. But that doesn't work out at college. You can do it or else . . . I am sorry. I wanted to be here with you this summer. You don't know how I wanted it!"

So I let him go, comforted by that remark, I suppose. But before he went Amelia Adams was here almost constantly. They discussed, of all things, mathematics. She brought books over, and they would sit out on the terrace, leaning over the wicker table there. She looked like a schoolteacher, that's sure. I believe it annoyed me, thinking that she knew more than Philip about something. But of course his knowledge was much broader. If you stuck to one thing, as she did, of course you were more proficient in it. I see that contradicts something I once said to Philip.

Bessie would bring them milk and cookies. "He'll wear his brains out, that boy will," she said.

He also made a little clay head of Amelia before he went back—"went," I should say. It was one of those elongated things that some find charming. I don't see much point in distorting human features in art. But here was this very long head, a longer neck, hair not upswept like a queen's at all, but hanging down, flat and straight. It was ugly, but Philip liked it. I saw Amelia looking at it, puzzled, as well she might be. Then I saw her give Philip a smile that surprised me. She was always so sullen-looking, but this was a warm, delighted, grateful smile. For what? That monstrosity of distortion? No, I don't understand the young. How could she feel flattered, grateful, for that?

Well, he went. One day while he was gone Amelia came down. She ordinarily kept out of my way, but this time she came to see me. She brought a pailful of huckleberries. She wore blue jeans, her shirttail hung out, and there was a huckleberry stain on one cheek. She looked like a gamin. "Mother isn't in the mood for making a pie. I thought maybe you or Bessie would be," she said.

"Yes, we would be," I said. "Thank you."

I thought right off that I'd make a pie and take it down to Jen.

"Sit down, Amelia. I'll empty the pail," I said.

When I came back she was still standing. "I'm too dirty to sit on anything!" she said. Then she surprised me by saying, "Is Philip really at Princeton, Mrs. Boone?"

"Why, of course! Why do you ask a thing like that?"

"I don't think he's there."

"Well, he is." I went and got a postcard I'd had from him.

He'd said he was going to work hard and wouldn't write letters. "Here you are," I said. There was some campus view, and on it he had written, "At my Augean task! Love, Philip."

"Oh," she said. "Odd."

She gave me a brief smile, went away.

That bothered me, but the postcards came every few days with amusing messages.

It was in the middle of August that one day I had an air-mail letter from Guatemala with no address on the outside. I couldn't imagine who'd sent it, but I opened it and it was from Jerry Baker.

"Dear Mrs. Boone," he said, "You will find this impossible to believe, I know. I did not know till this morning that you were unaware of Philip's activities this summer, that you considered him safely at Princeton. He is with me here in Guatemala. It is a completely harmless expedition, but you may be sure I would not have undertaken it with Philip had I known the facts. We start home in three days. Please do not misunderstand me—I do want Philip to be free, free from you, if you will forgive the bluntness, but of course this is not the way one attains freedom. Isn't it up to you to free him, Mrs. Boone? It has been a happy summer, but some of the happiness has gone out of it since I've discovered the truth. You see, people do not behave this way without reason. There's no use going on about it, I suppose, but I am upset and worried at the moment. We do not think alike about many things, but in this I am agreed with you—nothing good can come of deception. Philip will be with you shortly. Sincerely, Jeremiah Baker."

I went and took out the postcards, with their gay messages. "Sorry I'm not there for blueberry muffins!" one said. Another said, "Don't let Bessie or anyone touch my statue of A." Another said, "Working as never before. Worn to a thin shadow."

Hurt? Of course I was hurt—a little frightened too, I think. I was beginning to see that the little boy who had lied to Miss Gray hadn't changed at all. I told myself I didn't believe Jerry, that he had put Philip up to this. I even excused Philip for wanting to keep up with a boy who had a lot more money than he did. But I was frightened. Now perhaps he would be put out of college for his failure in mathematics. And then what? But I didn't tell anybody, not even Bessie, who was getting everything in shape for Philip's return. Not Jen, who was so thin and jumpy that summer. Not Amelia, either. I did wonder whether I had been firm enough with Philip, whether I had made things too easy for him, but I had really expected him to do well always—I hadn't excused him for any mistakes he'd made, had I?

Then he was there, not worn to a shadow at all, but tanned, looking like a golden god of some sort. There was nothing apologetic in his greeting, no look of apprehension or guilt.

"Well, off the treadmill!" he said. "Is the fatted calf roasted?"

"Did you pass your exam?" I said.

"Oh, I think so—I really think so—but I haven't heard yet. They like to keep you in suspense!"

He chattered on about the summer, giving details he didn't need to. "You know what almost threw me off—blue examination papers! They've always had yellow ones. But they were *blue*. I sat there and wasted ten minutes because I couldn't make myself write on blue paper!"

But after dinner I said, "Let's walk up to the corner."

He came willingly enough. I waited till we got past the wall and then I said, "Philip, I know where you've spent your summer. Guatemala. So stop lying about it. I'm angry with you, son."

He took my hand and drew it up against his cheek. "Not with *me*, darling!" he said.

I pulled my hand away and I said, "Yes, with you. Did you have to make up this math, or did you not?"

"Oh, I have a make-up when I get back. But I can do it. Look, Mother, didn't you ever feel you had to get away, just away from everything familiar? No, I guess you never did, did you? It isn't that I don't love this place, and you—you know I do. But now and then I get this feeling that I have to get away—see what I'm really like, all that. You do want me to be myself, don't you? Not a blueprint of you?"

"Aren't you evading the point? Why not tell me you wanted to go to Guatemala with Jerry?"

"Oh, you'd have thought I wasn't happy here with you— and it wouldn't have been that at all. It was just— Well, I wanted it all on my own."

"You took elaborate means to make it so."

"I suppose Jerry wrote you. He said he thought he would, but he didn't tell me he had. That was a betrayal, don't you think?"

"If I were you, I wouldn't talk of betrayals, Philip," I said.

"Mother—"

"Yes?"

"I'm not a boy any more. I'm really not. Some things I have to decide for myself. I think I'll quit college."

"Well, I think you won't. If you want to be considered a man, act like one."

That was almost what I said to Walter once. Funny.

"And if I flunk out?" he said.

"You won't. If you spent as much time at your lessons as you spend getting out of doing them, you'd get along all right. I don't like this, Philip. I'm truly angry—I'm not fooling. I can't excuse you for this. It was childish and foolish. You are not going to slide out of college just because it seems difficult in spots."

"You're disappointed in me," he said in such a sad voice. "I suppose you ought to be. But you don't know how I've tried so that you wouldn't be. I'm not a scholar, Mother."

"Nonsense! You've got brains; you can do anything you set your mind to. Even Jerry says that's true. And, yes, I'm disappointed. I don't begrudge you money for schooling, nor even for legitimate pleasures. But I haven't the kind of money that allows for trips to Guatemala on what was meant for schooling."

"I'll pay you back," he said. "But it was better than schooling—it was wonderful, really. Or it was till Jerry got put out with me. He'll forgive me, though."

You see, you couldn't get at him, not really. He slid over the important things. He tried to make you feel sorry for him; he counted on forgiveness. The irritating point was that he did make you sorry for him. I felt I hadn't given him enough. But I didn't feel he hadn't been free. I didn't feel I'd hung onto him, as Jerry indicated I had.

Something did come out of that, though—something good, or so I thought then. The next morning Philip walked up to see Amelia. He came back quite soon, looking troubled, angry —well, more troubled than angry, because he had one of those faces that can't show violence.

"Wasn't Amelia home?" I asked.

"Yes," he said, and went on upstairs.

Then he just stayed home till school started. He never went up to see Amelia, and she didn't come down here.

"Have you lost your shadow?" I asked Philip.

"I never had a shadow," he said. Then he smiled at me and said, "That's true, you know—I have no shadow. I can't be very solid, can I? Maybe I'm just a ghost slipping through your life."

"I was referring to Amelia Adams," I said. I wasn't in a mood for his fancies.

"Oh, yes, of course I knew that. But she was never my shadow, you know. Maybe I was hers. She's acquired other interests, may we say? You've done a good deal of worrying over a girl you think of as a child—and a dirty child, at that—haven't you? Well, stop worrying. She's like you, a stickler for cold truth. She doesn't know gradations at all. I hope you're pleased. But I didn't ditch Amelia, darling. She ditched me."

I am not as consistent as Philip has said, for I found I was angry at Amelia for daring to turn against Philip, who had certainly showed her more kindness than anyone else ever had. But she didn't come near, and Philip didn't go over there, and presently he was gone for another year.

I started out to tell about how this business of Besten came out. I shy away from it, for some reason. It doesn't *belong* in our lives, and yet there it is and can't be skipped. I saw Besten and I don't forget him. And probably if I hadn't been worried about Philip, I would have seen sooner that Jen was making herself sick about this mess she'd gotten herself into. The first time it came to light was one day when I saw Jen going somewhere in a suit. With this suit she always wore a high-necked blouse and the diamond brooch. I said, "You've left off your brooch." She looked at me as if I were a stranger and said, "My brooch?" Then she got into the car and drove off.

In the fall Jen had a spell of real sickness. The doctor said it was "general debility," whatever that means. But she was sick all right. I took things down to eat, went every day, sometimes twice a day, to see her. I tried to amuse her, tell her about Joe's attachment to Bessie, things like that. Then one day she put out a thin hand and touched my arm.

"Cornelia," she said. "You've got to help me."

And it was that Besten again. She was supposed to go to town on Saturday and meet him. She had nothing to take him, but she had to go. So of course I said I'd go, and I asked about the place, how to tell him and all. She'd been giving him anything she could get her hands on for months. I was furious, but I didn't think I couldn't handle Besten. I was glad of the chance. I didn't care what happened to him, or John, or anyone but Jen. I'd been a fool not to see what was making her sick. In the first place, I couldn't see why a genuine blackmailer would bother with the little that Jen gave him. She'd be small potatoes to a man who made his living that way. But I got a picture of a man who put every tiny bit of scandal he ever heard down in a little book, and saw to it each bit paid off.

I went to the city Saturday morning, went straight to this restaurant and in. I didn't have any trouble recognizing him. He sat there at the back, an elegant man around forty, with a cynical, smooth face and a small mustache. He had on a blue tie and a gray suit, as promised.

I walked right back to him and said, "Mr. Besten?"

He gave me an appraising look and said, "I'm afraid I don't have the pleasure . . ."

"I'm Cornelia Boone," I said, and sat down. "I'm the next door neighbor to Jen Deemster, and her best friend. She's sick, and I came in her place."

"What a pity—that she's ill," he said.

"Your pity is overdue," I said. "She wouldn't be ill if it weren't for you, Mr. Besten, or whatever your name is."

"Oh?" he said. He had the most brazen smile. "Perhaps it's her conscience. That can make one ill, I've heard. Did you bring anything from her?"

"No, I did not. And she isn't going to bring you anything else either. You've come to the end of this little adventure, Mr. Besten. If my friend hadn't been foolish about her husband you wouldn't have come this far."

"Could I order you some lunch?" he asked. "They have quite respectable salads here."

"Thanks, no. I'm just delivering you this message—Jen's done with you. Not another cent will she give you, and that's final. She may be afraid of the police, but I'm not."

"I can well imagine you're not," he said. "But you're quite different from your friend. There were two young men who talked about the police. It came to nothing."

"But I am not those two young men. You don't frighten me, because I know the truth, which is nothing like your insinuations. You wouldn't have an easy time in court, you know."

"Oh, I have no intention of being in court," he said. "Perhaps if your friend had been as forceful as you, things might have been different. But you don't think the Judge would believe her at this stage, do you?"

"My son said you were a man who ought to be shot. You are, you know. Or a slower, more dreadful death would be more what you deserve. You see, the truth is that the Judge would forgive his wife, no matter whether your insinuations were true or not. It's just that Mrs. Deemster fears for his health. But he's quite able to bear the hearing of the truth that has nothing except innocence in it. He will be no more than moved by his wife's efforts to save him embarrassment. You see, Mr. Besten, you don't know the Judge, but I do."

He fiddled with a spoon on the table. A fat waitress kept moving about. She had very slim ankles, which surprised me when I looked downward from all that bulk. There was a window with a deep ledge, set high in the wall. On the ledge stood three pots of geraniums. It was that sort of place, like a country kitchen, simple and bright—not the background for melodrama.

"You're not the woman I'd have taken for a friend of Mrs. Deemster's," he said in that smoothly irritating voice of his.

"Well, I am her friend. I must go now. You understand this is the end, don't you?"

"I understand that you want me to think it is. That's as may be. Why don't you go out and get a policeman and have me arrested right now?"

Why didn't I? Well, there was no evidence at all except my word against his. I didn't have his last letter to Jen, not anything. I knew I couldn't make it stick. Yet perhaps I should have done it anyway.

"Mr. Besten," I said, "you know as well as I do that I could not convince a policeman at the moment. But you also know that I could do so another time. I would not be so stupid as not to have evidence by me. But understand this, I am a ruthless woman when crossed. Ruthless. And I would do anything, and I mean *anything*, to protect my friend."

"I believe you," he said, but he kept on smiling. "You look

ruthless, which was what made me wonder about your friendship with Mrs. Deemster, who at least has the manners of a lady. You know, I think she likes having lunch with me. She's charming, isn't she?"

He was loathsome. I got up and said, "One more letter and I shall call the police. That is all I have to say."

I walked out and left him there, fiddling with his spoon, smiling his smooth, infuriating smile. I understood, though, why the boys hadn't got further. He didn't frighten that easily.

I drove back home, stopped at Jen's. She looked at me hopefully.

"He is a dreadful man," I said. "I tried to frighten him, but he is not a man who feels anything. But you must never, under any circumstances, agree to give him anything else. You see what it's done to you, don't you? I wish you had given me his last letter. I would have called the police then and there."

"Oh, no, you can't do that, Cornelia. Then it isn't over. It is going to be the death of me."

She looked so ill, her eyes big and dark, her red hair against the pillow limp and lifeless-looking.

"It is over. I will see to that. Just get well and forget it," I said.

"But you see—you must see—he never lets anything be over. If he says he will go to John, that is exactly what he will do. What does he care about John, or anything?"

"Jen, promise me, that if you get another letter, you will let me see it. Promise me that. . . . And you'd better get up, Jen. This is more of a worry to John than any blackmailer would be."

She looked at me strangely, raised herself up, swung slowly out of bed and stood up. "Thank you. I needed that," she said.

She stayed up, too, but she looked so thin. I think she lived in a trance those days, but she stayed up. Yes, it must have been a trance, because of what happened. She did get a letter, but she didn't show it to me. It sympathized with her on her illness, gave her time, three weeks, to recuperate; then—same time, same place.

It was Anna who called me. "It's the Judge, Mrs. Boone! Something awful's happened to the Judge! Come down, won't you? Quick, too, Mrs. Boone!"

The Judge had walked out of the court, gone toward the little room where he kept his robes, and had a heart attack and died. Jen collapsed. I was the one who had to go to town, take care of everything.

"There was this man, see—he come up to Judge Deemster and begun to talk to him—and all of a sudden the Judge went down, all in a minute, just like that!" the old man who swept the halls told me.

"What did he look like, the man?" I asked.

"Well, I didn't take notice—a nice-looking gentleman. He went off to get the doctor, he said, but I never see him come back."

Jen was up when I got back. She didn't break down. She got through the funeral. It was after the funeral she showed me this letter she'd had. "I won't go. That's over, at least," she said. But I saw the date on the letter and I saw that somewhere she'd lost a week in her life. This Saturday of the appointment wasn't to come, it was past. She thought John had had the heart attack she'd always feared, and that was that. I never told her. I burned the letter. Once later, she did say, "He must have heard John died. He's never written since." And that was all.

I was afraid Jen might move away, but she didn't. I like to think it's because she wants to stay near me, but I don't know that. We're close, but Jen's changed since those days. She was always the elegant, dignified lady with the judge; but with me she was sometimes hoydenish, as if she had spirits that had to be released somehow, spirits left over from those days on the stage maybe. But after the Judge died she was more dignified than before, even a little haughty sometimes. She never sent her hat sailing down the room, or played jigs on the piano. She's more beautiful than ever, takes more pains with her clothes. It's a pity she stopped laughing, though, when the Judge died.

14

I HAVE TRIED not to anticipate. Books that do that annoy me. Bessie just brought me tea, and I've been sitting here by the window with it, reading over what I've done so far. It is all true, and yet so much remains unsaid. The world is gray today. The sky seems swollen with snow, and Bessie, who always knows what weather is coming, says we will have a heavy fall tonight. I feel like the sky, swollen with all the memories. Not a pretty comparison, but true!

Now I am coming to Fanny. Could it be that I've evaded talking of her? It is incredible that year after year went by without thought of Fanny or any attempt to communicate with her. But I went on the theory that it was better so, that you shouldn't let a child be torn between parents. I had let her go, and that was that. Or was it that I knew she wouldn't be torn, that she would always cling to her father, and that that was the way I wanted it, that I preferred being alone with Philip? I won't say I never thought of her. Of course I did occasionally. But except at odd moments, such as when Philip mentioned the organdy dress, I didn't *see* her.

Well, there was one other time. There's a little path through the woods, and past the woods there's a clearing where you can always find mushrooms. One day Jen and I went back there after mushrooms, and we sat on a log at the edge of the field and talked. It was a beautiful clear day. And Jen said, "Fanny loved toadstools. They were pure magic for her."

Right then I did see Fanny, lying flat on her stomach out by the old apple tree near the woods. Under this tree were three toadstools, and Fanny was looking at them in a very serious fashion, almost as if she were talking to them. She didn't look exactly childlike, but her legs were bare and she had on blue socks and sandals. Yes, I saw her as she was that day.

It was coming on spring when they came, Walter and Fanny. I was out in the garden. I heard the car, but I thought it was the milkman coming to collect. Bessie came down the drive and said, "There's someone to see you, Mrs. Boone." She had a startled look.

"Who is it?" I asked her, and she said, "I don't know, Mrs. Boone. It's a man and a girl."

I went up the drive and in at the back door. I took my time washing my hands; then I went into the living room, and Walter and Fanny sat there on the sofa. Of course I realized at once that it was Fanny, but I wasn't prepared for what she had grown into. She was as beautiful a girl as I have ever seen, tall, black-haired like me, but not like me otherwise. Walter was very thin.

I said, "Hello, Walter. And you must be Fanny."

She said, "Yes, I'm Fanny."

Walter said, "You are looking well, Cornelia. Nothing seems to have changed. Fanny, will you take a walk around the garden? I would like to talk to your mother alone."

She stood up and walked away. She was extremely graceful.

I watched her go, and then I said, "What brings you back to the old homestead, Walter?"

I saw then that he held a book in his hands. It had an odd jacket, with limbs of a tree on it, all twisted together in a way that made them not a tree at all.

He held out the book to me and said, "It's for you, Cornelia. You see, I did it."

The title was *The Ginkgo Tree*. I admit it gave me a queer feeling, holding the book. There was something about his voice that made it seem there had been a long, long struggle toward the writing of this book—something that made me confused. For the first time I began to see that his life apart from me had been not only the dreary routine of the office, but filled with something else.

"Congratulations," I said.

"Thank you. Sit down, Cornelia. I have something to ask of you."

It was strange, sitting down with Walter, as if I'd never been his wife, slept with him, quarreled with him, and all.

"I don't want to be melodramatic," he said. "But I am dying, Cornelia. I doubt whether I'll last six months. Mate is married. She would take Fanny, but it would be inconvenient for many reasons. She loves Fanny, and Fanny her, but the man Mate has married has three children already, and Mate knows it would make for complications to bring a girl so loved among these other children. That is the situation. I didn't think I'd ever ask anything of you again, Cornelia, but I wish you would take Fanny. She will not be a trouble to you."

. "How do you know you are dying?" I asked him. You know, even then I could not keep a little scorn from getting into my voice.

"You may be assured I do know," he said. "It would be fine if you could love her a little," he said, "but I do not ask that. She has her own life well in hand and won't demand anything from you except a roof over her head and her meals. I have saved a little toward her college, but it will not be enough. However, whether she gets to college or not, she will be educated. She will never stop being educated. It is a great trouble to me, leaving her, and yet I am not afraid for her. She will be safe, even with you, Cornelia. Sorry, I meant to keep very calm."

I looked down at the book, at those queer, twisted tree limbs, at the words *The Ginkgo Tree,* so black against the turquoise. The funny thing was that I could have started quarreling with him right where we left off. It was just as if the years between had never been, and yet I knew they had been, for here was Fanny, grown into something incredible out of that sullen child with the eyes that looked right into you and found nothing good.

"Safe, even with me?" I said. "You sound as if you thought I might corrupt her in some way."

"I said—sorry. No, you couldn't corrupt her. How is Philip?"

"He's at Princeton. He's fine," I said.

"Good. Will you do this, Cornelia?"

Then I looked at him, at his thin face, and I knew it was true, he was dying. There was death in his eyes. You can't refuse a dying man.

"If it's necessary," I said. "But you surprise me, Walter, wanting her here."

"Yes, I'm surprised myself. I think it's because you are so strong, Cornelia. I feel someone must take over who is strong. Fanny is very precious to me."

"Does Fanny know you are ill?"

"Yes, she knows. She understands everything. You'd better know that she does not want this, though I have never spoken against you to her. But she will make no fuss. She is strong too, Cornelia, perhaps even stronger than you. She could go to school in the village. This is her last year. Or she might take the bus into town if there is one early enough."

"When did you want her to come?"

"Now. Today. I have her things in the car."

"You seem to have been very sure that I would consent," I said.

"No, Cornelia, I wasn't sure at all. In fact, I feared otherwise. I suppose I have been a little desperate, with time running out."

He didn't sound desperate, just very, very quiet. Then he looked around and said, "It's all exactly the same."

Then it was that Jen came, walking in without knocking, as she always did. She was in the room and had started toward me when she saw Walter.

She stopped dead still, said, "Why, Walter! *Walter!*"

"Hello, Jen," he said.

She went to him quickly then, held out both hands. "How good to see you!" she said. "How really wonderful!"

She looked at me—wondering, I suppose, whether he were back for good. Then she said, "Thank you for your letter after John died. I did thank you—but I do again. It made me cry when I'd thought I never could again."

I said, "Fanny is coming home, Jen. You will be pleased to hear that, I daresay."

"Fanny? Wonderful! Where is she?"

"In the garden."

Then she saw the book and she said, "Oh, Walter—Walter, you did it!"

"Yes," he said.

She took the book from me and looked at it as if it were something priceless. "Why, bless you!" she said once. "Bless you, Walter!"

Odd—I didn't like having Jen hold that book in her hands.

Then she gave it back to me and said, "I must find Fanny," and went out in a rush.

"Then it's settled?" Walter said.

"Yes. I suppose you'll want to come to see her often?"

"No, I think not. Perhaps once or twice, no more. Cornelia, you've never missed me, have you?"

"I suppose it would please you if I said I had," I said. "But no, not excessively, Walter."

"I thought not. I've often missed you, though. But it was better all around that I left. I haven't regretted it—only that it might have been different if you'd cared for me. It might have been so different."

"Let's not be sentimental at this stage," I said. "Of course it might have been different if we'd been different. We were what we were, and that's that."

"I'm glad Jen is still here. I thought she might have moved away."

I didn't answer that.

"I'll get the things and be off," he said then.

He brought in two bags and a box of books. I wanted to help him carry them, but he brushed off my offers. "I'll go see Fanny," he said then, and walked down the drive. I didn't even see his good-by to Fanny. He came back presently, held out his hand, said, "You won't be sorry. Thank you, Cornelia."

He drove off. It seemed to me he let Fanny go very easily, but I suppose he didn't, actually. They came up the drive then, Jen and Fanny. Jen held Fanny's hand in hers, and Fanny's face was clear of any expression at all. She looked like someone in shock. But oh, she was beautiful! I couldn't believe that she could look like this. It was in the days of long bobs, touching the shoulders. She had bangs and straight hair, just curling under at the ends, and the loveliest face—pure, you might call it. Philip had been beautiful from babyhood, but Fanny had grown out of ugliness to this. No, she hadn't been ugly, just plain and solemn.

Fanny said to me in a distant voice, "It's kind of you to let me stay."

"Why shouldn't I let you stay?" I said. "Aren't you my daughter?"

It wasn't the right thing to say, and I knew it as I said it. She just looked at me, and then we went in and I took her up to the guest room, which I gave her with hardly a thought.

I wanted to ask Jen to stay for supper, but I didn't. She couldn't be with us always, and we might as well get over the hard part right off. Jen was still there, though, when I came downstairs after showing Fanny her room. She had the book in her hands, reading the first pages standing. When I came in she put the book down again.

"Life's funny, isn't it?" she said. Then she smiled and said, "Now that was a profound remark, wasn't it? You're lucky, Cornelia."

She went away then, and I was left alone with Fanny—and

Bessie, of course. I went out and told Bessie that Fanny was staying, to set another place at the table.

"That's fine, just fine," Bessie said. "You rattle around here all alone, Mrs. Boone."

So there we were presently, at the table. When Bessie came in I introduced them. Bessie just said, "Hello, dear," and that was all.

I couldn't get over Fanny's face, which I can't find any word for but "pure"—like Joan of Arc's, only not so peasantish as Joan's. Aristocratic pure, you might say. She didn't stare at you as she had when a child, though, when her lids lifted, the same look was there. She often lowered her lids, though. She had very long lashes and eyebrows with an upward sweep, like a bird's wings.

I decided to take the bull by the horns and get the things said that had to be said.

"This isn't easy for you," I said. "Nor for me, when it comes to that. I don't suppose you like me. I'm not an ogre, though, and we must try to get along. It's embarrassing, picking up after all these years, but, the circumstances being what they are, we'd better be as friendly as possible. Now, school. Do you want to finish in town? I expect you do."

"It would be better if I could. But it doesn't much matter."

"Of course it matters. There's a bus at seven-thirty. Could you manage that?"

"Oh, yes. It won't be for more than a month. I graduate then."

I had a minute there of confusion, of not knowing how old my own child was. "Aren't you young to be graduating?" I asked, but, as I say, I couldn't think whether she was or not.

"I'm going on sixteen," she said.

"At least my children are reasonably bright," I said. "That's a relief. Well, we'll see that you get off on that bus, then. I'll take you to the Corners to get it. Now, what do you want to call me? It can't be 'Mrs. Boone,' can it? And I daresay 'Mother' would stick in your throat. You can't call anyone Mother that you can't even remember having seen before, can you?"

Those lashes swept up, and she looked straight at me out of those gray eyes. "But I do remember you," she said. "I remember you perfectly."

"You couldn't," I said. "You were four years old."

"I do, though. And I was almost five. I called you 'Mummy' then, but that doesn't seem to fit now, does it? You don't seem like my mother, but I don't mind calling you so. It would be easier all around, wouldn't it?"

"Yes, easier," I said. "But you don't have to."

Then she folded her arms in front of her on the table's edge and looked at me. "I'll do anything, so that Father doesn't have to worry," she said. "It doesn't matter what I call you for a few months, does it? I won't be here after that. But I want him not to worry about me. That's the only reason I am here. I will do anything you say, call you anything you want me to, for a little while. If it was for forever, I wouldn't, but for a little while I can do anything. I have never deceived Father, never, but this is a lie, my being here at all, for he thinks he can leave me here forever. I couldn't stay here, you must know that. But for a little while I will, and I will be no bother to you."

It was a kind of shock, having her speak to me like that. It might have been myself speaking, so firm it was.

"You can hardly go out on your own at sixteen," I said.

"Yes, I can."

"Nonsense!" I said. "But we'll forget that for now. Just be free here to do as you like. For the time being, at least, this is your home." I did try to be sensible and friendly, but it was embarrassing.

"All right, Mother," she said. I gave her a quick look, and she was looking at me with mockery—yes, mockery. Her eyes said she didn't mean that "Mother" but that she was strong enough to say it. I admit that it gave me a jolt, hearing it from her.

"Philip is going to be surprised," I said.

The mockery went away from her face, and she was a child with a face wistful and young.

"Oh, Philip is never surprised," she said.

Then she said she'd put her things away and, if I didn't mind, she'd read a while and go to bed early. She had a little homework to do, she said.

So I said, "Good night," and she said, "Good night, Mother," and went up the stairs.

The whole thing was fantastic. It seemed as if I were in a nightmare. Everything about my life had changed in a few hours. I knew Fanny didn't like me, for all her politeness. That "Mother" showed that as clear as crystal. But she did love her father and she would do anything for him. And that remark about Philip—didn't it denote that she had been seeing him all these years? "Never surprised"—didn't that mean she'd known him forever?

I took the book Walter had given me and went up to my room. It was a relief to be there by myself with the door shut. I suppose I was curious as to what Walter had written. I remembered how he had said he would put the ginkgo tree into a book sometime, and here it was.

I began to read the book. It began: "The leaves were falling from the ginkgo tree . . ."

It was almost two when I finished the book. I would have to get up at six to see that Fanny got off to school. I've said often enough that I have no passion for literature. But I know fine writing when I see it. It wasn't anything to do with our life, but it was the story of an adolescent boy—oh, he didn't seem at all like Philip. Except that there was this ginkgo tree in the garden, there was nothing familiar. The father was dead, and this boy lived with his mother, who was possessive and passionate. The boy lived in a world of fantasy because he couldn't face the mess his mother made of her life. The story ends where it began, under the ginkgo tree in the fall, but the boy has grown up and accepts the mother for what she is. It was a sad story, but it had beauty in it, a good deal of pain, such as the young feel.

I went to bed, but the story kept going through my head. I did not see myself in that mother—of course not. I had never looked at any man since Walter, and, in spite of Jerry, I was not possessive. And the boy was dark and not handsome at all, not remotely like Philip. But the people were vivid and real and you didn't get them out of your head. And you would have thought Walter had loved the countryside, so beautiful and real did he make it. It wasn't true, of course. He cared absolutely nothing for the land and must have looked up flowers and trees and so on from a book. It was a fake, writing was, when a man like Walter could make you see the hills and the flower borders, the woods, as he did—Walter, who hated to so much as rake up leaves. And right there I remembered that day when I'd seen Walter lifting the rake and leaning against it, all in slow motion. And I thought, Maybe he was really sick—which just shows how soft that book or something must have made me.

You know, as I read that night, I almost forgot Fanny was in the house. But I was up at six, had my breakfast, and took Fanny to the bus. She was very quiet, and so was I. I hadn't slept much, and everything still seemed a dream.

When I got back I came up to my room, and I picked up the book again and looked at it. It still seemed strange that Walter had written it—impossible, really, that a man you had lived with could have had such thoughts as these. And then I saw the flyleaf for the first time. "For Cornelia," it said. I just stood and stared at it. For *me!* Why for *me?* I kept asking. Maybe he thought this justified all these years away—I didn't know. But I had a queer sensation of breaking up into little pieces. Why? Why to *me?* He hadn't loved me, that was sure. He couldn't have gone away if he had. . . .

I remembered when he had asked me to marry him. We were just walking down the street, and it was snowing. He put out a hand, and the snow fell on it, and he said, "You're as cold as the snow—will you marry me?" What a strange proposal! But I said I would. I wanted to. I don't know when I stopped wanting him. I think it was that time Philip was sick and I was annoyed with Walter for pretending to be sick himself. I think it was then, but I'm not sure. It might just have been growing all the time in me. Some marriages just never should have been, but when you're very young you don't understand anything like that. Nor did I understand that dedication. "For Cornelia"—why not to Fanny? Why not to his sister?

Well, it's too late now ever to find out.

NOTHING has been the same since that day Walter brought Fanny here. For years I had had no thought except for Philip—and Jen. I suppose the bitter truth is that if I had known Fanny would turn out as she did I would never have let her go. Shameful words, those are. Still, I believe a good deal of nonsense has been talked about the love of mothers for children. Women are filled with the legend of mother love and they are ashamed ever to admit that they have no especial feeling for this or that child. But children are people, and you just don't like all people.

I was confused that first day. The book had upset me, and the cool way Fanny had announced her intentions of going away as soon as possible. Walter had said she might be stronger than I was, and I know it gave me a feeling that I ought to prove that wasn't true, and at the same time a kind of respect for Fanny.

I sat down to write Philip the news and then couldn't write it, though I was used to telling him everything that went on here, even the smallest things that Joe or Bessie said. Why did I hesitate to tell Philip? I wonder. Did I feel it was a betrayal of him that I was pleased with Fanny? I got up from the desk and went into the room I had given Fanny, the guest room where Jerry always slept. There was the little room that had been hers when she was small. Why didn't I give her that? The guest room is a good room, with a cherry drop-leaf table and a spool bed and a good bureau with brass handles. There are two chintz-covered chairs and a secretary desk, something like mine, in one corner. The rugs are white chenille. I had spent much thought and money on that room. Yet I had not hesitated to hand it over to Fanny. There was not much sign of her presence, except for a couple of notebooks on the desk shelf and a picture of Walter on the little table by the bed. The picture flattered him, made him look distinguished. I looked in the closet, and her clothes were hung neatly there. On the floor of the closet was the box of books, not unpacked yet.

Bessie came up for cleaning and found me just standing there.

"She's a real lovely girl," Bessie said.

"Yes," I said.

"She don't look a bit like your boy."

"No."

"Well, it's nice to have somebody young in the house," Bessie said. "Always makes a house more natural like. Wonder if you'd like these white rugs out of here? There's those rose-colored ones you've got rolled up in the attic. White shows the soil awful when they're used regular."

"No, we'll leave the white ones," I said.

Twice we'd put the rose ones down when Jerry had been there. But somehow I wanted to leave the white ones for Fanny.

"Well, it's your house," Bessie said.

I wanted to go down and see Jen, but I didn't. I had a feeling I had to be alone that day, that I'd maybe talk too much if I went. Yet I wondered if Jen had seen that dedication in the book, and I wanted to hear her talk about Fanny. Maybe I wanted her to talk about Walter.

We generally had supper at six, but the bus didn't get to the Corners till six twenty-nine, so I told Bessie we'd have to have supper later till school was out. She didn't like it much, but she said if it had to be, she supposed it had to be.

I drove to the Corners and waited for the bus. Fanny got off and came right to the car. She had on a cotton dress, white, striped with red, no hat.

We sat down to supper almost as soon as we got home. Fanny said, "I could get here on the four-fourteen, but I wanted to see Father."

That was something new in this house, telling the exact truth about something. She must have known I wouldn't approve, but she wasn't going to have any deception about her movements or her feelings.

"No reason you shouldn't," I said.

"I can see Bessie doesn't want to wait this late," she said.

"Well, it won't hurt her to wait."

"I don't want to upset your routine."

"Nonsense! We can change our routine—good for us!"

Why didn't I try to argue the case with her, try to make her see it was an emotional indulgence, going to see her father? I'm sure I would have with Philip.

"Who's taking care of your father?" I asked her.

"Oh, Aunt Mate had a housekeeper by the day. She's staying on for now."

"Then he's alone nights?"

"Yes."

You know, I almost said he might as well come here to die, but I stopped myself in time. We'd finished, and there was no reason to open up old wounds, even if he was dying. He didn't want to be here, and that wasn't changed just because he was sick.

"Is he still working?" I asked.

"Mornings," she said.

Then she looked up at me and said, "Do you mind if we don't talk of Father?"

She looked so crisp and cool in the red and white dress, so young and so lovely. But there was something in her eyes that stopped me in my tracks, something that told me I had no right to talk of Walter and should hold my tongue.

"No, I don't mind," I said. "I wasn't trying to pry. Who's this man your Aunt Mate has married?"

"Mr. Brewster. He's a school principal." Then she smiled in a quite friendly way and said, "It's wonderful, really wonderful, for Aunt Mate. He's so kind, and he *loves* her. He doesn't just want her to take care of the children—he *loves* her."

"Well, that's nice for Mate. I never thought her very attractive, but I daresay she has brains."

"But you don't love people for their brains, do you? It's her heart he loves her for. She didn't want to leave Father and me, but we made her. She doesn't know quite how bad Father is, and Father says she mustn't know—it would spoil all her happiness."

"I should think she might have waited a little while," I said. "After all, she is obligated to your father, isn't she? He's been looking after her for some years now."

She stopped smiling and let her lids go down. "No, we're obligated to her," she said quietly, "greatly obligated. And of course she couldn't wait—why should she? She's forty-six years old."

I would have thought her older. She'd looked that old when I first saw her. She was stiff and spinsterish even then, with her hair pulled straight back and a mouth as straight as a ruler. I didn't see why anyone should have loved her for her heart; she didn't look as if she had one. But I saw I was bothering Fanny and I gave up on Mate. I didn't see their obligation to Mate, though. She was delighted, I'm sure, to get her brother under her wing. And I'm sure Walter must have carried the expenses of the household, such as they were. A schoolteacher couldn't have managed a family by herself.

"You must feel quite free to have your friends here," I said.

"Thanks, but I don't want anyone," she said. "You really needn't think of me at all. I don't need to be entertained. I have to study very hard till examinations."

"I only hope Philip is doing the same," I said. "Have you seen him lately?"

"Of course," she said. No explanation—just "Of course."

It was strange to have someone so direct in the family. Philip had seen her—recently, too, it seemed—but you would never have known it from anything he said. All these years, far away as he was in Princeton, he had kept seeing her. It made me very angry for a moment.

"Oh. He didn't tell me," I said.

"Well, he wouldn't, I suppose. But there's no reason he shouldn't see me, is there?"

"None, I suppose. No reason to hide it, either."

"He likes to hide things," she said. "That's the way he is. And you wouldn't have wanted him to come, would you?"

"I thought it better not. The way things have been, it would certainly have been better not. But I'm not as unreasonable as I daresay Philip has made me appear."

She said slowly, "No, I see you're different from what I expected. I thought you would hate having me here. You don't, do you?"

"Of course not. I'm delighted to have you. I didn't send you away, you know."

"No, I knew that, and yet—and yet, you didn't try to keep me, either, did you?"

I wanted to say I had tried to keep her and failed, but I couldn't. She was so forthright, so honest, you couldn't pretend anything with her.

"No, I didn't," I said. "But that was a long time ago, Fanny. I couldn't expect you to understand all the ins and outs of old difficulties. It was a trouble between your father and me—I couldn't go into it now. We just didn't get along in harness, that's all. I'm not blaming him—or myself, either."

"I could understand," she said. "I'm quite grown-up, Mother."

"Yes I see you are, but not grown-up enough for that. Let's just leave it that I'm glad you're here, shall we?"

"You mean you've missed me all these years?"

"Of course I've missed you," I said.

"*Really?*" she asked in a puzzled way.

"I'm not made of stone," I said. But I saw I was getting in too deep, that I couldn't tell her the exact truth or she would hate me forever. I didn't want her to hate me. But it's true that I found her lovely, someone to be proud of, and that if she had still looked like herself at four I would have felt quite different and said something else.

"There isn't much point in hashing over old mistakes," I said. "You're here, and you're my daughter, and I'm proud of you and very pleased to have you with me. Let's not think of the past and we will get on better."

We went into the living room, and she sat down for a few minutes before she went off to her homework. She looked around the room and said, "I remember the piano. And the luster pitcher on the mantel. The sofa has a different cover, hasn't it? It used to have red and green stripes."

It was true, there used to be a slipcover on the sofa with dull green and terra-cotta stripes, some white in it. But it didn't seem possible that she would remember it.

"And the rugs. I remember the rugs," she said. She was sitting on the gold-covered stool by the hearth. Her red and white skirt flared out, and she was resting the palms of her hands against the stool.

"You must have a remarkable memory," I said.

"Oh, I have. I remembered Jen too—Mrs. Deemster. She used to laugh a good deal. She took me for walks in the woods and we saw a snake."

Then she jumped up suddenly and said, "I have to work now!" and ran off upstairs.

I thought that probably Philip had kept alive these memories in her, for children of four don't remember much, but it gave me an odd feeling. It sounded as if she had been missing this house all the time; it made me unperceptive, and even cruel, to have thought she wouldn't. "How do you know

Fanny is happier where she is?" Philip had asked me once. And how did I know, except for knowing she loved her father best? No, I had never thought that she would miss me or the house, and that is the truth. But there had been something in her voice that said I hadn't understood her at all, that she had remembered everything and kept it in her heart for this very time. And what had she thought of our separation? What picture had she had of me in her mind, that she had been able to say she thought I would hate having her here? Had that been Philip's fault? Or Walter's? Yet Walter had said he had never spoken against me to her. It must be Philip.

It was unnatural not to see Jen. Yet I hesitated—it came hard to discuss Fanny with her, knowing how she had felt about the child's leaving. Then Jen came up.

"How about giving me some lunch?" she said.

"Fine!" I said and went to tell Bessie. When I came back to the living room Jen was standing by the window that opened on the terrace, just looking off toward the hills across the little valley.

"I suppose you've been laughing at me for taking Fanny in," I said.

She turned, sat down in the corner of the sofa. "Laughing?" she said. "No, not laughing. I suppose I'm curious, being human."

"Mate's married, Walter's ill—that's the size of it. Under the circumstances, I couldn't refuse."

"Very ill?" Jen said slowly.

Odd—I didn't say, "He thinks so," or anything caustic like that. I just said, "Yes, very ill."

She gave me a surprised look, knowing, I suppose, that Walter must be ill indeed to have me admit to illness. Then her eyes filled with tears. But she said only, "She's very lovely, an enchanting child."

"Child" didn't seem the word for Fanny.

"Yes, she's turned out surprisingly well," I said.

"Oh, I'm not surprised," Jen said. "You shouldn't have been, either. Have you read the book yet?"

"Yes, I've read it. It's nicely written, but it won't sell more than a few hundred copies. I don't really know why he felt he had to write it."

That was not giving the book its due. I tried to add something. "It is good enough so that I sat up most of the night reading it," I said. "Thank heaven it's not autobiographical! Would you like to borrow it?"

"Of course."

I went upstairs and got the book. Jen said, "All right— good-by. I won't stay to lunch. I want to go home and read it this minute."

But at the door she turned. "Cornelia—" she said.

"What?"

"Oh, nothing. Take good care of Fanny."

She went off. I must say I waited to hear her opinion of *The Ginkgo Tree.*

After she went I began a letter to Philip. "You'll be surprised—or will you?—that Fanny is here for the time being," I said. "I daresay you know all about it. . . ." I tried not to make much fuss about it. Philip had a queer streak in him— he just didn't like my making much todo about anyone else. I suppose he was jealous. But I'd always liked his feeling that way. It made it seem I was very important to him. So I told him and let it go at that. I didn't tell him about the book, I don't know why.

He phoned on Saturday noon as soon as he got the letter— collect, as usual. "Hello, Mother! Could I talk to Fanny?" he said.

"It's for you," I said to Fanny, and over her face went something of terror. "It's Philip," I said quickly.

"Hello, Philip," she said.

Then he must have gone into a long speech, for there was quiet a long time.

"Yes," she said then. "Yes, Philip. All right." And she hung up.

"I hadn't finished talking with him," I said.

"I'm sorry. He hung up," she said.

"What did he want? Anything?"

She turned and looked at me, almost as if she were sorry for me. "He wanted me to go away from here," she said. "That's what he wanted."

I laughed. "Yes, I can imagine," I said. "That sounds like Philip. He likes everything to be secret, even his friendship with his own sister. You'll find he won't be so fond of you when he can see you without melodrama, my dear. He's a very sweet boy, but he does like to be mysterious."

That wasn't kind to Philip, and I was ashamed of it. But I could just imagine Philip trying to make something dramatic out of Fanny's being here. He couldn't let things be simply what they were.

Fanny kept looking at me till I became nervous and said, "That's the way he is, Fanny. But I love him very much. Loving him doesn't make me see him other than he is, though."

"You've left out his kindness," she said.

"Kindness?" I said. "Yes, he's kind, but not in any simple way. He's been kind to Amelia Adams, a very ugly girl who lives next door. He can't possibly find her attractive, yet he's kind to her—chiefly because I don't like her and he feels her family doesn't understand her. He would give anyone anything, but it rarely costs him anything. He liked sneaking off to see you without my knowledge. If you're right here, you'll find you don't excite his kindness much."

"You're cruel," she said, almost in a whisper.

"No, I'm not cruel. I just accept the truth," I told her. "I've lived with Philip longer than you have. I love him, but I see him."

"But you don't love anybody," she said. She had on a dress of some old-fashioned material like calico, tan, with little blue figures on it. She looked at me just as she had when she was four. Then she said, "But I won't go away."

I was hurt, I admit. And I was angry too, partly because she was so strong and grown-up. She didn't like me, she believed I was cruel, and yet she was going to do what she'd promised her father she would do.

I was ashamed that I had tried to belittle Philip, even if I had done it for her own good. For, no matter what she said, I did love Philip. I had loved him from the day of his birth, and I'll love him till I die. I thought she would find out the truth of what I had said when Philip came home. Strange, though— I had begun to love Fanny too. I wanted her to like me and stay with me even after Walter died. Now I had presented myself to her in a false light, and she was the kind who would remember that, believe it to be the true light—though of course she might not have done so without Philip's help. Yet how

could Philip turn her against me, after all we had meant to
each other? It was just this love of the mysterious in him, this
love of conspiracy.

Fanny had gone upstairs after that last remark, and I didn't
see her again till lunchtime. When she came for lunch she was
very polite and calm.

I forgot to say that Jen called up the night after she'd taken
the book. About ten o'clock, it was. All she said was, "Cornelia—you must be so proud!"

On Sunday, Joe brought up the Sunday *Times* as usual.
And there in the book section, on the very front page, which
they usually save for the writers already famous, was a picture
of Walter and a review, a full-page one, of *The Ginkgo Tree*:

> The story of adolescence has become all too familiar.
> From Joyce to Salinger, authors have been elaborating on
> the pains and joys of growing up. *The Ginkgo Tree*, by
> Walter Boone, does not vary in theme from the story we
> now know so well, but it has a difference that may well
> make this book a small classic in its author's own time.
> The familiar pain is there, but there is also an awareness
> of outward things that is rare in the young, a perception
> of meanings that makes the youth, Johnny Cole, someone
> new and strange and unforgettable—yet completely cred-
> ible. The difficult emotions of the young are played out
> against a world completely sophisticated, sifted for mean-
> ing through the intelligence of the boy Johnny, an intelli-
> gence that comes out as real, not a figment of the author's
> imagination. He has too many talents, and too little guid-
> ance, too little specialization. The mother is as dreadful a
> creature as this writer has seen in fiction in a very long
> time, and yet she too is to be pitied, sometimes even
> liked. . . ."

And farther on it says:

And through all this ugliness of emotion, the outside world remains beautiful, calm, real. Even the chairs in the Cole house are remembered for their coverings. And one could walk in the garden, look out on these hills through snow or sun or fog. This is a world deeply known and felt. . . .

I must say I was astonished. I sat there and looked at the picture, which was the same one Fanny had on her bureau. That was Walter, whom I had married and lived with and borne children for. He looked completely familiar and yet at the same time someone I had never known at all. Now this is not to my credit, I know, but I have to say it. I thought, sitting there, about that dedication and felt a kind of excitement. I have never made any bones about liking successful people, have I? I hadn't, up to then, felt that writing a book necessarily meant success. But now the critics were saying this was an exceptional book, and it stirred me that they were saying it.

Fanny came down the stairs, and I said, "Come here, Fanny. You will be pleased by this."

She came slowly, but she came, saw the page and the picture. She picked it up and read it, never looking at me as she did so. I saw her face change, all the coolness going away from her eyes. Once she raised a bare arm, rubbing it across her eyes, as a very small child might do. It moved me, that gesture.

"It's fine, isn't it?" I said. "They really like it."

She dropped the book section onto the table. "But I knew it was fine," she said. "He's been writing it for three years. He had so little time—he's been ill. But he had to keep on with his job; he couldn't take time out. He couldn't even do a page a day. He was afraid he wouldn't get it done. He was so afraid!

. . . He didn't even take time or money to go to the doctor —and then it was too late. He has a cancer and they can't help him now. But if he'd just had some money, if he hadn't wanted so much to get the book done, if he'd not tried so hard to earn a living . . . If I'd just been older, so I could understand—I'd have got a job. He was always so patient, he always pretended it was just his hobby, that he didn't expect anything to come of it—and then, when they took it, I knew how much he'd wanted it. I can't stand it—I just can't stand it!"

I hadn't known there was that much passion in her. It was frightening.

"But they did take it," I said. "He got what he wanted."

"But he ought to have had a whole life of writing! It's wicked!" she said.

"Please, Fanny. Don't cry. He's had this much, anyway. Be grateful for that."

"Grateful?" she said. She turned and went away from me up the stairs.

16

THAT WAS a spring one doesn't forget. The garden had never been better, and I liked it that Fanny should see it that way, in all its glory. The daffodils came on, the narcissus, then the iris, the lilacs.

"What do you mean, going on sixteen?" I said one day. "Your birthday was in March, your fifteenth birthday."

"That's going on sixteen, isn't it?" she said.

"You must be some sort of prodigy, getting through school at this age."

"I've got a high IQ, if that means anything," she said. "But I got off to a good start with Aunt Mate. She used to say a lot of time was wasted on things that didn't matter, that some things we had to have in our heads, and the sooner we got them there the better—and no matter whether we liked them or understood them at first. So she taught me to read and my multiplication tables before I went to school at all. Everything was easy after that. But they didn't want to have me skip grades for fear I wouldn't be adjusted socially and all that. Aunt Mate got very high and mighty about it, though, and I did skip grades. Silly not to, don't you think? A waste, really.

If you're grown-up ahead of time, you just are. Staying back doesn't make your brain any different."

It was the longest speech she'd made to me, except maybe the one about Walter. I said, "I suppose they mean emotionally adjusted. They used to talk about that at Miss Gray's school."

"Oh, they don't know what they mean! I don't see how it helps your emotions to be kept in kindergarten when you ought to be in the third grade, and could be. It's silly to talk about your 'age group,' just silly. You like the people that think the way you do, no matter how old they are or how old you are. Miss Cooper tried to explain to me that it wasn't good to be an intellectual snob, that I wouldn't be liked and I'd never be happy. But I'm not a snob and I've been happy till now. And people like me well enough. I don't even care whether a lot of people like me."

I was fixing a bowl of narcissus for the table. I finished and carried it to the dining room.

"Next time may I do it?" Fanny said, coming and looking at the flowers. "We didn't have a garden in town, and I don't know flowers very well."

"Of course," I said. "Fix some for the living room right now, why don't you?"

It was pleasant talking with her. She went off to the garden with a pair of shears swinging beside her. When she came back she had just one spray of white lilac. It had two clusters of flowers. She got out a thin crystal vase and put the lilac spray in it, placed it on the round table. Very simple and beautiful it was, too.

"You're as good at it as Philip," I said. "He has a knack for flowers too."

I remember that because of what came after it and because it was as peaceful and friendly a moment as we'd had together.

The phone rang, and I answered it.

"Hello. Jerry Baker speaking, Mrs. Boone—from Princeton. Is Fanny there?"

"Yes. What is it? Do you want to speak to Fanny?"

"No. I just wanted to know if she was there."

"Is something wrong?" I asked him. His voice was too held in, queer.

"Yes," he said. "Don't get excited—but something is wrong. Could Fanny get down here quickly, do you think? Could she get that train at seven for New York? I would meet her there. Philip has had an accident of sorts. He's going to be all right, so don't panic. But he wants Fanny."

"I'll bring her if necessary. I'll start at once," I said.

"No!" he said. He was very sharp. "No, you're not to come, Mrs. Boone. It's Fanny he wants."

"Look here, don't talk that way to me. Of course I will come if something has happened to Philip!" I said.

"Mrs. Boone, listen to me. Philip does not want you to come. I think he will come home in a few days, but right now, send Fanny. I will meet that train. Good-by, Mrs. Boone."

"Wait! How badly is he hurt? You can tell me that," I said.

"Not badly. He will be all right."

"Was it a car?" I asked.

"No. I have to go now. Good-by."

He hung up, and I stood there, shaking, as scared as I have ever been.

"What is it?" Fanny asked. She stood there by the table with the lilac, just waiting.

"Of course I'll go. What does he think he is, ordering me not to come?" I said. "Philip's hurt."

"Philip?"

"Jerry Baker says for you to come. But I will take you. Can you start right off? After all, I'm his mother—why shouldn't I come?"

But the words came banging through my head—*Philip doesn't want you to come. Philip doesn't want you to come.* . . . Had he got into some trouble he didn't want me to know about? He was always so anxious that I should be proud of him.

Fanny was staring at me. Then she went out and got some sherry, brought it to me, and said, "Drink it!" I drank it, too, and sat down because I couldn't stand up.

"Get my bag from my room," I said. I had quite suddenly accepted Jerry's orders, I don't know why. Fanny ran upstairs, brought the bag to me. I had about twenty dollars in it. "Joe will take you to the train," I said. "You'll just have time. Jerry will meet you in New York. Do you know Jerry?"

"No," she said.

"Well, how did he think he'd know you, then? He never mentioned that. He's over six feet tall, dark and ugly, thick black hair, gangly. He's probably seen your picture. He says it's important that you come. Now, if Philip is injured but able to be moved, I want you to make arrangements to have him brought home. I can wire money if necessary. It means you'll be missing school, but it can't be helped."

I tried to sound sensible and competent, but I don't know whether I did or not.

"Just in case Jerry misses you, take a cab to Penn Station and

get the next train for Princeton. Philip is probably in the infirmary. Have you any money of your own? Here is twenty
dollars—that will at least get you there. Borrow some from Jerry
if you need to. Get ready, I'll call Joe and ask him to take you
to the seven-o'clock. I'll have Bessie make some coffee and a
sandwich."

She came down with a little duffel bag, in the same cotton
dress, no hat. She drank the coffee standing up, but couldn't
eat the sandwich. I remember thinking, She's scared too. She
isn't as grown-up emotionally as she thinks she is.

Joe honked the horn, and she said, "I'll call you as soon as
I get there. The very minute."

And then she was gone. I said, "You ought to have a hat
on," but she was gone.

Bessie brought me some coffee, said firmly I was to drink it
and then lie down. I wasn't going to do Philip any good taking
on.

I hadn't taken on, as she put it, and that made me angry. It
seemed to me I had been very calm and sensible. But I was
frightened. I drank the coffee and went upstairs and just
walked up and down, counting the minutes before Fanny
should get there. Once I thought, He's never wanted Fanny to
be here; maybe this is just one of his tricks to get her away. But
Jerry had sounded very sober. No, it was something else. But
the hurt that he hadn't wanted me went deeper and deeper
every minute. . . .

Three hours to get to New York—how far to Princeton? I
didn't know exactly. It couldn't be too far. But she might not
call before midnight. It was still daylight outside, and midnight
seemed a very long way off. I wanted Jen to come, but I didn't

call her. I just walked up and down and waited, and the minutes went by like hours.

Once I remember thinking that it had been wrong to send Fanny. Not because she couldn't manage anything, but because never over the years had I once worried about her, never thought perhaps she was ill and needed a mother. It was true, though, what Walter had said—Fanny was strong, and I let her be strong that time. She didn't like me, but I used her strength all the same.

She didn't call till one. Her voice sounded tired. "Everything's all right. Don't worry," she said. "Philip will be home in a week or so."

"But what happened?" I asked her. "What happened?"

"I can't talk about it now. But you needn't worry. He's going to be all right. He sends you his love."

"Are you staying there?"

"No. I'll come back day after tomorrow—on the noon train."

"Look, Fanny, I have to know what's happened. I have to know," I said.

"He just got cut in an accident and lost a lot of blood. But really, he's fine."

"Can I talk to a doctor?"

"He isn't here just now. I have to go now, but you needn't worry, truly. Could someone meet the train?"

"Of course. Give him my love."

That wasn't much good as far as information went. But she had seemed quite sure he was all right.

Then I had to get through the next day. I did see Jen then. She comforted me some. She said of course they'd have had me come if it were serious. I could trust Fanny to tell the truth. But I thought about Fanny, just a young girl, without a hat, in a cotton dress, landing in Princeton, helping Philip through trouble.

It was a worse trouble than I had thought, much worse. I have never recovered from that trouble. Fanny came back as she had said she would. I met her myself at the train. She didn't look as young as I'd remembered her. There were circles under her eyes, as if she hadn't slept, and she just said she couldn't talk till she got to the house. Nor did she, anxious as I was to know everything.

When we got to the house she said, "Let's go up to your room, shall we?" I knew by her voice that this was something that not Bessie or anyone should hear. So we went up to my room, and Fanny sat in the window seat, where Jerry had once sat and talked so outrageously to me.

"I don't want to tell you, but it's no good not to, is it?" she said. "Philip tried to kill himself."

I just stared at her, feeling life flowing out of me. My Philip, with all his grace and beauty and brains—*Philip*.

"He's all right. He will be all right," she said.

"But why?" I asked. "*Why?*"

"He's always been so desperately unhappy," she said. "You must know that."

"Philip?"

"You didn't know that?"

"No—why should he be unhappy? He's had everything."

Now it was Fanny who said, "Philip?"

Then she said, not in a grown-up way at all, "I'm so tired. Could we talk tomorrow?"

"Yes, you must be tired," I said. "But I have to know, Fanny. You must see I have to know."

"He read Father's book," she said. "He thought it was about him, only he— Well, he said, he'd never have as much courage as Johnny in the book. He said he wasn't going to come out of it that easily and so well. He thought, What was the use of trying any more? He just couldn't make it."

"He isn't remotely like Johnny," I said.

"Yes, of course he is," she said. "He's very like him."

"Nonsense! And I'm certainly not Johnny's mother, either."

She didn't answer that. I knew I should let her go, for she was terribly tired, and of course she had been through something very bad, something she was too young for, in spite of her high IQ. I suppose I just couldn't bear it all alone.

"I called Father," she said suddenly. "He's down there now. I hated to trouble him, but I had to. They're so alike, you know. I—I didn't know what to do, you see. I had to call him."

She slid off the seat then, stood up. "I have to go to bed," she said. "I haven't had much sleep. I'm sorry. I can't make you see how it is, can I? Philip isn't the same person to you as he is to me—maybe we're all two people, like that, I don't know. But when I talk about him, I see you don't know who I mean."

"All right, child. Go to bed," I said.

"I'm sorry," she said, and went off. She walked stiffly, as if she could hardly stand upright, not gracefully, as she always had.

That was a dreadful thing to make a young girl go through. But it was dreadful for me too. I wondered how Jerry had happened to be there, and I was terribly angry with him for asking Fanny to come. I was angry too because Fanny had called Walter—why not me? It sounded as if Philip didn't love me at all, and yet I knew he did. He just hadn't wanted to hurt me. But to call him "desperately unhappy" didn't make sense to me. He liked to get his own way, but he was always *happy*. He had a hundred interests; flowers and music and sculpturing, writing poetry, girls—everything interested him. He might not want to *be* anything, but he still liked everything. You couldn't get desperate enough to want to kill yourself when you were so interested in life. He always liked the melodramatic, and maybe it was just one of his gestures, like sneaking off to see Fanny when he was just a boy. But it was a horrible gesture and might have ended everything. Maybe his work was going badly at school—maybe it was as simple as that. . . .

Yes, that was a nightmare, that spring—that summer too.

Fanny slept all afternoon. I took her some supper and she said, "Thank you," but nothing else. She went off to school in the morning as always. She was very quiet all that week, though she wasn't unfriendly. She seemed actually to pity me.

On Friday she did say, "Father's back. Philip's all right now."

"Your father was in no shape for traveling, was he?" I said.

"No, of course not. But he says it doesn't matter."

Then, on Sunday, Jerry brought Philip home. Philip walked from the car. I saw him coming, and for just a minute there I couldn't rush forward to meet him. His wrists had bandages on, and he looked pale and somehow fragile, though he'd been healthy enough for years. Then I did run out the door.

He just grinned at me and said, "Well, you've still got me on your hands, darling!"

"I should hope so!" I said. "Come on in!"

"Hello, Fanny," Jerry said, and there was Fanny, just standing there, her hands behind her.

"Hello," she said.

They came in, Jerry carrying bags in and up to Philip's room. I didn't quite know what to say. But Philip took care of that. He laughed and talked and said something to Bessie that made her laugh. Then he said, "Jerry'll be putting all my things in the wrong drawers," and went slowly up the stairs.

Fanny watched him go. At the landing he turned and looked down at her, smiled at her in the same sweet way he had always smiled. Fanny's eyes filled with tears, but she smiled back at him just the same. When Jerry came down he said, "Let him rest. Don't push him or fuss over him—just let him rest." He walked all about the room, nervously; then he said, "Oh, I forgot! Fanny, he wants you to come up and play some records for him!"

He was too careless about that, as if he thought maybe I'd object if he made too much of a point of it. But I said, "Run along, Fanny. Let us know if he wants anything to eat."

She gave me a look from under lowered lids, then went up the stairs. Then we heard the sound of music, faintly, through a closed door. I'd hardly had a word with him.

Jerry said, "Let's go out on the terrace, shall we?"

I went with him because I didn't know what else to do to fill the moments just then. Jerry sat in the bamboo chair with the high curved back, his feet stuck straight out in front of him. "Mm! Smell the lilacs!" he said. At the corner of the terrace was a very old lilac bush, white.

"How did you happen to be in Princeton?" I asked him.

"Shall we call it a premonition?" he said with that faint, mocking smile of his. "Actually, I wasn't there till it was all over and he was safe in the infirmary. He called me up Sunday and asked me if I'd seen the *Times*. 'That's my old man!' he said, and hung up. I went out and got a *Times*. I thought his father must be dead, and I looked in the obituaries first. Then I looked everywhere else but the right place. The book section was on the floor, and I looked down finally and saw Mr. Boone's face, and the name under it. Then after I read the review—which was remarkably favorable toward a new author, wasn't it?—I remembered Philip's voice, which hadn't sounded boasting, or even glad. I didn't do anything about it till the next afternoon, though. It was a premonition, or a feeling he needed me—I didn't quite know how or why. So I drove up, and there he was."

I couldn't answer him. It seemed too cruel that everyone had known about Philip, had been with him, except me, who loved him more than all of them put together. I've always felt sure what to do or say. This was the first time that I hadn't been able to find words. Jerry didn't say anything, either, for a long time. We could still hear the music faintly going on and on. The air was soft, as if rain were coming. Two chewinks walked about under the cedars. Yes, I still remember those chewinks.

When Jerry spoke he said something quite different from what I expected. "Why did you ask Fanny to come home?"

"Her father was ill. It seemed necessary," I said. It was none of his business.

"Yes, I could see he was ill. I wasn't prepared for Fanny."

"Not prepared for her?"

"Oh, I'd heard of her forever, ever since I first knew Philip. She wore a little knitted hood and mittens—red—when she was little. Naturally, I knew she wasn't that child any more, but I always thought of her as not more than eight or nine, still wearing the red hood. When I asked him how I'd know her at the station, he said, 'She'll just be the only one alive in

Grand Central!' And she was. . . . I've never thought I'd marry. I haven't had very good examples set me. But I plan to marry Fanny someday, Mrs. Boone. Get used to the idea."

"She's not sixteen yet. But she'll never marry you, Jerry, you may be sure of that."

"Oh, but she will—in time. This has been a shock to you, Mrs. Boone. I'm sorry."

"Yes, it's a shock," I said. "Not about Fanny—that will never be. But I find it hard to understand what Philip has done."

"Well, he loves you very much."

"What kind of an answer is that?"

"It's the only answer. But he loved his sister too, you know. I think he never knew his father much, till he read his book. I can see that Mr. Boone would seem very quiet and distant beside you. But you see, Mrs. Boone, he has been afraid all his life that you would send him off the same as you did Fanny. An unreasonable fear, you'll say, but there it is. You were all the order, all the love in his life—and yet you had let Fanny go away. He's never felt he could live up to your expectations for him. He's never felt sure your love wouldn't stop suddenly."

"How monstrous!" I said.

"Yes, perhaps that is the exact word," he said, and then was quiet.

The music had stopped, and it was very still. The scent of the lilacs came heavily.

"I have never thought of anything but Philip's happiness," I said.

"Oh?" he said, and stopped.

"He must know that. He's had everything he's asked for all his life. He must have known it would kill me if anything happened to him. Fanny says he saw himself as the boy in Walter's book. That's preposterous. There's no likeness at all."

"But of course there is," Jerry said.

"And he sees me as that dreadful, promiscuous woman?"

"She was more than promiscuous, wasn't she? She was possessive and she was insensitive. Oh, no, it wasn't you! Your passions don't run toward other men. But you ought to have seen something of what Philip was suffering, Mrs. Boone."

I felt such a rush of hate toward him—yes, hate. To tell me what I should feel for Philip!

"You've certainly encouraged him in his suffering, haven't you?" I said.

"I made it easy for him to see his sister, if that is what you mean. He needed someone to feel sure of. I've tried to let him be sure of me. He looks at so many sides of a thing that he will never seem as strong as you, Mrs. Boone. But you shouldn't underestimate him."

I got up, went into the house and up the stairs. I couldn't bear another word from Jerry Baker. I went to Philip's room. The door was shut, but I opened it gently and stepped inside. Fanny was curled up in the deep chair, her eyes shut. Philip slept too. His arms lay outside on the covers, and all I could see at first were his bandaged wrists. I couldn't bear the sight of them and I wanted to pull the cover over them, but I just stood there and looked at him. He looked so innocent, asleep —beautiful and innocent, but pale.

Jerry had said dreadful untrue things to me, and I would never forgive him for them, but he had frightened me too. I felt for a minute that I ought to send Fanny away, that I ought to make Philip know beyond any doubt that I loved him with all my heart. How could he doubt my love? I went very softly over to the bed, bent, and kissed him, but he did not move. Underestimate Philip? These young people felt they had to have some Freudian explanation for everything; they made things complex just for the sake of unraveling them. Things like that I thought, looking down at Philip asleep. Why couldn't they let things be simple? I had a queer feeling of being an intruder. Even asleep, they seemed to put me out.

I didn't talk any more with Jerry Baker. He slept in Philip's old room and went off early in the morning, taking Fanny to her bus.

Philip came down about ten, let Bessie fuss over him, went out on the terrace, and sat there, just looking at the hills. It had rained in the night but was bright now, with everything wet and shining. I went out to him after a while and I said, "I'm not going to preach at you, son. Only you came close to breaking my heart."

He smiled at me so slowly, as if the real gaiety had all gone out of him.

"I'm sorry," he said, and that was all.

I was glad to have Jen come then. She joined us out there, greeting Philip warmly, saying, "And what on earth have you done to yourself?"

"An accident in the laboratory—fantastic, really. But he's all right, thank God!"

Jen sat and talked cheerfully, telling a funny story, catching Philip up on the local gossip—nothing serious at all. She mentioned Fanny casually, said she was the loveliest thing seen in these parts in her time. And then she fell silent, and none of us could find much to say. I saw her look toward Philip's wrists, frown a little; then she got up quickly, said, "Bless you! Come see me, Philip!" and was gone.

She knows, I thought. Jen knows.

Philip didn't talk, and after a while I couldn't stand the quiet and said I had some work to do and left him there.

PHILIP didn't go back to Princeton. He didn't even talk of going. He sat outside for hours at a time, doing nothing at all.

I would come with a book and say, "Want to read for a while? I'm caught up on chores."

"Yes, I'd like that," Philip would say. So I'd sit and read to him as I used to when he was a boy. Only it is not easy to read outdoors, where there are so many things to watch, and sometimes I would feel that Philip's thoughts were far away, that he heard nothing I said. After a while the bandages were gone, but there were those thin red lines on his wrists, and my heart would sink every time I looked at them. I didn't reproach him; I tried never to talk of the reason for his being there. Jen came quite often, and I would let her sit with him alone. It's odd, that, for I don't like missing conversations, missing Philip.

Once I heard her say, "Are you going to be able to make your examinations?"

"No," Philip said. "I will never take another examination."

"That's a pity. You're almost through—only another year to go. It would be a pity."

"Oh, I don't think so," Philip said. "It just doesn't seem important any more."

"I know. I really do know, Philip," Jen said. "After John died, I had this feeling that I was finished, that nothing could ever happen to me again that would matter. In a way, it's still true—but not as true as I thought. I like, for instance, sitting here talking with you. I still like your mother dropping in for tea with me. I like just being alive."

"I daresay I'll stop feeling like Lazarus in time," Philip said.

They didn't know I was right there by the door, and presently I felt guilty and went away.

Fanny still stayed till the late bus. It annoyed me a little, when Philip obviously waited for her to get back. I said something to her once. "Would it be too much to ask if I urged you to get the early bus home for a while?" I said. "It would help get Philip over this bad time, child."

Fanny put her books down. "Sorry," she said, "but I couldn't—not now. Philip understands that."

It was too much to ask of the child, and yet it certainly couldn't have been good for her to spend time every day with a dying father. Philip would be easier than Walter. But Fanny went on as always.

Then she was to graduate. I said, "Don't you have to have a dress for graduation?"

She said no, they were wearing caps and gowns, rented ones.

"Well, don't we get an invitation?" I asked her.

She hesitated. "Of course, if you want one," she said. "It won't be very exciting, though. I think you'd be bored."

Philip smiled at her, said, "We're coming." She flushed and went up and brought down two invitations, dropped them on the table.

It was the first effort Philip had made to do anything.

Well, there's no point in describing a graduation ceremony; it was just like all others. You'd have thought Fanny would look young with the rest, but she looked as old as anyone, and more beautiful than anyone. We were halfway through when I saw Walter and Mate sitting across the auditorium from us. Walter's face was shockingly thin. His hair was grayer than it had been when I had seen him. Mate didn't seem to have changed at all over the years. It was then I thought, Why, I never wrote to congratulate Walter on the book! Why hadn't it entered my head? I wonder. I could have done it quite easily and sincerely the morning after I'd first read it. Now it wouldn't be easy, and yet I knew I must do it. Fanny might never forgive me if I didn't. Yet that book had brought sorrow to us, and perhaps wasn't as far away in theme and character as I'd thought at first.

As soon as the graduation exercises were over, Philip said, "Let's get out. We can wait in the car."

I was glad to get out. I didn't want to meet Walter and Mate. But we sat in the car a long time before Fanny came. It's strange, I see now, that nothing had been said to Philip about Walter's illness. He couldn't help seeing Walter was ill, and perhaps I took it for granted that Fanny would tell him the whole story, being one for truthfulness past necessity. Then we saw Fanny coming with her father and aunt. They stepped off the walk, stood together on the grass a moment, then Fanny flung her arms about Walter and kissed him. She came quickly toward the car.

"It won't be six months, I'm afraid," I said. "Your father looks dreadful."

"I think I'll go speak to him. Do you mind?"

"Why should I mind?" I said.

He didn't answer, but got out of the car, crossed the parking lot, and walked up to his father, put out his hand to him. Somehow their figures were alike—tall and slender, both of them, with a grace few men have. I had never thought of Walter's being graceful before. Fanny got into the car, and I said, "I hope Philip doesn't take on your father's illness as his own personal tragedy. He's in no shape for it."

"Neither is Father," Fanny said.

"Sorry, Fanny. I didn't mean to hurt you."

Philip was coming back. He never said a word about Walter, just got in and we started home.

"We were very proud of you, winning the scholarship and all," I said.

"Oh, it was no more than to be expected of Fanny," Philip said. "Only don't think college is going to be different from high school. Don't get your hopes too high, honey!"

Fanny didn't answer. After a long time Philip said, "Don't mind me. I'm just a disillusioned old man." Still Fanny was silent.

When we were home I went up to my room. I had this feeling I must write to Walter, and at once. But Fanny came to the door, and I said, "Come in. Did you want something?"

"Yes," Fanny said. "It's about going to town. I won't be going in early any more, but I do want to be in town afternoons for a while. I must. I could go at noon, couldn't I? And be back at the same time as always? I have money for bus fare."

"You must do as you please," I said. "But I think this is harrowing, Fanny. I do not think your father will expect it of you."

"No, of course not. I expect it," she said. "If it isn't convenient, I will manage somehow."

"Oh, we can get you to the bus. I was just thinking of you, child."

"Thank you," she said, and went to her room.

So I wasn't in a very good mood for writing to Walter. He ought not to have subjected Fanny to these visits. But I got out paper and wrote. "Dear Walter," I said, though he was not dear to me any more, "I have been remiss in not thanking you sooner for the book, which seems to be a smash hit, as they call it. I congratulate you on your success, though I realize you do not think highly of success. Perhaps, having it, it will seem more important to you. I thought it a fine, well-written story, but it has had some evil effects on our household, as no doubt you know. Philip has insisted on seeing himself as the hero, though it is obvious to me he is nothing of the sort. I apologize for Fanny's sending for you in Princeton—she should of course have sent for me, but naturally she is in the habit of turning to you. I hope the strain was not too much for you. Fanny is a charming girl and we are glad to have her here. Your mind can be at rest concerning her. Sincerely, Cornelia."

I wasn't satisfied with it, but it was the best I could do at the moment. I had wanted to ask him why he had dedicated the book to me, at least to say something about the dedication, but I couldn't make myself do it. It would seem I was personally affected by it, instead of just being curious. So I sent that letter, but I never had a reply.

I've thought since of many things I should have said to Walter. It wouldn't have hurt me to seem warmer, no matter how I felt. I was moved by that book but, after all that had happened, I couldn't make myself say so. I ought to have told him I was fond of Fanny, I ought to have thanked him for being with Philip in his trouble. I don't suppose he expected warmth from me, and yet, when he was dying, I should have forgotten old and present hurts.

It was too much, what happened in that year. Philip did his best not to upset me. He seemed very calm, really. But all summer those lines showed on his wrists, and every time I saw them I would feel a cold chill. He began to work in the garden, insisting that Fanny help him. Sometimes I would hear them laughing out there. After lunch he would drive her to the bus, and then he'd just seem to wait till she got back again. It helped, having her there, because I found it hard to talk with Philip. I was so afraid I would say something that would hurt him. Sometimes he'd go down to Jen's by himself. He didn't do anything else but work in the garden and read.

Then he got a letter from Jerry. He read it out on the terrace, and I came out with a glass of milk and found him with the letter in hand.

"Would you want Jerry here for a couple of weeks, working on a piano piece?" he asked. "He'd like to come, but it would be noisy."

"He always seems to come whether I want him or not," I said.

He shoved the letter into his jacket pocket, lifted the glass of milk. Then he said, "I suppose he wants to look after me. But I don't need him, so if you'd really rather not have him I'll say so."

It was inconsistent of me to feel sorrow for that remark. But it was as if Philip didn't care about anything, even his old friends, any more.

"Why, I don't mind, if you want him," I said. "I've never made any bones about not liking him. He knows it as well as anyone, and if he can stand being here, I suppose I can stand having him. But he'd better leave Fanny alone, I will say that. He says he's going to marry her when she's grown up. That I would not have, Philip."

"Do you think you'll have anything to say about it?" Philip said.

"I certainly will!"

"If she has to marry anyone, it might as well be Jerry."

"Philip!"

He smiled, said, "Of course I'd just like her to stay here with me forever, but it won't be that way. She'll have to work out her own destiny. We can't manage her, Mother—you must see that."

"I certainly don't want a temperamental, rude musician for her—and I won't have him," I said.

"Jerry's the best. The very best," Philip said, but in such a mild, far-off voice.

"I thought you just said you didn't need him any more."

"To look after me, I said. But I'd hate thinking of a life without Jerry in it. He's my friend, Mother." Just what he'd said to me when he was a little boy.

"Oh, well, tell him to come," I said.

Yes, I was willing to have Jerry there if it would please Philip. He had made me feel sad. It had always seemed, when he came home, that he was terribly glad to be here, that this was the place he loved best in the world. Oh, of course he'd done other things, gone away when he could have been here, I know that, and yet there was always that gladness at getting here at last. He was always so relieved that nothing had changed, that he could count on home to be always exactly the same. Well, he was here now, and never went anywhere except to take Fanny to the bus or to Jen's, and yet sometimes it seemed as if he weren't here at all. He was gentle, friendly enough, and yet—well, it's hard to say how it seemed. But sometimes when he sat looking at the hills I remembered that little poem about the bird and I would feel he had flown away —from me, from home, from everything he'd ever known. He didn't act ashamed of what he'd done, he was just quiet and distant.

And at the table that night Philip said suddenly, looking at Fanny, "Jerry's coming."

Fanny had on the red and white dress that always looked so crisp and cool. She looked up at Philip and said, "That's nice." But over her face went a wave of emotion that frightened me. She held herself off so, and now her face was open, full of feeling.

"It is, rather, isn't it?" Philip said, and laughed.

So Jerry came, and at first he didn't seem to notice Fanny much. Oh, he cast her an occasional remark, but he wasn't intimate with her at all. He was deep in music, spending hours every day at the piano. He pulled a little table close to the piano, and his score lay on this table. You would hear the same phrase over and over and over till you wanted to shout at him to stop. But Fanny would come sometimes and sit on the stool by the hearth and hug her knees and just listen. Once I heard her say, "Stop! That's it!" and Jerry laughed and said, "If you say so."

At night, late, I would hear his voice in Philip's room, going on and on, Philip not doing much of the talking. I don't know what they talked about, night after night.

But one night, toward the end of his stay, Jerry said, "Fanny, want to pay a call with me?"

"A call? On whom? Mrs. Deemster?" Fanny said.

"No. On Amelia. She's an old flame of mine."

"Then you'd better go by yourself," Fanny said.

But he reached down, took her hand, and pulled her up. "I need you along," he said. "Want to come, Philip?"

"No," Philip said.

"Very final, that sounded," Jerry said.

"Yes, final," Philip answered.

So Jerry and Fanny went off up the road together. "Want to come down and see Jen with me?" Philip said suddenly.

"She's got company from town," I told him.

"What of it? She wouldn't put us out, would she?"

"Some of John's cousins. It wouldn't be any fun," I said.

He went to the piano and played a while—lazily, not too well. Then he picked up a book and sat reading it.

Then we heard voices coming up the drive, and they came in, Amelia with them. She had changed some, held her head up instead of dipping it in that shy fashion of hers. Her hair was cut short as a boy's, and she wore a cotton dress instead of blue jeans.

"Hello, Mrs. Boone," she said. "Hello, Philip."

"Hi," Philip said. "How are you?"

"Fine," she said.

"We're going to have a sing, now that's over," Jerry said. "Where's that book of folk songs, Philip?"

Philip got the book, and Jerry said, "Gather round!" and began to play "On Top of Old Smoky."

Now, I didn't have any use for Amelia Adams, and I wasn't pleased to see her there, but I must admit that I enjoyed hearing them sing. Their voices were not trained, just young and clear and true. Philip always had a lovely voice, and Fanny sang well enough too. Amelia had a soft, clear alto. They sang "Green Grow the Rushes, Ho," and I remembered Philip's singing it when he was little. Philip stood the other side of Jerry, a little apart from the girls, but he sang with them, and it made me feel good to have him make the effort. Yes, I was sentimental that night.

They must have sung for an hour. Then I went out to the kitchen, made coffee, and got out crackers and cheese and a fresh loaf of bread and some jam. They came to the kitchen, and we all sat around the table, eating and talking. Nobody said anything very important. But after that Amelia said she had to go.

"All right—come along, Fanny," Jerry said.

"I'll take Amelia home," Philip said. His voice was hard and quick and angry, not like his voice at all.

"All of you come," Amelia said.

"No," Philip said. "I will take you home."

Jerry just shrugged and let them go. He said to Fanny, "They don't want us."

"Funny," Fanny said, "she doesn't look at all as I expected. Philip told me about her long ago—but she doesn't look as I expected."

"Come with me. I'll show you something in Philip's old room. Or maybe you've seen his head of Amelia?"

"No, I haven't," Fanny said.

So he took her upstairs and I suppose showed her that head that they said looked like a queen. When they came down, Fanny said, "It's wonderful, isn't it?" I was annoyed and didn't answer.

It was a long time before Philip came back, and then he just said, "Good night, all," and went up to his room.

Yes, something always went wrong when Jerry Baker visited us.

"That was stupid, Jerry," I said. "Philip had forgotten all about her."

"Forgotten her?" Jerry said. "He'll never forget her as long as he lives. Philip is very faithful, Mrs. Boone."

The next day, after Fanny had gone to town, Philip said, "You said something about college, Mother. But I'm not going back, you know."

"Of course you're going back!" I said. "It's just another year. You can surely make up what you've lost, can't you?"

"I don't know, but I'm not going to. Let's not argue it. I'm just not going."

I thought, He's ashamed to face his friends, and I said, "Go somewhere else if you don't want to finish at Princeton."

Jerry gave me a sharp, cruel look and said, "Princeton is as good as anywhere, Mrs. Boone."

"Better than most," Philip said. "But I feel through with college, Mother. So don't make any plans. Or don't you want me here?" He said it very quietly.

"Of course I always want you here, but I must say I think it foolish not to finish and get your degree. I'm sure Jerry thinks so too. I remember how he raised Cain to see that you stayed in Endley."

"That was long ago," Jerry said. "It's up to Philip, I should think."

Philip said, "Oh, you think I'm afraid to go back, Mother? Well, you are quite wrong. I'm not afraid of anything or anybody. Strange, but that's the truth. I don't intend to stop studying, you know. But I am through with college. Just through."

"It's not so easy to get a job without a degree behind you," I said.

"Oh, I'll manage," Philip said. "Don't worry."

"You needn't think you'll just play around with Fanny, for she'll be going off to college herself in September."

"Will she? She told me she couldn't go while Father lived. She said she wouldn't go, in fact. . . . In any case, Fanny has nothing to do with it."

In spite of what Philip had said, I did think he was afraid to go back. I didn't blame him for dreading it, and I would have tried to see that he got transferred somewhere else, but I thought he'd regret it if he didn't finish somewhere. It was like giving up in the middle of a race.

I tackled Fanny that night on her decision. "What's this I hear about your not going to college this fall? Of course you are going. Your father would want you to. He thinks highly of education and he's planned for you to go and saved toward it. And now you have your scholarship too. He would be more disappointed than anyone if you gave it up now."

"But I haven't given it up," Fanny said. "Only I can't go this fall, that's all. I can't, Mother—you must see that."

"I'm afraid I don't."

She turned away from me and said, "No, I don't suppose you do. But you see, I *love* Father. It isn't anything he asks of me. I *love* him."

"Well, you don't have to stop loving him even if you go to college," I said. "It's wrong for you to watch him die. Wrong."

"Why?" she asked. "Why is it wrong? He'd watch me, wouldn't he? You'd watch Philip, wouldn't you? When you're

dying you've got to have someone who loves you there. You've
got to."

You know, till that moment I hadn't really taken in the fact
that Walter was dying. Oh, I had believed him, but somehow
it all seemed apart from me, not my business. But when she
said that about Philip, I understood her. For of course I would
have stayed by Philip, because I loved him. I saw I had been
stupid not to see that someone could love Walter as I loved
Philip. And I seemed to see Walter lying in a shabby room,
watching the door for Fanny.

"Yes," I said, "I suppose you've got to." She turned and
looked at me, surprised. There was real feeling in her face, a
sudden friendliness, and it touched me.

"We'll talk of it later, child," I said, and went away. I went
to my room and I started reading *The Ginkgo Tree* all over
again. I don't know why I did that. It had been on the best-
seller list that week, and that surprised me. This time I tried
to see the boy Johnny as Philip, but he wasn't, not to me. Yet
both Jerry and Fanny had said he was. And this boy was desperate, and it seemed that Philip must have been too. I tried
to see myself in the dreadful mother, but I couldn't. I looked
at that "For Cornelia." I'd never mentioned it to Philip or Jen
or anyone. But I remember sitting there looking at it, not feeling that sort of pride I'd felt in it at first, but something else I
couldn't name.

Fanny didn't have to put off college, for Walter died the
fourth of September. It would have been natural for Fanny to
break down then, after all the strain of the summer, but she
didn't. Walter had all his affairs in order. Mate took charge of
the funeral. It seemed odd that there was nothing for me to

do for the burial of my husband. I didn't even go to the funeral—that's always seemed strange to me, and maybe wrong. But when I said something about our driving in together, Fanny turned on me and said, "You're not *going?*"

"Naturally I'm going," I said.

"No," she said. "You can't. How could you?"

"After all, he was my husband," I said.

"Mother," Philip said, "you don't really want to go. Why should you? Why don't you just skip it? Everyone knows you didn't live together. No one will expect you."

Perhaps I was just being conventional—I don't know. Philip made it seem silly to go. But I felt determined till Fanny said, "Oh, do as you please. It doesn't matter. Not any more. He loved you so terribly much all his life, and you didn't go to see him once while he was sick. Not even once. He won't know you're there, but go if you want to—if it makes you feel any better."

I just looked at her, and then I went away and I didn't go to the funeral. They took Jen with them, though. Just a friend, not a wife—that was cruel of Fanny. For of course Walter hadn't loved me at all. Would he have left me if he had? You'd think that I was to blame for the separation. Had Walter liked dramatics, then, as Philip did? Had he made Fanny believe such nonsense? I looked at the book again, at those two words on the flyleaf. I remember thinking, Suppose it's true? Suppose it's *true?*

I was still upstairs in my room when they got back. It was Jen who came up to me. I was just sitting there, feeling numb, not myself, and Jen came over and knelt beside my chair, leaned her head against me, and said, "Oh, Cornelia! He's *dead.* Oh, Cornelia!"

I wanted to say it was nothing to me, but I couldn't. She took it for granted that I grieved as she did for John. I wanted to cry, but I didn't.

After a while she got up, said, "We'll miss him so, Cornelia. We'll miss him terribly." She bent and kissed me and went away. And then I did feel tears coming, but whether they were for Walter or because I was moved by Jen's love, I don't know. "Come out to the terrace, Maud—or whoever you are," Walter said. . . . "You're like the snow—will you marry me?" Walter said.

18

FANNY herself came to me and said, "I'm sorry about this afternoon. I'm really sorry."

"Forget it. It was better that I stay home."

"I'm sorry," she said again.

We sat in the lawyer's office, Fanny and I, and found out that Walter had left any royalties from his book to Fanny, everything else to me. There was nothing else, it seemed. His small savings had all been swallowed up in those last weeks, and in the funeral. There was no word of Philip at all.

As we went out I said, "He had a son too."

"Philip helped him write the will," Fanny said. "He said he didn't want anything—he said he'd always had more than his share. He—he said the book was his bequest."

"And when did all this happen?" I said.

"In Princeton. They had time for talk there."

"A pretty subject for discussion, when Philip was so near death himself!" I said.

"Maybe that's why it came up."

"It isn't that I begrudge you anything—and I am afraid it

216

won't be too much anyway. It's just that for a minute I resented Philip's being forgotten," I said. "You're quite welcome to anything that comes from Walter's writing. But the income from a book is very limited, Fanny—it may see you through a year of school, but that's about all, I'm afraid."

"I can work summers," Fanny said. "I may have to take it slowly, I don't know. It won't matter."

"Oh, I'll see you through, no matter what. Your father may have thought I didn't care for the finer things of life, but I have always expected that my children would be educated. I'm well aware that you have some prejudices against me but I don't believe you should let them stand in the way of a proper education."

We were walking along the street now. It was a cool day, though the sun was shining. Fall seemed already to have come.

"Mother—" Fanny began in a hesitating way.

"Yes? What is it?"

"Did you love Father?"

She embarrassed me by her directness. She often did that. I said, "Well, isn't that a personal question, child?"

"I'm not a child. I wish you wouldn't call me that," Fanny said. "Yes, it is a personal question. You don't have to answer it. But I thought—the day of the funeral—that maybe I'd been wrong all this time. That maybe you did love Father. You've been kind to me; I'm grateful, and I shouldn't have spoken to you the way I did. I don't like not understanding things, and it's always seemed so strange about you and Father. Philip used to come when I was very little, and I didn't understand it even then, why he had to run away from school to see me. I think I thought you must be some sort of monster. But you aren't. Only Father was so special—he was wonderful, really he was. So I couldn't see what the trouble was, how you could have helped loving him. Because he did love you—he always loved you. And when he used to get so tired at the writing—one night I went in and he was asleep over his papers. I woke him up and begged him to go to bed, and he said, 'I must finish this. I must, you see, darling. It's a promise I made to your mother. I must keep it.'"

You know, I was tempted, tempted to say that of course I loved him, to fix up some sort of excuse for our separation, but I didn't.

"I'm afraid you misunderstood your father," I said. "I suppose it seems to you now, while you are young and full of ideals, that true love never dies. Well, it does. People marry who never should have married. Your father and I were two such people. We didn't like the same things, have the same values. It rubbed on our nerves, and that's the truth, Fanny. We couldn't live together any longer. But we bore each other no ill will."

"But why did he take me?" Fanny said.

Now that was a question I wished she hadn't asked. I knew why, in a twisted kind of way. But it wouldn't sound good to Fanny, this Fanny who was so graceful, so lovely, so exactly the kind of girl you would like for a daughter. It wasn't why he took her, but why I let him take her that she wanted to know, and how could I tell her that?

"It was fair, wasn't it?" I said at last. "We parted amicably, and each had one of you children. I don't like this discussion much. It's no good going over old quarrels, old troubles."

"But it's still a trouble," Fanny said. "It's always been a trouble. I've been happy. Aunt Mate was so good to me—and Father was wonderful. But I've always wondered how it happened, how it could have happened. You see, I remembered you. You didn't like me, I thought—you wanted me away from you. I used to cry at first, but I got over that. But now you do seem to like me and you've been kind. I am confused."

I couldn't say, could I, that it was true, that I hadn't liked her back then, that she made me uncomfortable, that she was disobedient and defiant, that I welcomed having Philip alone with me? No, I could not possibly say that to her, because I had become fond of her.

"Fanny," I said, "I can't talk about it. You'll have to take me on faith, I'm afraid. Your father went away from me, not I from him. I didn't send him away, and that's all I can say. I do want you with me—I want it very much indeed. Philip has always been very fond of you. It isn't true, what I said once, that he wouldn't be so fond if you were close at hand—though I thought it true when I said it. He needs you. It would be cruel if you went away from him now when he needs you so much."

"I'll stay if you want me," Fanny said.

I was relieved, and yet not quite happy, for there was something in her voice that said she did not understand her own decision, that said she still wondered and would wonder forever.

"Good!" I said.

After we were home, Fanny went out to the terrace and sat there with Philip. They talked in soft voices, talked a long time. Philip didn't get excited, just leaned back lazily and talked gently. I did want to know what they were saying, I must admit. Afterward Philip came slowly into the house alone, sat down beside me on the sofa.

"Were you listening in?" he asked, smiling at me.

"Of course not. I'm not an eavesdropper," I said.

"You've got Fanny all mixed up," he said. "You've got her wondering whether she hasn't misjudged you all these years. Do you think that's fair?"

"Oh, not you too, Philip!" I said.

"But you see, Mother, I understand you," he said. "I wish you'd let her go—she'd be safer."

"I'm not keeping her anywhere she doesn't want to be," I said. "Don't you want her here?"

"Naturally. She's my little sister. But that doesn't mean it's good for her. It isn't. She might come to blame Father, and that would be dreadful, don't you think?"

"Well, I've been blamed enough, it seems to me. Don't you think it might be nice to have it the other way for once? And I am her guardian, it seems. And while we're about it, I'm a little tired of hearing from all sides how unhappy you've been. You know very well you haven't been unhappy. At least, if you have, it's been none of my making. You have always seemed to love your home and me, and I've certainly tried to make a good home for you. So let's keep things straight and not drama-tize something that just isn't true."

"I know. I know you love me, and I love you too, Mother. Don't get angry with me. But I understand our love, which is more than Fanny does. She doesn't know a mother can love one child and not another—she doesn't see how it's possible. And if you've been hurt all these years without her, she feels she has something to make up to you. Well, she hasn't. She doesn't owe you a thing, does she? You really ought to make that very clear to her, Mother."

"Fanny and I understand each other."

"Do you? I doubt it, darling. Fanny isn't devious, like us. She wants everything clear as crystal."

"Maybe you're devious," I said. "I'm not."

"I'm trying not to be," Philip said. "You must see, Mother, that I am trying very hard not to be. We'll never be happy, any of us, unless we keep things straight and clear. And I don't think you ought to deceive Fanny about your love for her. You've never even missed her."

"I love her very much," I said. I was surprised to have that come out—and truthfully, too.

"Yes, now. How could you help it? That's not the point, is it?"

"I don't know what the point is," I said. "You don't, either. You're just trying to make things difficult. Don't talk about deviousness to me!"

Then I caught sight of his wrist, and I said, "Philip, don't quarrel with your mother. I don't think I can stand it. Let's just be happy together and wipe the past out."

"I don't know how we can do that. It's part of us," he said. "But I don't want to quarrel with you. I know I haven't been very satisfactory, and it's a pity, isn't it, when you so wanted me to shine like a star? All I want is that you be truthful and gentle with Fanny and not bind her here against her desires."

"I'm not binding anybody—not even you," I said. "Am I?" I was tired of that sort of nonsense.

"I'm not blaming you, but yes, I'm bound," Philip said. "But I see I'm bound and I accept it."

"What on earth are you talking about?" I said.

He was silent a long time, and then he said, "Sorry, Mother, I can't tell you because you just don't hear me."

He got up and strolled slowly out of the room. I could hear him talking with Bessie and Fanny in the kitchen, quite cheerfully too.

Queer, wasn't it?

They were invited to Jen's for supper that night. "Not you, Cornelia, this is just a party for the young. Do you mind? We see each other every day. Shall I ask the Adams girl too?"

"Oh, do!" Fanny said.

"No, don't," Philip said.

When they came home, quite late, I said, "Well, did Amelia come?"

"Yes," Fanny said. "Philip was awfully rude to her."

"I don't mind," I said.

"I wasn't rude," Philip said. "I was just truthful. She has a passion for truth, you know. She ought to appreciate it when she hears it."

"But she's in love with you," Fanny said.

"Amelia? Well, hardly," Philip said. "Quite the contrary. She loathes me. I asked Jen not to invite her."

"You used to be great friends. You told me so."

"That was in the long, long ago. We change—we do change, you know."

"I don't think Amelia would ever change. And I do think she's in love with you. You were cruel."

"Well, maybe I felt like being cruel. Maybe she was cruel too, in her way. You don't know Amelia. I do. Yes, we used to be friends, but we aren't friends now. She was a nice little girl, too. It's a pity."

Fanny laughed. She didn't laugh often, and when she did it was a delight to hear. "What a liar you are!" she said.

"You mean, what a liar I used to be. In my early-Amelia

days, that was. You must listen for overtones—you would hear in Amelia's remarks that she still doesn't believe a word I say. She never will, and that's that. And if I feel like being rude to her, I will be rude."

"But the head—the head up in the little room. You couldn't have done that without liking her very much. And people that love each other are often cruel—that's true. I don't know why it's so, but it is. I like her; she's so different from anyone else, beautiful in a queer way, like the statue you made."

"Yes, she has nice planes," Philip said in a quieter voice. "We used to say she looked like Nefertiti—you know, long in the Egyptian way. Mother used to think she was ugly because she was untidy, but of course she never was that. She was nicer untidy, actually. But don't try to make anything out of it, my dear sister, because there's nothing left of our friendship, and it wasn't kind of Jen to ask her."

"Have it your own way," Fanny said.

It turned out that Fanny went with Amelia when she left for MIT that fall. Mr. Adams drove up, and they offered to take Fanny. I'd planned to go myself. I thought it would be good for Philip, but there didn't seem any excuse not to let her go with Amelia. "Such a charming girl!" Mrs. Adams said on the phone. "I hope it won't bore her to travel with our little bookworm."

Fanny kissed me good-by, which pleased me. But then she clung to Philip as if suddenly she couldn't bear to go. I saw Philip look away over her head—such a strange look. Then he held her away from him, a hand on either shoulder, and he grinned at her. "For heaven's sake, you're a big girl now!" he said.

"I didn't know how much I was going to miss you," Fanny said. "I don't suppose you'll even write to me."

"Haven't I always?" Philip said. "But you needn't expect a letter every day. I'm a very busy man."

So she laughed, and then the Adamses drove in and she was gone, looking grown-up and lovely in her new suit.

"Well, I hope she has fun," I said. "She's had a hard year! I must say she stood up under it very well."

"Do you think so?" Philip asked.

I was closer to Jen than ever that year. After Fanny left I went down the hill to her house, feeling, I must say, a little limp.

"They're all growing up," Jen said. "Queer, isn't it, how we never feel we're older? Inside, we always feel just as we used to when we were very young. 'That's the real me,' we say to ourselves, and it's queer that other people don't see us that way. We're what they mean by 'middle-aged,' but I always feel we're two girls talking together."

"Well, we're not too ancient," I said.

"That's what I mean. Maybe we're ancient as all get-out to them. Philip and Jerry flatter us and make us think we seem young to them—but do we? I wonder. I think the girls are more honest—Fanny and Amelia. I think they know exactly how old we are; they know we're a different generation."

"Oh, I don't know," I said. "Fanny told me herself that she thought 'age groups' were silly, that you made your friends with people who thought as you did, no matter what the age was."

"Yes, but even so she might not think us *her* age, you know."

"You're certainly feeling your years!" I said. "I think we're pretty brisk for being so close to eternity."

"I am, at that—feeling my years, I mean. When they were all down for dinner that night, I suddenly felt old and sad, hurt for them because they were so young and so vulnerable. They hurt each other in queer ways, and if they were older they couldn't do it. I think it was Walter's dying that made me so sure life was short. John was older, but Walter was just my age. I kept feeling, But he was so *young!* And of course he wasn't any younger than I am. I remember when I first came here, how kind you both were to me, how friendly, and how I felt Walter had such promise. You think young people have promise. I always thought Walter would write something fine someday—no one ever loved good books as he did. Well, he wrote something fine, and now he's dead—over, a whole life, just in a breath. . . . And now here they all are, looking so young, so heartbreakingly *young,* and they don't know how fast time goes, how much they ought to be putting into it, or it'll get away from them with nothing done. I know I sound depressed—I think I am depressed. Philip and Amelia were hurting each other; they ought not to. There just isn't time enough for that. But maybe it's just that Philip has been so hurt himself and is striking out at someone—I don't know. I just know I do feel sad today, sad and old."

That was nonsense, because Jen looks young to this day. She has grown more handsome every year. But I must say she made me feel sad too. I've always been one to look ahead, but I suppose Walter's going stopped me for a bit too. It had been a tough year all around, and I didn't feel quite up to coping with everything those days.

"What are you trying to do?—make me cry?" I said. "I don't believe in it. And I don't believe in mourning over the years passing, either. I just want to go on with the next one."

She gave a little grin at me—out of her youth, it was—and she said, "Yes, bless you, that's the way you are. You're very good for me. Do you want tea or coffee?"

19

I SEE I became a little mawkish about Walter's death. I must pull myself together. The truth is that I have missed Walter, though I have never admitted it to anyone. The world has seemed not quite the same without Walter in it. Now why that should be, under the circumstances, I don't know. I presume, too, that when Jen talked of him I remembered him more just because she was so fond of him. Once or twice I remembered what Philip had said—that he'd thought when he was a boy that Jen was in love with Walter. It wasn't true, for she loved John. Only perhaps she did have a kind of love for Walter too. He was her kind of person. Perhaps she didn't even recognize her own feeling for him.

Walter ought to have married someone like Jen. She would have fed his ego, nursed along his books, admired him for his bookishness. But he married me. I don't understand any more how he could have done so, except that there's no sense in young people when it comes to marrying. At the time I thought it natural enough. I suppose I even liked his fine speeches, admired him for his education, but I hadn't lived with fine speeches then. But even now old sentences of his come to me at odd times. I'd had the bedroom papered in pale yellow, and Walter said, "Yes, it's lovely. A lovely shell we have. But what's the kernel, Cornelia?" And Walter wasn't religious any more than I am, but when I said something about a little dud of a minister that was in town then, he said, "It doesn't much matter—we all make some sort of peace with the universe. What does it matter whether we call it God or the Brotherhood of Man, or just Nature? Just so we don't take the strangeness and the wonder all out of the world. The Reverend Deems isn't very bright, but he's made his peace." And once he took my hand and led me down through the back yard and said, "Look. A hummingbird moth." I stood there and watched it with him. It dipped like a hummingbird in the phlox. "I wonder if he thinks he's a hummingbird," Walter said, and laughed very softly. I've never been much interested in moths, but I remember that one. I've even wondered sometimes about people, whether they think, because they look like this or that, that they are this or that. Does Jen see herself always as a great actress? Did Walter, just because he played with writing, see himself as a famous author?

That was the year the war started for us. Queer, I knew boys were drafted, I even knew Philip had registered, but I never thought of him actually in the Army. He never talked about the war at all. After Fanny went he spent a great deal of time in his room, reading and writing. Sometimes he went in to town and came home with a great armful of library books. "What on earth are you doing?" I asked him. "Homework," he said. Sometimes he went out and walked up the road, walked slowly, going nowhere.

Fanny didn't come for Thanksgiving. "Good for her!" Philip said, but naturally he was disappointed.

Then there was Pearl Harbor, and Christmas was coming on and Fanny was home and she and Philip were trimming the tree. "This is a family heirloom—cherish it!" Philip said when he hung the bird of paradise on the tree.

Jerry had been asked, but he didn't come till New Year's. He was in uniform, and I must say he looked better than I'd ever seen him, really a man at last. Philip just stood and looked at him and said, "So," and turned away.

"Yes, so," Jerry said. He looked at the tree and said, "So you did get it trimmed without me!"

He threw his cap on the sofa, sat on the stool, and looked at the tree. "Same old angel, same old bird," he said. "Nice— eh, Fanny, my love?" Then he said, "I brought you a present, honey. It's that box by my bag. Handle it gently. It's fragile."

Fanny didn't move, and he said, "Go on—get it!"

Fanny got up and fetched the package. It was just a brown corrugated flat box—no Christmas wrapping on it. "You have to imagine a red bow," Jerry said.

So Fanny opened it, and it was a record. "With all my love," Jerry said. "Play it!"

Fanny looked up from the record, straight at Jerry. She looked so beautiful, standing there looking at him. Her hair was still long, and she still wore bangs. Her brows had that winged look. She was a child, but she looked at Jerry as if she were a woman.

" 'Sonata in B Minor' by Jeremiah Baker," she said.

"For Fanny Boone," Jerry said.

Philip brought the player down and put the record on. He looked excited—more so than in a long time. It was that thing Jerry had worked on here. I remembered bits of it. But when it was all put together it was quite impressive. It started with slow, single notes—but then it seemed to grow till it filled the whole room. At the end there were just those single slow notes again. I'm not a musician, but I suppose that was fine music. I know we sat there after those last sad notes, and no one said anything.

Then suddenly Fanny, who was so controlled, jumped up, turned with a sweep of her red skirt, and knelt on the hearth beside Jerry and said, "Oh, Jerry, am I your love?"

"Yes, you're my love," Jerry said. Then he got up, as if embarrassed, began to whistle, and carried his bags upstairs.

"If only—" Fanny began.

"If only what?" Philip said.

"If only Father could have heard it," Fanny said.

"It's *The Ginkgo Tree*," Philip said. His voice was tight.

"What do you mean?" I said.

"What I said. That's the theme—*The Ginkgo Tree*."

He gave a quick smile at Fanny, followed Jerry up the stairs.

"I'm afraid I don't see the connection," I said.

Nor did I—except that *The Ginkgo Tree* started and ended with the same words.

Now, I was wrong about Jerry Baker's talent. Philip had said I would hear of him and I'd denied it. Lots of young people think they have talent, and Jerry wasn't happy at home and used music as a means of getting away from his folks, or so I thought. It seems I was wrong, for Jerry Baker has become known already. And I think I knew, hearing the record, that I'd been mistaken. I did think it was a pity that the music had been so moving and had induced Fanny to act like a young infatuated fool. Musicians are notoriously unfaithful, and I couldn't wish worse for Fanny than that she cling in a childish way to this man so much older than herself, who would certainly not cling to her till she was really grown up.

At the table Philip said, "I thought you were coming for Christmas."

"I was. Didn't you get my wire? I spent Christmas with my mother. Father's trying to get a divorce, and it set Mother back a bit."

"I thought you were a fully emancipated young man," I said. "Didn't you say so once?"

Jerry looked at me in that way he has—I call it cruel—and he said, "I said I'd got clear away. But I'm not emancipated. I don't suppose I ever will be."

Philip never said a word that I heard about Jerry's being in uniform. I did mention it, asked him where he was stationed, all that. He told me, but he didn't elaborate any. He only stayed the one day and night, and then he was gone.

"See you in the South Seas!" he said to Philip.

"No. You won't," Philip said.

Then Jerry took Fanny's hands in his, just looked at her. "Good-by, my love," he said.

He didn't kiss her, just looked at her, then dropped her hands and got into the car and drove away.

We didn't see Amelia that Christmas, and all too soon Fanny was gone and we were by ourselves again. "Will you leave the record here?" Philip asked Fanny, and she said, "All right, Philip. If you want me to."

He played it over and over, up in his room. I got so I knew it all the way through. Those single notes are still in my head —I could go to the piano and play them myself.

Then one morning right after that, Philip came down ready to go to town. When I asked him where he was going, he put his hand up against my cheek, and his eyes were strange. He seemed to ask forgiveness for something. "It's my hearing," he said. He hadn't even told me he'd had his questionnaire. I stared at him and he patted my cheek, then he kissed me and went off.

I didn't give up my son in the war. Quite the contrary, Philip never went to war. I felt sick that day, waiting for him to get back. Everyone hates war. I hated war, and yet when Philip told me he was a conscientious objector I was shocked. I suppose I showed I was shocked. Never, by a word, had he told me what he had been thinking.

"I couldn't say I was a Quaker, could I?" he said. "Nor a Jehovah's Witness. Very odd, don't you think, that you can't have principles unless they come out of a definite religion? . . . You look as if you'd wanted me to die, Mother. Or did you just want me to be a hero without dying?"

"Don't be a fool, Philip," I said. "Of course I didn't want you to die—I didn't want you to go, when it comes to that, but it could have been managed in some more respectable way, couldn't it? You did have those attacks when you were young; you're not really *fit* to go."

"I'm fit as a fiddle," Philip said. "But I'm not going to kill anyone. That's my final stand. I'm just not going to kill anyone, even if our country is overrun and we're made a subject race. Funny—once I would have, you know, just to please you, Mother. But once you've been dead, things look different. I'm not going to be sent to prison, though. You'll be amused to know I am going to work on improving a dairy herd at the State University."

"Philip, you're a citizen. You have responsibilities as a citizen," I said. "I'll go to the board and tell them about how sick you were when you were young. But you can't say you won't serve."

"They know all about every sickness I ever had," Philip said. "They even know about last spring in Princeton. Very thorough, they are. In fact, if it's any comfort to you, I think that turned the scale. I'm not a very good psychological risk for the Army. Sorry, but this is the way it's going to be."

"It's escape," I said. "You have no more right to escape your duty than anyone, son."

"No, I suppose not," he said. "Let's leave it that I *am* an escapist, if you like. Only, if I could do it respectably you wouldn't mind, would you? But for once I establish my own respectability, Mother. And I am never going to kill anyone."

He didn't go to the war. He did work with dairy herd improvement at the University. I've never understood it. How can you want your fellow men to despise you? And he must have known they did. And how could he have borne the work, which was nothing he was suited for or cared about? He did get a little leave from time to time, but he wouldn't discuss war with me or anyone. He grew thin and hard and looked as if he were in a dream. Even when Jerry was wounded, he didn't change. I held my head up but it was a great trouble. I talked of it only to Jen, and not much to her.

"You'd think I was disappointed that he wasn't going off to die," I said to her. "But it's not that, Jen. The day will come when he will see himself as a coward, and that will be more dreadful than anything that's ever happened to him. I can't bear the thought of that time."

"But he's not a coward," Jen said. "Do you think this is easier than fighting? It isn't. I don't know whether the principle is right or not—I just don't know. Philip is so—so *civilized*.

He doesn't believe civilized people kill each other. And should they? You can say we can't help it when we're in danger, but isn't it that all principles go by the board when a war is actually in progress? You've always thought Philip took life too easily. Well, he isn't taking it easily now, you may be sure. He's dead serious."

"He's no better than other young men. He hasn't any right to escape his responsibilities," I said.

"You'd be pleased enough if he had a short leg or something that would keep him out, wouldn't you?"

"That's not the same thing. Of course I'd be relieved, but he wouldn't be a byword in the town then."

Jen was knitting, which was something she'd just started since the war began. She stuck her needles into the scarf, put it down in her lap, and said, "Cornelia, you're not like that. Don't pretend you are."

"Like what?"

"I mean caring what people say. Philip's doing what he thinks is right, without considering the consequences. If ever he needed your love and faith, he needs it now."

"It's just because I do love him that I'm sick about this," I said.

"I know," Jen said very gently. I stopped talking about it.

Maybe I have always thought too highly of courage. Maybe I have cared too much about the world's opinion—not for myself but for my children, for Philip. When I saw him, he was thin and grave and tired-looking, and my heart would ache with my sorrow for him—perhaps some with shame, I don't know now. I didn't see why he made life so hard for himself and for us all.

I didn't tell Fanny. She wrote fairly often, but just short letters, telling about her work, about the professors, things like that. She now and then wrote privately to Philip, but Philip didn't show me her letters. I suppose she said more to him. I didn't know whether he had told her or not. He had, though. She came home for spring vacation and I saw she knew all about it.

"Aren't you well, Mother?" she said. "You look tired. Sorry—you don't like people to say that, do you?"

"No. But I am tired," I said. "I've never been so tired."

"Don't worry about Philip," she said. "He can't do more than what he thinks is right, can he?"

"If I only thought that was all it was," I said. "He's not the martyr type, Philip—he's afraid, and it will break him in the end. He might listen to you, child; he won't to me."

"But he's not afraid. It would be easier to go. He's not at all afraid. You mustn't ever say that, or think it, either."

"Yes. Jen said that. But it just isn't true."

"I thought you always thought Philip was right, no matter what."

I suppose I nearly always had thought just that, but I said, "Not no matter what, Fanny. But I'm thinking of his good now, too. I've always done that."

She hesitated, putting her fingers down tight over the arm of the chair where she sat. Then she said, "I don't know how to talk to you, Mother. I never have known. I guess I just don't understand you. It's—well, as I said once before, when we talk about Philip, we don't talk about the same person."

"I'm not so hard to understand," I said. "I'm just straightforward and honest, I hope. I call a spade a spade. I happen to know my son, and I love him too. That doesn't prevent me from knowing that he runs away when the going gets tough.

He wanted to stay home because he was afraid of going away from me to Endley. Then when things got bad at Endley—he did get into serious trouble there—he would have run away from Endley too. And at Princeton—what did he do there? I know Philip, and I see this for what it is, Fanny. It's another escape, that's all."

Fanny gave a sigh, then gathered herself together again and said, "But he didn't leave Endley, did he? He told me all about that. *You* wanted him to leave, wasn't that the way it was? I remember when he came to me. I was just coming out of school, and there he was, waiting for me. He told me what he'd done and he said, 'I don't know why I do such things. I must have a devil in me. If they put me out, I'll kill myself.' Yes, that's what he said. And afterward, the next time I saw him, he was so wildly happy because he wasn't leaving. If he'd been afraid, he would have been glad to leave, wouldn't he? He said Jerry fixed it. Oh, he was so happy that day! We went to the museum, and he said such funny things all afternoon. And he isn't afraid now either. You have to believe that if you really love him."

"Well, I don't go around telling anyone else how I feel," I said. "Of course I stand back of him."

But I didn't do what Fanny did. Philip was there for Saturday night and Sunday and when he came down for breakfast Sunday morning, Fanny said, "Good morning, slacker!"

"Aren't you supposed to present me with a white feather or something?" Philip said.

"Got to catch a white bird first," Fanny said.

"Davkes' have some white leghorns," Philip said.

"Oh, this must be a white swan, or an eagle at least! Yes, a white eagle, that's it."

"Jerry's out of hospital, did you know?"

"Yes, I know. Is the record in your room?"

"Help yourself," Philip said.

That night she went out to the car with him, hanging on to his arm. They laughed, and at the car he kissed her.

When she came back I said, "At least I never called him a slacker to his face, Fanny."

"Better than behind his back," Fanny said and ran upstairs, and then I heard those slow notes beginning for the thousandth time. After a while I followed her and found her there in Philip's room, just standing by the player.

The music stopped. She went on just standing there, and I said, "I don't know what will happen to Philip if anything happens to Jerry."

She looked around at me blankly. Then she said, "But nothing can happen to Jerry."

"Something could," I said. "Why not?"

I don't know why I dug away at her like that. I suppose it made me angry that Jerry was doing his duty like anyone and Philip was going off to an airplane plant every day. Even the record made me angry, for it meant work done, something accomplished, while Philip, who had more real talent than Jerry, did nothing. But then something in Fanny's face stopped me. Something bleak came into her gray eyes, some doubt of the everlastingness of life, something old and full of pain.

"No," I said, "nothing will happen to Jerry. He was born lucky."

I'VE NEVER known how much Bessie knew about me and mine. What she thought about Philip's not being in the war, I don't know. She never said. But she fussed over him just as always—over Fanny too, when she was there. Fanny got a job that summer and went in every morning with Philip.

I can tell only about those rare times when Philip came home. Weeks, months went by when I did not see him at all. But one afternoon I do remember. Philip and Fanny sat out under the big maple and I cut grass around the trees, grass Joe should have taken care of. Amelia Adams came walking up the road from the valley.

"Hi!" Fanny called out. "Come see us!"

Amelia had on jeans, as she used to when she was younger. She stood there in the road an instant, hesitating, then strolled up the drive, stopped in front of them.

"Hello," Philip said. "Take a chair."

She sat down cross-legged on the grass, but she didn't look friendly. Philip said, "Actually, this tree is sacred to Amelia and me, to our early love. You ought not to sit here, Fanny."

"Oh, don't move, Fanny," Amelia said. "It's just any tree now."

"How faithless you are," Philip said. "You were such a nice little girl, too. I was really fond of you."

"I liked you too," Amelia said. "In fact I thought you were wonderful."

"He is. He really is," Fanny said.

"Well, he was healthier then. He didn't have any allergies or anything wrong with his heart or flat feet or anything. He was quite attractive," Amelia said.

"No, the body disintegrates—but I still read poetry beautifully," Philip said.

"Yes, I can well imagine you do," Amelia said. "But sometimes life is prose."

"Oh, never, sweet Amelia! Never say it. You might make it so."

"It is so," she said flatly.

"But it was nicer when it was all poetry, wasn't it? You know, you look quite familiar in those jeans. I almost feel I've met you somewhere before."

"Stop," Fanny said. "Stop it."

"Stop what?" Philip said in his laziest voice.

"You know what. Being so dreadful to each other. I could hate you both for it. Have you forgotten how we walked in the park and you told me how to do long division and how you told me about walking to the creek with Amelia? And how you said she was the only girl you'd ever liked, except me?"

I went on clipping, but I looked around and saw that Amelia looked pale and angry.

"Oh, of course I remember. I have the gift of total recall," Philip said. "I forgot to tell you, though, that she was a black-hearted Puritan—or maybe I hadn't realized it yet. You know, I still like her, though. Funny, isn't it?"

"No, it isn't funny at all," Fanny said.

"I think it is. I often have a good laugh, all by myself, over Amelia. Jerry and I had it all planned out, how I'd marry Amelia, and he would come to board with us—and he'd furnish the piano. Amelia wouldn't mind the racket, because she's the understanding kind—she goes to the heart of things. She listens. Don't you, Amelia?"

Amelia didn't answer. Philip said again, "*Don't* you?"

"I hear you," Amelia said. "But it's just words, words that don't mean anything at all. You're all words, and charm—but you're nothing inside. You're no good, Philip, so don't waste your charm on me. It just doesn't take, any more."

"Oh, I could make it take if I tried. If I really cared to try," Philip said. "But I don't. And if I were you I wouldn't say what I was or wasn't 'inside.' Those are just words too, you know. You used to know without any words at all. I daresay you'll turn into a Curie or something, you'll concentrate like all get-out on something, and you'll dry up and forget you're a human being at all. In fact, you've forgotten already. But don't talk about what I am inside, for you couldn't ever possibly know, child. You've forgotten the language for the inside story—if you ever really knew it. And now, would you just as soon run along and leave Fanny and me to our fantasies? You've broken the rhythm."

Amelia got up. She stood there, head bent in the old way. Only now her hair was short and didn't flop over her face. But I did remember that that was exactly her old posture.

"Excuse me for intruding," she said.

"Oh, we don't mind a hello, just in passing," Philip said. "But run along now."

She went down the drive and up the road toward home.

"Oh, Philip," Fanny said. "How could you?"

"How could I not? She's like one of those chiggers that get under your skin and you can't ever get it out."

"Why do you try to?"

"Because I won't be despised by Amelia Adams. She considers me a fool, a liar, and a coward. And it's true, she's going to turn into a scientist and she's going to be as unyielding as iron."

"She loves you."

"You said that before. It isn't true. You're the only one I know who knows what love is—you know that isn't love, Fanny. Well, Father knew too."

I went farther off, to another tree, not wanting to hear any more. They hadn't even seemed to notice I was nearby. Now, I don't like Amelia, but even I thought Philip was hard on her. Of course she was angry with him for his pacificism and his laziness. Who wouldn't have been? At least she had that much sense, but still I didn't like anyone turning against Philip. And I was hurt, too, by what he'd said about the ones who knew what love was. Didn't he know I knew? He must.

It's hard to think of those years, the rationing, the sameness, the war news, the months and months of Philip's working at something he didn't like.

Where were all his dreams now? . . . "What were your dreams?" Philip asked me once. I did have a dream, I suppose, and I ought to have admitted it to Philip. I did want to go to college, and maybe that's why I was so determined Philip should have a good education. Father thought college was a waste, not practical, he thought we couldn't afford it. Business school was all he would give me. I suppose I have always held that against Father. I remember Mother coming into my room, sitting on the bed and putting her hand on my hair. "I'm sorry it can't be college. I'm so sorry, Cornelia," she said. She was always so tart with me, but she was gentle and loving that night. I don't know why I remember that now.

The weeks and the months and even the years went by somehow. I didn't have to worry about Philip's having to capture some beachhead, I didn't have to wait for news from the war office, as so many women did. I suppose I felt guilty that I didn't have to worry. Somehow we lived through that time, but I don't know how any more. It is not easy to be always on guard against the scorn and pity in people's eyes. People were always telling me about this one or that one in service, about someone's being killed or wounded or home on leave. And then would come this embarrassed lowering of eyes, a reddening of face.

I met Lucia Adams in the village one day. "Isn't it dreadful, trying to shop?" she said. "I'm worn out trying to find some meat. There's a little place over in Plessyville—now and then you *can* get a roast there. I've managed to get hold of a couple of ration books, too. And with the girls away, I save up. Did I tell you Susan was engaged? He's such a lovely boy, a lieutenant in the Navy. I do love these military weddings, don't you?"

"I can't say I know anything about them," I said. "And a lot of them will end in disaster, I imagine. Perhaps a little glamour will suffice them, I don't know. But when the husband gets killed, or doesn't come back—or even if he comes

back, he'll be changed and she'll be changed—the glamour
will be off and they'll have to start fresh. I don't know whether
any young people have that much courage."

Yes, I dared to say things like that to people.

"Well, it's the courage they have that makes them go off
to war in the first place, isn't it?" Lucia said. "They'll have
enough to carry them through, I fancy. I'm sure Susan and
Lawrence have." Then she flushed, as if embarrassed, only I
think she'd meant to say exactly what she did say.

I heard quite a few remarks like that over the years—remarks
that were hard for a proud woman to take. But I took them, I
kept my head up, and I didn't nag at Philip any more. I just
tried to keep going on an even keel, did what I had to in the
way of rationing and the like—never used the black market as
Lucia did. Maybe I would have if I hadn't had those words
from her—maybe it was just anger at her that kept me from it.

Dreadful and long those years of war, too dreary and yet too
full of pain to talk about. And then Jerry came home. It just
happened that Philip was here that day. I hadn't seen him in
three months, and it would have been better if he hadn't come
then. But there he was. Jerry hadn't sent word that he was coming—the war wasn't quite over yet—but on this Sunday a car
came in with a woman at the wheel. I just got a glimpse of her
at the wheel and knew there was someone with her, but I didn't
see who it was. Then the car stopped and the door slammed.

"Who's that?" Philip said. Fanny was there too. She was
mending a hole in the sleeve of a jacket. The door opened
without anyone's knocking, and there was Jerry, in uniform,
but with one sleeve limp and thrust into a pocket. I must admit that sleeve gave me a turn.

"Jerry! You old so and so!" Philip said, jumping up from the stool. Fanny just sat there and looked at him, and the jacket she was working on slid to the floor. Then Philip put his hands on Jerry's shoulders and he said, "Damn them! Damn them all to hell! Damn them!"

"All right, kid. Turn it off," Jerry said, but I've never forgotten how gentle his voice was. "Hello, Mrs. Boone. Hi, Fanny. Could I bring my mother in for a few minutes? We can't stay long."

"Of course," I said.

Fanny hadn't said a word, even to his greeting. The jacket lay there on the floor, and I picked it up.

The woman came in—a little, pretty woman, with big, tragic eyes and a good many lines in her face, though she was so pretty. I said, "How do you do? I'm Mrs. Boone, and we're very pleased to see Jerry's mother. Come sit down."

She said, "I did want to see you all! You've always been so kind to Jerry!"

Her voice was quick and nervous, and when she sat down, her hands wouldn't keep still. It was easy to imagine her an alcoholic, though she seemed sober enough that day.

"Well, here we all are," I said. "Are we what you expected?"

She looked around at us all with those quick, darting glances of hers. "You're all lovely," she said. "It's always been such a comfort to me to have Jerry so at home here. I just haven't been able to keep a home going, I've been ill so often. Such a pity. A boy does need a home. . . ." Her voice trailed off and I saw Jerry give her a smile, a really nice smile such as he had certainly never given me. She hurried on, "Would it seem an intrusion," she said, "if I asked to see the whole house, and the garden? Then I could think of what it was like when Jerry was here. I declare, he does think this is his home—you've been so *kind*."

Philip had been looking straight at her, his face, so thin now, with a strange expression on it. "Come along, let me show you everything," he said. She got up and went with him toward the kitchen, and I heard them talking to Bessie.

"Mothers are always curious," Jerry said. "Is all well here, Mrs. Boone?" He didn't even look at Fanny.

"Yes, well enough," I said. "Are you through with the Army?"

"I will be soon. I haven't been discharged yet."

I simply couldn't mention his arm. I had no patience with Fanny's feeling for Jerry, but I did wish she would say something.

Then she did. She got up, went over, and knelt down by his chair, put her face against his sleeve, and began to cry. "Oh, Jerry! Oh, *Jerry!*" she kept saying.

"Oh, come now, Fanny!" he said. "Let's not have any dramatics!" His voice wasn't even kind.

"Come walk in the garden with me," she said.

There was a little pause then. When Jerry spoke his voice was stiff, not even friendly. "I think I'd better wait for Mother here," he said.

"You mean I'm not your love any more?" Fanny said.

"I'm afraid I mean just that," Jerry said. "So get up and stop weeping."

Fanny stopped moving—stopped breathing, it seemed. She leaned back after a minute, put her hands flat down on the floor behind her, and she said, "Look at me. Say that again. You can't."

He looked right at her and he said, "You're a nice girl, Fanny—but let's put away childish things, shall we?"

She did just that. She stood up and held her head up and looked quite grown-up, a little haughty, even. "As you like," she said. "Shall I get some tea, Mother?"

"Would you?" I said. I would have preferred to do it myself, but I saw she wanted to get away.

Yes, young people can be terribly cruel.

"You could have let her down a little more kindly than that, couldn't you?" I said.

"Is there any kind way?" he asked. "You ought to be pleased."

"I am. But after all, you did encourage the child."

"She isn't a child any more," Jerry said. "Oh, there you are, Mother! The house is charming, isn't it?"

"Yes, Jerry. It's a real home," she said. "A real home."

Fanny brought the tea, and we got through it somehow. Once it came to me that a drink would have helped more, that that woman needed a drink terribly much. But somehow we did finish. We talked a little, and then Jerry said, "We'd better get on, Mother. We have quite a way to drive yet."

"How about a real stay?" Philip said to Jerry. "A month or two?"

"Perhaps—in the fall," Jerry said. "I'd like that." He didn't so much as look at Fanny, though he said good-by to her and to me politely. He even went out and spoke to Bessie.

After they were gone, Philip sat there on the stool, his head in his hands, saying, "Damn! damn!" over and over.

"He can still do his composing," I said.

"Oh, sure, sure," Philip said bitterly.

Fanny drifted away and up the stairs. After a while I heard those slow notes of the record beginning.

"He was pretty cruel to Fanny," I said.

"Well, what in God's name else could he be?" Philip said. He got up, went to the stairs, and called out, "Turn that off! Turn it *off*, Fanny!"

But the music went on, getting louder, fuller, the way it always did. Fanny didn't answer. Philip stood there, hanging on to the post at the foot of the stairs, as if he couldn't stand up without it. He just stood there till at last the record was done, those slow notes repeating themselves.

Bessie came in and took the tea things. "It's real nice seeing Mr. Jerry again," she said. "A pity about his arm, though—a real pity. I guess they get used to it, though."

"Yeah, a pity," Philip said. "It's hell, that's what it is."

He went slowly up the stairs. I don't know what he said to Fanny.

OH, BUT Fanny was proud the rest of that summer! She even spoke of Jerry sometimes, as if he were only a family friend, no one special in her life. She spoke of his mother. But she was tight-wound and you couldn't get close to her. . . . And then came the day when the whistles blew in the village and I went down to Jen's and we said, "Thank God!" for the war was over. It had seemed the bad dream would never end, but it ended, and Philip came home. Came home from improving dairy herds.

He didn't rejoice that the war was over. The first thing he said to me was, "Well, Mother, you can relax now. You won't have to apologize for me any more."

"Don't be stupid, Philip. I never have apologized for you," I said.

"I can read you like a book, darling," he said. Then he came over to me, bent and kissed me, and rubbed my hair into a tousle. "You've had a tough time," he said.

But after supper he went out by himself and walked a long time. He didn't even take Fanny with him.

Fanny came and sat with me, almost as if she really wanted to be with me.

"Why didn't you go with Philip?" I asked her.

"He didn't want me," she said. "I don't believe he needs anyone very much any more. He's gone away, even from me."

"I suppose seeing Jerry upset him," I said. "He's always worshiped Jerry, goodness knows why. And it is a pity, but still— Well, child, I told you the time would come when he'd feel shame, and I think the time has come. He's feeling that Jerry fought his war for him, and it hurts."

"No. I don't think that's it," Fanny said. "He hasn't changed his mind about the war."

"I think he has."

But he hadn't. I remember when some book came out, a popular book by a popular novelist—that wasn't so long ago— and in it the man said something like this: "The only noble profession for a man today is that of soldiering." I don't suppose those were the words, but that was the sense. Philip took the book and put it on the fire.

"And that is what we've come to," he said. "A man can be praised for saying that."

But that's getting ahead of my story. It was true that Philip didn't seem to need anyone in those days. Fanny went back to school. Philip didn't try to get a job; he just stayed home.

"Why don't you try getting something in your own line?" I said.

"Tired of having me around?" he said.

"Of course not. But you don't want to sit here with nothing to do."

"Oh, don't I? You'd be surprised!"

Then he asked me if I'd mind if he fixed his room up a little. He said he'd pay for it—though I don't know where he'd get the money from. And little by little he did fix it up, till it was as it is now. He spent a good deal of time in here. Sometimes I'd hear the typewriter going, but generally it was quiet. Some-times I'd see him sitting out on the grass, talking with Joe for an hour at a time. Or occasionally he walked down the hill to see Jen.

In October Jerry came, as he'd promised. He was out of uniform now. He planned to have an artificial arm, but he didn't have it yet. I didn't think it would be good for Philip to have him here; it would remind him too much of the last years and his own lack of participation in the war; but he didn't seem to mind that at all. He walked with Jerry, talked with him endlessly, got him going on music again. He said he was very good at copying score and he'd be his amanuensis.

"I am afraid I have nothing to say," Jerry said.

"Nonsense!" Philip said. "If not you, who?"

"I feel, no one. There's a silence settled on the world," Jerry said.

"Well, break it!"

And in the second week they did sit at the piano, or Jerry did, with Philip beside him, and that old experimenting be-gan again, with phrases played over and over. Only of course it was harder, doing it all with one hand. It made me sad to hear them, but I was glad enough to have them doing any-thing.

You might have thought Jerry's experiences in the war would make him write violent, bitter music, but he did noth-ing of the sort. He was working on something very gentle, simple as a lullaby. It was called "Requiem for a Child Killed by a Bomb"—a horrible title. But I didn't even know it was called that till afterward.

Jerry stayed on into November, but when it came near Thanksgiving he said one morning that he had to be off.

"Oh, nothing is calling you," Philip said. "You must stay till Christmas at least."

"No, I must go. I have things to tend to," he said.

"Fanny'll be disappointed," Philip said.

"Oh, I doubt it. I'm an old story to Fanny."

"Don't be a fool!" Philip said. "Are you trying to be noble, or what? You know Fanny's madly in love with you and always has been. You'll never be an old story to Fanny."

"Well, maybe I'm an old story to myself. Fanny is very young—now she seems very young indeed. And nobility's not in my line, you know that."

So Jerry went off—to Philadelphia, I think, where he had been studying music before the war. Fanny called up and asked if she could bring a friend for Thanksgiving. It was the first time she had done such a thing, but of course I said yes. She brought a young man, Joe Levison, a law student at Harvard, a man with a quick tongue and a quick mind too. He was obviously in love with Fanny, and she seemed friendly enough toward him. He went out of his way to be polite to me, and also, I think, to show me how brilliant he was. Philip didn't warm up to him much, but he watched him all the time with a sardonic eye.

Levison said something about having had his law studies cut into by the war, and Philip said, "I wouldn't know anything about that. I sat out the war."

Levison stared at him, and Philip explained more carefully, "I was a CO."

"Well, of course any civilized human being wanted to be just that," Levison said. "Naturally."

"But not many had the courage to be," Fanny said sharply.

"No, true," Levison said. "But when it comes right down to it, most of us are conformists."

He tried to be diplomatic and tactful about it, but you could see he thought Philip a queer egg. He laughed and said, "I actually sat out the war myself—I got stuck in Washington."

"But in a uniform," Fanny said.

"Oh, yes, in a uniform," Levison said. "But I do admire any-one who has the courage of his convictions. And what are you doing now?"

"Oh, writing a bit. Actually not much of anything. I am a very lazy man."

"What sort of writing?" Levison was a persistent young man.

"Oh, I skip about from this to that. I'm versatile," Philip said. "If you'll excuse me, I think I'll run down and see Jen."

"We'll come too," Fanny said.

Philip acted as if he didn't hear her, went off, banging the door.

Levison said, "I wasn't being polite, you know. I do admire someone who is a genuine pacifist and acts on his beliefs. I used to talk like a pacifist myself, but when it came right down to it I couldn't act."

Fanny said, "I know. Not many did."

He wasn't such a bad young man. I see I am being a little caustic about him, but he wasn't bad. He was intelligent and he was devoted to Fanny, that was plain to see. And he had good manners.

But at Christmas, Philip said, "I thought we might have to suffer your young lawyer for Christmas."

Fanny had fixed her hair in a different way that year. She had pulled it back into a knot at her neck. It changed her looks but didn't make her less beautiful. She turned and looked at Philip and said, "Suffer? Joe doesn't make anyone suffer. He's very kind and very nice. Is there any reason I can't have a friend or two not passed on by you?"

"None at all. Have a dozen. In fact, I'd like it better if there were a dozen."

"Look here," I said. "I won't have you two quarreling. That I won't have."

Fanny turned and smiled at me. "Oh, we're not quarreling," she said. "But I can't have anyone telling me what friends to have—not Philip or anyone."

"Just so you don't marry Levison," Philip said.

"And I might even do that," Fanny said.

Philip was polishing the brass andirons. It was a job he always did. He put down the chamois on the hearth and he looked up at Fanny.

"I thought you loved Jerry," he said.

"I've put away childish loves," Fanny said.

"You mean you'd ditch him because he lost an arm? Oh, no, kid, you wouldn't do *that*."

She sat down suddenly on the stool beside Philip. "He's ditched me," she said flatly. "Of course I love him, but he doesn't want me any more. If it were just his arm—it isn't that. He isn't trying to be noble, you know. He just doesn't want me any more. So what am I going to do? Sit and mourn for something I can't have? No, I'm not going to do that. I'm going to live somehow, and probably with someone, even if not Joe Levison. Someone. I'm not going to waste my life."

Philip began to polish again, quickly and angrily. "Have it your own way," he said.

"You'll get over Jerry, child," I said. Yes, I tried to comfort her. There was something too desolate about the way she sat there on the stool.

"I'm lying," she said. "Of course I'll never get over him. Never. I thought he meant it. I know he's older, but I didn't think that had anything to do with it. I'll never get over Jerry. But all the same . . ."

"If I were you, kid—not that you've asked for my advice—but if I were you, I would wait a bit. A man has to get the war out of his system, you know. You're not so ancient you can't wait a bit."

"I could wait forever," Fanny said. "Only it's no good."

"Oh, it's good," Philip said. "He loves you all right. He probably thinks he can't earn a living—I don't know. But Jerry doesn't change."

"He looked at me as if he really thought I was a child," she said. "I don't change either. Here, I'll polish that one." And she took the chamois and began to polish the other andiron.

I couldn't tell her that everyone changed.

"You'd both better be a little more realistic," I said. "Jerry is too old for you, Fanny. He was always kind to you and teased you because you were Philip's little sister, but he's old. In fact, he's always been old. He was too old for you at fifteen. He's vastly too old now. He showed you quite plainly, in front of my very eyes, that he didn't want any nonsense of that kind any more. I thought he was a little rough on you, but better that than let you go mooning after him forever. Much better."

"But Fanny and I are two of the old ones too, Mother," Philip said. "We're quite as old as Jerry."

"You don't act it," I said.

"You must let us act it," Fanny said then. "I see what Philip meant—I really begin to see it now. You must let us act our age, Mother."

"Well, I've never stopped you," I said. "It would certainly please me more than anyone to see a little maturity around here."

That's true enough. I like to see people who stand on their own feet, answer questions for themselves, take responsibility. I'm that kind myself. I've never dreamed about the time when I'd be mature, I've just acted as if I were. That sounds odd—like the remark about the hummingbird moths. Have I acted that way and therefore thought I was that way? I wonder. Fanny is the same. Yes, perhaps she is like me in that. Philip is different, with a kind of laziness at the very core of him—a lack of decision, you might say—that makes him have no authority. Or is it as Jerry said, that Philip sees all sides of a thing and therefore only seems to lack decision? Once Walter said to me, "Oh, yes, in a black and white world, I suppose that's true." I've forgotten what we were talking about, but I do remember his saying that, and not knowing quite what he meant. I do know right from wrong—and why shouldn't anyone? Philip has always seemed to feel there were infinite gradations in right and wrong, that you could never have the right to say, "That's wrong." But that's not true. You know, all right, though you wriggle around excusing yourself forever and a day.

I see I'm leaving out the very considerable success of

Walter's book. Some book club took it, there's been a paper-
back edition, and there were foreign sales. I think there's
been about twenty thousand dollars come in from it, which
has been very nice for Fanny and gives her independence. It
has seemed strange to me, this success, for *The Ginkgo Tree*
is what you'd call a precious sort of book, literary as all get-out,
subtle—not much plot or outright drama. It's of a special boy
with a special problem. It's always bothered me that I haven't
understood this. It's bothered me, that first review in the
Times. How did they know it would be a success?

Of course I'm pleased, for Fanny's sake. Not that she
wouldn't have been independent without it. She would have
been. I must say I thought that showed spirit, that she determined to make a life for herself even if Jerry didn't want her.
But she never asked that young Levison down again. She did
ask others, though, and the house took on considerable life in
that period. A couple of times she brought girls, but Philip
didn't warm up to them much. I liked having people in the
house, different people—not always just Jerry Baker. I thought
it was a sign of health.

It was in the spring that Philip had a letter from Jerry. He
heard from him fairly often, but rarely read his letters to me.
This time we were still at the table when the mail came, and
Philip went out and brought the mail in, dropped it down by
my plate. I gave him his letter, and he sat there reading it.

"What's the matter? Bad news?" I said.

"That tears it," Philip said. "He's taken an apartment in
Philly and has his mother with him."

"So much for the young man who got clear away," I said. I
couldn't help being that way about Jerry.

"Oh, he's away, all right," Philip said. "But he's merciful.

He can't help that. When the divorce went through, she went off the deep end. He can't help being merciful."

"I wouldn't want to be pitied by Jerry," I said.

"No. Nor I. It would be like being pitied by God. Maybe he just loves her. Maybe it's as simple as that."

"You couldn't love an alcoholic," I said.

"You mean you couldn't. But Jerry's not you, Mother."

"No, thank heavens, he's not. And I don't envy his mother, being taken in by him. Though I suppose he sees it as a duty and ought to be commended."

"I'd take her in myself, if it would free Jerry of her," Philip said. "But of course it wouldn't. And maybe she'll straighten out with him. Who knows?"

"I know. She won't. She's weak as water, you can tell by looking at her. She had Jerry before, didn't she, and it didn't stop her? No, everything will be spoiled for her, and Jerry too. He won't be able to compose, and she'll live off him—"

"Oh, he won't stop composing. He's stronger than that. Only it'll be tough. I'd wanted him here this summer."

I suppose I could have said I'd ask his mother too, but I didn't really see why I should let myself and all of us in for that. It was, after all, Jerry's problem. But I think it pleased me a little to have Jerry, always so strong for freedom, for "getting clear away," stuck with his alcoholic mother. He'd find out it wasn't quite so easy, being responsible for somebody else. Oh, I did pity Jerry some for losing his arm, all that. But he'd always been a thorn in my flesh. He'd been running around, free as air, all his life, and it was easy for him to be righteous for other people. And now he wasn't quite so free, and I did have the feeling that it would be good for him to see how it felt.

It wasn't long after that that one morning Philip came and put a check down before me. It was to him and for twenty dollars. "You see, we're a family of authors," he said. "Isn't that elegant?"

"But what's it for?" I asked.

"Oh, just a little essay on music," he said.

"And what do you know about music?" I asked him.

"Quite a bit, actually. Since we're partners, ten of it's yours."

"I think you need some new shoes," I said. "We'll skip sharing this one."

"Don't you even want to read the essay?" he asked.

"Naturally I want to read it. Is it published?"

"Yes. They pay on publication."

"Why didn't you tell me before?"

"I don't know. I wanted it an accomplished fact, I suppose. Are you pleased? Say you're pleased, Mother!"

"Wait till I read it. I'm pleased you're doing something, I'll say that—though the life of a writer isn't what I'd like for you, if you want the truth. You won't make much of a living out of essays on music, son."

"No, I don't suppose I will. Does it seem terribly important? Oh, I'll make a little, maybe more than you think. I'll try to pay my way, if that's what's worrying you. But do you mind if I don't care awfully about making a lot of money?"

"Well, what's money but a sign that you're ambitious? We'll live, I daresay, if you never earn a penny, but I wouldn't want that kind of a life for you. I don't think life means very much without ambition."

"Oh, I'm ambitious! Never doubt it! But not so much for money. I'm afraid you'll have to get used to that, Mother. Would you like me to take a garret room somewhere else?"

"Don't be silly! Where's the essay?" I said.

He brought it to me. It was in a little magazine, one of those prestige affairs that the highbrows read and that don't pay much for material. It was a clever little essay, very erudite. I didn't know half the time what he was talking about with his musical terms thrown in so freely. It certainly wasn't anything that would ever be popular.

"Sounds like a gabfest with Jerry Baker," I said. "Well, congratulations, Philip. But I must say that you'll never pay your way, as you call it, with articles like this."

"Oh, I see. You wouldn't feel like being proud of me, then?"

"Of course I'm proud of you. I always am. But I'm a realist, son."

He took the magazine from my hands, looked down at the pages. He had a sudden tired look, as he'd had after he came back from Princeton that awful time.

"I'll do better next time," he said. "I suppose it isn't much."

"Oh, it's fine, for that kind of thing," I said. "I didn't know you knew that much. Don't take it away. I want to show it to Jen."

"Must it be *shown* to somebody?" he said. He went away, taking the magazine with him. I felt upset because he hadn't believed I was proud of him. I didn't want him to be a writer, but if he was going to be a writer I did wish he'd do something that would be read, that would make him successful and bring in a little income too. Yet he made me feel I'd failed him, and that hurt.

I had a special supper that night. "This is a celebration!" I said. He smiled at me, but he didn't talk about the article any more.

The next day a telegram was phoned to the house. Philip

had gone off walking somewhere so I said I'd take it. It was from Fanny and said something like this: "Darling CO. It's wonderful. You're wonderful. In a tailspin of delight. Bless you forevermore. Love, Fanny."

When Philip came in I said, "You had a wire from Fanny. Here it is. I've never known her to be *that* enthusiastic before."

"No, she did go out on a limb, didn't she?" Philip said.

"I must say I could get along without that 'CO.' Does she have to do that?"

"It must be. She did it," Philip said. "Did you think I'd mind?"

"I do," I said.

"But it was to me," Philip said and took the slip of paper upstairs with him.

I suppose it was just because she was young, for there wasn't anything to get that excited about. But in a way I was glad she was excited, because I did feel I hadn't been excited enough and that Philip had felt it. Yes, I've always known that I should have been more pleased, but you can't take it back afterward.

JEN CAME IN one day, bringing daffodils, though I have
great clumps of them myself. "It's spring," she said.

I put the daffodils in a big white bowl of mine and
then sat down with Jen.

"I've done something odd," Jen said. "Now I've done it, I
almost wish I hadn't, for I don't think you'll like it."

"Well, what is it?" I asked her.

"I've asked Jerry Baker and his mother for a visit."

"Jen! Whatever for?" I said.

"Hard to say. Only Philip told me about his mother, and I
couldn't seem to bear it that Jerry had shouldered that all
alone. Philip said he wasn't coming here, and I don't suppose
he would, under the circumstances. Probably he won't come
to me, either, since he's first of all your friend and used to coming to this house. But I don't do much that's useful any more
—I just had a sudden notion that that would be useful. I do
like Jerry so much, and I could take his mother under my wing
for a bit and leave him free."

"You must be out of your mind," I said. "Did you ever cope
with an alcoholic, Jen?"

"No, I never did. But it can't hurt me to try for a few weeks, can it? He hasn't said they'd come yet—he probably won't. But I thought I ought to tell you I'd done it. Do you mind?"

"It's your business," I said. "I think I do mind some, though. I think it won't hurt Jerry to have some responsibility for a change. He's always ducked responsibility. I could have asked them here, but I honestly didn't think I should, or even ought to consider it. And I don't see really why you should be willing to let yourself in for such complications."

"But I don't think he has ducked responsibility. You don't either!"

"Oh, I know he did his duty in the Army, and goodness knows I pity him for losing an arm. But up to then he certainly hadn't been very close to his mother. He didn't live with his folks or anything. He seemed free to wander around wherever he wished."

"Then you don't like it," Jen said.

"No, but it's your business. Of course you can have any guests you like. But I think you'll be very sorry if they should ever come."

"Maybe so. I suppose I worship talent. I can't bear it when the young aren't able to use their talents. This is a crucial time for Jerry. He got off to such a brilliant start—and then the war cut in, and it must be hard to get going again. Some of them never do get going. But Jerry mustn't stop, Cornelia; it would be too heartbreaking. Besides, I think it's good for him to be near Philip."

"Oh, do you? I wish I could agree, but I can't. I think they've been very bad for each other. I don't think he'll come, Jen—on account of Fanny, I mean. Fanny has this schoolgirl infatuation for him, and Jerry's trying to cure her of it. He just wouldn't want to be near Fanny, I'm sure."

"What a pity! They're made for each other," Jen said.

"That's ridiculous. And I heard him brushing her off—and not too gently, either. I'm not imagining it."

"I suppose he's self-conscious about his arm."

"Jerry? He's not self-conscious about anything. He knows what he wants and goes for it. No, he doesn't want Fanny, and a good thing for all concerned it is, too."

"Oh, *Cornelia!*" Jen said. "Don't pretend you're so tough. You're not at all—not really. You know very well it would break your heart if things didn't come out right for Fanny. And aren't you proud of Philip? He's on his way—and a good way too."

"Do you think so? Not a very remunerative way, Jen. It seems very queer sometimes that I'd have such an introvert for a son. Anything to keep him just sitting up in his room, that's all he asks. I think it's a pity, actually. I do, Jen."

"Well, he had a father too," Jen said.

"I'm beginning to know it," I said.

Funny, though, I never did think of Philip's having a father. I'd always had the feeling that I'd produced him all by myself. Silly, but true. And when he was young he certainly showed no signs of likeness to Walter. He was all outgoing and happy, not shut up in himself at all. But at this time, I admit, I saw a likeness—a shutting himself away from reality, digging into books and his own mind like a hermit, which was the way Walter would have liked to live if I'd let him; the way he did live, I expect, when he got away from me. Well, it killed him. If he'd kept on here and got outside more, cared for things here, he might be alive today. Or would he? I'd better think that one over. Already he was getting so he didn't join in with me on anything, didn't care about the house and grounds, preferring to settle down with a book or his writing. Maybe it would have come out just the same.

"Philip's a natural born critic," Jen said. "A poet, too, but perhaps a critic first. I think he's going to be a very fine one. He doesn't talk off the top of his head, but he knows deeply what he's talking about. He shows that, even in that small article. None of those pat phrases critics know so well, that gobbledygook that says nothing at all. Don't you hate gobbledygook? I do. Well, you may be sure Philip will never talk that language."

"Oh, he writes well enough, but there's no audience for that sort of thing," I said.

"Oh, I think there's an audience—maybe small, but good."

Well, Jerry wrote a nice enough letter to Jen but said he couldn't come. I expected that. But I made the mistake of telling Philip about the invitation. "But he isn't coming—of course not," I said.

"Why 'of course not'?" Philip said.

"Well, in the first place he knows better than to dump his mother on anyone for any length of time. He knows that can't be done. I give him that much intelligence. And besides, he's not in the mood for this part of the country right now. He wants to evade Fanny, I expect."

So Jerry didn't come that summer. Fanny got a part-time job in the library, so she was only home nights. She was very sober that summer, reminding me often of herself as a child. But she made no complaints about anything, seemed interested in her job. She was closer to Philip than I was, reading with him nights, listening to music, walking with him. I think he read her what he was writing, though she didn't talk about that.

Toward the end of the summer Jen went away. She never made visits, and it surprised me. Nor did she tell me where she was going. I know now that she went to Philadelphia. And after Fanny went back to school, Jerry and his mother came to visit Jen. It upset me some.

Jerry came to call almost at once. "It seems very odd not to be here," he said. "As Mother says, this seems like home. But Mrs. Deemster made it seem like a favor to her, and she has always been so kind. You'll come down to see Mother, won't you?"

"Yes, of course," I said.

"Where's Philip?"

"He went to the library. He'll be back soon."

"Well, I'll see him. I just wanted to say hello to you."

He went down the hill, which did seem strange, after all the time he'd spent in this house.

I went to call. I said, "How nice to see you, Mrs. Baker!" But she didn't look as well as when she'd come to call on us that time. She seemed to have shrunk and she didn't look straight at you; she kept looking away as if she were very nervous, even frightened.

She said, "Come sit by your mother, Jerry," and seemed to cling to him.

Jerry was nice to her. He didn't act as if she were any different from any mother; he didn't seem to coddle her or condescend to her. And after a while she got over the nervousness and talked a little. Jen said how lovely it was to have company in the house, things like that. But it was all a little uncomfortable and strained—for me, at least.

Philip spent a good deal of time down at Jen's, and Jerry came in and out here too. Mrs. Baker came once for lunch with Jen, and it went off reasonably well.

"I've been trying to get them to stay all winter," Jen said. "It would be so wonderful for me."

"That's awfully kind of you," Mrs. Baker said. "But Jerry has to get back to his work. Besides, we've imposed on you quite long enough. It's been lovely, though—just lovely."

"Lovely for me," Jen said.

But of course something happened; it was bound to. Jen had carefully put away any liquor there was in the house. I don't suppose there was much anyway, for the Judge was an abstemious man and Jen never seemed to care for so much as a cocktail. But there were a couple of bottles of cooking sherry in the kitchen—not right in sight, but they were there. And it must be that Mrs. Baker discovered them somehow, for one night she crept downstairs in the middle of the night and drank both bottles, every bit. Then she went outside in her dressing gown—all lace and satin, it was, and on her feet just some mules—and she wandered down to the valley road, singing and talking, till Mr. Fipps, coming home from his night shift, almost ran into her. It was a very cold night, and she really had almost nothing on.

Fipps didn't know where she belonged, and she wasn't in any shape to tell him. He knew we had city folks here sometimes, so he took a chance and brought her here.

I heard him banging on the door and I got up, but Philip was already running down the stairs by the time I got out into the hall. I looked at the clock and saw it was three in the morning. I thought Jen might be sick or something. Then I heard Fipps say, "Does this lady happen to be staying here,

Mrs. Boone? Found her down the valley road—looks like she's had a drop too much!"

Philip said, "Yes, yes, Mr. Fipps, bring her in."

Mrs. Baker's hair was all tossed around. It was black, and there was quite a lot of it. In that silly dressing gown, she looked— Well, I don't know what. I thought of Medusa, with all that hair and everything. She was still talking and laughing.

"Thanks a lot," Philip said. "We'll take care of her. Mother, get a blanket, will you?" So I ran up and got a blanket, and Philip wrapped it around her, all the time talking to her gently.

"You just lie down here and rest," Philip said. He got her to the sofa, and she flopped down, but she was still talking.

"Silly, silly, silly," she said, "but I found it all right. . . . Silly, silly Jerry—poor Jerry, poor, poor Jerry, thinks his mama's a little dotty. Poor Jerry, poor, poor Jerry . . ."

"Make some coffee," Philip said. "Fast, too."

He was very sharp. I made the coffee as quickly as I could, and Philip said, "All right, Mrs. Baker, this will warm you up. You don't want to have pneumonia, now. Come on, drink it down!"

But she gave a push and knocked the cup out of Philip's hand, all over the sofa. "Get some more—never mind the sofa," Philip said. But my sofa had a lovely cover. Coffee is hard to get out.

I brought another cup, though, and this time Philip held it firmly, lifted her up, and saw that she drank a little. She stopped talking so steadily.

"Come on, now, get some sleep," Philip said. He wrapped her up, asked for another blanket. "I think we ought to have the doctor," he said.

"She'll sleep it off," I said. "It will upset Jerry, won't it, calling the doctor in?"

"I don't know whether she'll sleep it off or not. She's chilled. It's bitter out tonight. No, call him. I'll take the responsibility."

Mrs. Baker wasn't asleep. She lay there staring at us, her eyes glazed the way drunk people's eyes are. But she had stopped talking.

So I got Dr. Melling out of bed. He was a little gruff, which isn't surprising, but he came. He looked at her, said, "She's just plain drunk. Been having a party?"

"No," Philip said. "And yes, she's drunk, but it's more than that. She's been wandering around outside without much on, and she's shaking with chills."

So the doctor got out his stethoscope and looked her over. He frowned. "Yeah," he said. "She's sick, all right. Can't we get her into bed?"

"She isn't staying here," I said. "Someone brought her here."

"Well, she's staying here for now," Dr. Melling said. "That's for sure, Mrs. Boone. Philip, could you help me carry her upstairs?"

So they took her up and put her in the guest room—or Fanny's room, rather. I know it seemed sort of an insult to Fanny, putting her there, but Philip didn't ask, he just took her there.

"Know where she belongs?" the doctor asked.

"Yes, we know. We know her," Philip said. "She's a friend of ours, really."

I don't know what Melling thought of that, and it was unnecessary, too. After all, we are respectable people and have never had drinking parties in this house. But I didn't say anything.

"This is habitual, Doctor," Philip said. "It's not just because someone had a party."

"I see," Melling said. "Looks it, I must say. Well, here's a prescription. Can't get it before the drugstore opens, but get it as soon as you can. Lungs don't look too good. I'll drop in again after I've had my breakfast."

He has very sharp eyes, Dr. Melling, and he looked around as if he were memorizing everything in the room, then took us in too. "She ought to be in a hospital," he said. "Want a nurse?"

"Mother and I'll look after her," Philip said.

Mrs. Baker had fallen asleep with her mouth open. I must say she didn't look too appetizing. After the doctor went Philip said, "You'd better sit here for a bit. I'm going to dress and go down to get Jerry. I'll take over as soon as I get back."

I wasn't used to being ordered about by Philip, but I sat down by the bed and waited. Mrs. Baker's breathing was heavy. Her black hair was flowing out across the pillow. You couldn't see the lace and satin, so closely had Philip pulled the blankets up about her throat. Then, I don't know why, but all of a sudden, sitting there, I felt sorry for Mrs. Baker. I hadn't up to that minute. I'd thought she was disgusting. I've never had patience with people who have no self-control. But it may be that some people just aren't born with wills. I used to think they were and only failed to use them, but I'm not sure any more.

Anyway, I thought about her husband's divorcing her, and of how she'd been in this home and that getting cures and hadn't seen too much of her son—and of how it must have been down at Jen's, trying to be a lady and longing so for a drink, and of how ashamed she was going to be when she came

to and realized what she'd done, disgracing Jerry, insulting
Jen, and all. You could see how hard she'd tried not to let
Jerry down, how pathetic she was in being so glad to have been
asked. I thought I ought to have asked her here, for I
was tougher than Jen and I might have managed to keep her
sober. And I thought, too, that Philip would have been pleased
if I'd asked her. Yes, I was soft that morning, sitting there by
Mrs. Baker. And I thought too of how I'd have felt if my son
had come home from the wars with one arm gone, and my
son a musician too. Maybe if Jerry had stuck by her earlier she
wouldn't have been this way.

Then Philip was there with Jerry, looking white and very
grave.

"I'm so sorry, Mrs. Boone," Jerry said. He could see his
mother was asleep and that there was nothing he could do.

"It's all right," I said. "Don't worry, Jerry."

He gave me a quick, surprised look, then sat down on the
other side of the bed. He put his hand out and laid it on his
mother's forehead, drew it back again.

"Want to make us some breakfast, Mother?" Philip said. "I
want to run down to the village as soon as the drugstore's
open."

So I went down and fixed some bacon and eggs and coffee
and toast. Philip came down and helped me carry them upstairs, and we sat there in that room and had breakfast together, though Jerry just drank his coffee and took one bite of
toast, that was all.

"I think I can wake up Gruber by now," Philip said suddenly. "I'll be off."

Jerry let him go without any protest. "You can't help anyone very much, can you?" he said suddenly. "You can under-

stand everything, but when the breaking point is coming you
can't hold it off. I knew it was coming, you see, and I planned
to leave tomorrow—today, it is, isn't it? Could we get a nurse
around here?"

"Bessie and I can manage, Jerry. Just don't worry."

"Jen knew how it might be. She—well, no need to go into
it, is there? I suppose when people have their heart broken
over and over . . . Mother's had a very hard life, Mrs. Boone
—a terribly hard and unhappy life."

He didn't sound as if he were excusing her but just telling
me the facts, that was all. Yet Mrs. Baker had money, that was
sure, a smart son. Why was it any harder for her than for anyone?

"While we're about it, Mrs. Boone," Jerry said, "let's clear
up something. You mocked at me once for bragging about getting away from my folks. Perhaps you were right to mock, but
it wasn't quite as you thought. It was my mother who got me
away, you see, who insisted that I be on my own. Our home
wasn't a happy one—my father being unfaithful constantly
and in rather sordid ways, and cruel, to boot. But a lot of the
money was Mother's, or from her family. Father used it
to make more, of course. He did make a lot of money. But
Mother threatened to take her money out of the business unless I was let go. Father made her pay for that threat, I assure
you. She kept pretending it was all right, but of course
it wasn't. I think she had to drink or go mad. And in the end,
when Father had enough money so he didn't have to worry
about Mother's money, *he* divorced *her*. She used to be beautiful." His voice went off in a sad way.

I wanted to ask why she hadn't left long before, but I didn't.
And maybe she couldn't—how do I know? Maybe she loved

the man, even if I can't see how it was possible. Some people are like that, loving the wrong ones till death do them part— or divorce. Only it seemed she had seen what would happen to Jerry if he stuck to that home, and she'd seen he got away and lived his own life, which was remarkable, I suppose, when she was so plainly a weak woman. Maybe some people have one strong spot, even when they're weak every other way.

"We'll have her right in no time," I said. "Why don't you go get your sleep out? She won't wake up right away."

"I'm quite all right," Jerry said. "I'll look after her when she wakes up."

Yes, I was soft, for I couldn't leave him there alone with her. I stuck there—not talking, though—till Philip got back—no, longer than that; I waited till Dr. Melling came again, and by that time Jen was there too. Then I left the doctor there and went downstairs with Jen.

"That poor, poor woman," Jen said. "It's my fault. I ought to have thought of the sherry. How did she happen to be here?"

I told her about Fipps. So then she told me about a time in Philadelphia, in a restaurant. "So I knew how it could be," she said. "But I was so pleased that all was going well. Can she be moved down to my house? We can't have her muddling things all up for you."

"Oh, nonsense," I said. "And no, obviously she can't be moved. But she'll come out of it soon, I hope. There's Bessie. I don't know what she's thinking about all this hullabaloo; I'd better go out and smooth things over."

Well, Mrs. Baker had pneumonia, but pneumonia isn't as bad as it used to be, what with all the drugs they have nowadays, and she got better in time. We all took turns sitting with her. She was good and sick. Once or twice I thought she wasn't going to come out of it. Maybe it would have been better if she hadn't, for she certainly found life hard going. But she did get better. She was changed when she came to herself, not a bit talkative. Sometimes she'd look at Jerry in a tragic way, as if she were asking him to forgive her, but I never heard her ask him in words. He was very gentle with her, teased her some, read to her, carried her trays up and down.

Then one day when I was alone with her she said, "Mrs. Boone, how did I get here?"

I told her she'd been taken sick while out walking. I tried to make light of it.

"Oh," she said. "I did wonder. I've been a trouble to you."

"Not a bit of it!" I said. "We like having someone to look after!" No, I couldn't tell her what I really thought of her goings-on. She must have known she'd been drunk, but she didn't talk about it.

I'd thought the Bakers would be gone by the time Fanny came home for Thanksgiving, but it didn't work out that way, though Mrs. Baker had been up for an hour or two for several days and was talking about going. But the doctor said no, she was in no shape for traveling and wouldn't be for a week, or maybe two.

"We could take it slowly," Jerry said. "We really feel we ought to get home, Doctor."

"No, not slowly or any way," Melling said. "Your mother's weak as a rag, you must see that, my boy. Maybe in a week. We'll talk about it."

Jen said, "But she could come as far as my place, couldn't she, Doctor?"

Doctor Melling frowned and said he'd rather she went nowhere. She was doing all right, but you mustn't hurry things. Unless it was absolutely necessary, he preferred she stay right here. So of course I couldn't say she ought to get out. Then Fanny came.

"Philip," I said, "you meet Fanny and tell her what needs to be told. She can have your old room. It would have been better to have told her not to come."

Philip went off to the station and came home with Fanny. She had on a gray suit and gray sandals and looked beautiful. She went right upstairs and into her own room, where Mrs. Baker lay.

"Hello!" she said. "How nice to see you again, Mrs. Baker! Sorry you've been sick, but you look fine! Hello, Jerry."

"Hello," Jerry said.

"Mind if I take a few things out of my bureau?" Fanny said. "And don't think you're putting me out of my room, because I love the little back room and always have." She gave Mrs. Baker a brilliant smile, went to the bureau, took out some things, said, "See you later!" and went out.

We could hear her down the hall, talking with Philip, even laughing.

Jerry had stood up when Fanny came in, but he hadn't shaken hands or anything, and as soon as she'd gone he sat down again.

"Jerry," his mother said, "we must go. You must take me home."

"In a few days, Mother," Jerry said.

Of course it was hard for Jerry, having Fanny home—hard for her too, I daresay. But Fanny carried things off very well. She spent quite a lot of time with Mrs. Baker. She'd say to

Jerry, "Shoo! I want to visit with your mother—female talk—so get out!" And Jerry would go away and leave her there. Once when I happened in Mrs. Baker was talking about when Jerry was a little boy.

". . . he was generous in his own way, my dear, but, you see, most people are generous in some way. But it didn't happen to be music. It was so sad, sending the piano back. I suppose I cried too much. I do give way to tears—or I used to. I don't seem to cry so much any more. Only Jerry had such talent, it seemed such a pity. They had such a good music department at Endley, and so he went to Endley, which was a bit of luck, wasn't it? but it took some doing, and it did tire me out. I'm not very good at scheming, dear, not good at all. And when I knew he was coming here, and a good piano here and everything, I was so relieved. It did seem as if God were letting some things happen that ought to happen. God's never taken care of me very well, but I guess I haven't deserved it, you might say. I've got kind of a talent for doing everything wrong. But do you think God ought to have let him go off to war, dear? It does seem as if something slipped up there—giving him all that talent and then taking his arm off. . . . I'm such a dreadful mother to him, so dreadful. You know, I prayed I'd die this time. But God didn't see fit to answer. I suppose it was wicked of me, only I do hate it so, not being a good mother. I'm such a trouble to you all, don't think I don't know it—I do know lots of things that people don't give me credit for knowing. I just wish sometimes Jerry would put me out of his life, really put me out. It would be better—you'd know if you were a mother, child. . . . It doesn't seem to do any good to swear it will never happen again, for it always happens. You'd think I wanted to hurt my boy, but it isn't that. I'd die for Jerry, I really would—it's just something that comes over me, that won't let me have any peace . . ."

Her voice trailed off, and she shut her eyes. She'd been talking just to Fanny, not even seeming to notice I was in the room. And Fanny had listened so intently, never taking her eyes from Mrs. Baker's face. Now, Fanny has a strong and beautiful face, but not often did it look tender. It was tender then, so sweet and gentle. She leaned over and kissed Mrs. Baker; then she got up and went out past me, not saying a word to me.

I must say the woman upset me that day. It was then, I think, I did begin really to know that people are not all of a piece. So weak she couldn't keep away from liquor, Mrs. Baker was, and yet I did know that day that she loved her son terribly, the way I love Philip. I could have cried myself, listening to her.

After a while Mrs. Baker opened her eyes and saw me sitting there instead of Fanny. "I do talk too much," she said.

"Not at all," I said. "Sometimes you just have to talk to someone. I have a friend—well, of course you know my friend Jen—but anyway, she's always there, waiting to listen to me. I've been lucky to have a friend like that."

"She's lovely, your daughter," she said.

"Yes, she is," I said.

"You're a wonderful family. It's so good for Jerry to be with a family. He's so fond of you all. Could I have a mirror?"

I managed to laugh at her, and I said, "What for? To see if you've got thinner? That's a bad habit, Mrs. Baker, looking at yourself after an illness—not that you don't look all right."

I got up and fetched a hand glass, and she looked at herself in it so anxiously, so sadly. I don't believe she was vain, actually. You could believe it, what Jerry had said about her once having been beautiful. She wasn't beautiful now, except for her great sad eyes. She'd been sick and she showed it. Her skin looked dried out and yellowish, and there were circles under her eyes. She looked at herself for quite a long time, then laid the glass on the covers, face down. She didn't say a word about how she'd found her image.

"You have been so kind, Mrs. Boone. I can't ever thank you enough. I presume Jerry wishes you were his mother. I wouldn't blame him at all, you know."

"He wishes nothing of the kind," I said. "He's quite satisfied with the mother he's got, Mrs. Baker. He's been so anxious about you—"

"Yes, I know. Anxious," she said, and closed her eyes again. When you didn't see her eyes she looked sicker—worn out, exhausted.

That hadn't been a good word to use, I saw. "Because he loves you so much," I said.

She opened her eyes and smiled at me. In a way it embarrassed me, that smile. It was as if she loved me beyond measure for saying that to her, even while she didn't quite believe it. I'd been surprised at myself for saying it.

Jerry came in then and said Bessie wanted to see me, so I left her with Jerry and went downstairs. Yes, I went out of character there, I admit. I don't know what got into me.

ONE DAY when Jen was sitting with Mrs. Baker I heard
Fanny say, "I think I'll go over and see Amelia, if
there's nothing I can do here."

Jerry was sitting at the kitchen table, drinking a glass of milk
and Bessie was taking some cookies out of the oven. She
scraped off a couple of hot ones onto the table next to Jerry,
and he took one up and smiled at Bessie. Then he finished
the milk, said, "I'll come along, if you don't mind. Or would
I be in the way?"

Fanny was surprised, that was plain—or frightened. "Oh, I
know my way," she said.

"Of course. I wasn't going to show you the way, just keep
you company."

"Well, as you like," Fanny said.

"I like," he said soberly, got up, and they went off together.

I didn't like that, but they came back in an hour or so. The
record player was going upstairs, and Fanny said, "I'll go and
report to Philip. He pretends indifference, but he'll want a
report."

"And how was Amelia?" I asked.

"Snappy," Fanny said. "Very edgy, she was. I don't believe she wanted to see us at all."

"The academic life has hardened her," Jerry said. "A pity. She had great potentiality."

"Oh, she still has it," Fanny said. "She's just too stubborn to admit she has, that's all. I've never known anyone so stubborn, unless it's Philip—or you," she ended sharply, turning to Jerry.

"Me? Oh, I'm extremely malleable," Jerry said. "And when it comes to edginess, you're a bit edgy yourself."

"I know. It's rubbing up against stubborn people that does it," Fanny said. "You'd be surprised if I began to scream one day, wouldn't you? I might, though, I really might."

"I must hear you," Jerry murmured. "But no, that day will never come. You're too controlled. That's what I first heard about you, that you could manage anything at all, that you'd never go to pieces, no matter what happened. You were born that way."

"Says you. You don't know anything about me. Funny—you really don't. You think you do, you think you know what's best for me and everybody, but the fact is you don't even know what's best for yourself. Well, I must make my report." And she went off to Philip.

"She's getting very impudent, your daughter," Jerry said to me. "She needs an occasional spanking."

"Why didn't you let her go calling by herself?"

"Well, why didn't I? I don't know, Mrs. Boone."

"And she was spanked enough when she was little. She was a most defiant, disobedient child; there was really nothing to do but spank her. Maybe that's what makes her so decent now. I was certainly whipped often when I was a child, and though

I didn't like it at the time, I think it was no doubt good for me."

"Oh?" Jerry said. He took a cooky, ate it slowly. "And Philip? Was he whipped often?"

"No, he wasn't. Not Philip. He was an uncommonly good child. A little talk was all he ever needed. And if I were you I wouldn't start making deductions. Children are different—one needs one sort of discipline, one another."

"Quite," Jerry said. "There aren't any rules that always work, are there? And certainly Fanny doesn't show any resentment for having been spanked, does she?"

"No, she respects order."

"Doctor Melling says we can go tomorrow. I think I'll go down to Mrs. Deemster's and pack our things up. Mrs. Boone—"

"Yes, Jerry?" I said.

"Oh, I guess I can't make a speech. But I am grateful—more grateful than you can ever know. Mother thinks you've always been a sort of second mother to me. I haven't disabused her, and I thank you for not doing so. The truth is, you've almost seemed so, actually, this time, when there's every reason you shouldn't."

"I didn't have much choice, did I?" I said, which wasn't kind.

"Yes, you did—that's just it," Jerry said. "I've never underestimated you, Mrs. Boone. You've never wanted me to be friends with Philip. You've never really wanted me here. You've loathed the idea of Fanny's being interested in me. You've not troubled to hide your feelings much. And so I'm grateful—for you couldn't have been kinder if you had thought of me as your son."

"Well, you've always had a fixed idea I was some sort of monster," I said. "You can't expect anyone to feel warm toward that opinion. I've just been normally hospitable toward someone in trouble."

"Normally?" he said. Then he put out his hand and took mine, pressed it hard. "I'll go pack now," he said.

You know, I couldn't help liking him. He had always been my enemy, that I knew, but I liked him that day. He was really grateful. I even thought of going down to help him pack, but I didn't. Only it must have been hard, with one hand. But maybe Anna would help him.

They did go the next morning, right after breakfast. Mrs. Baker was still shaky, but she managed to get ready. She even put some make-up on. We all gathered round to see them off —even Jen, having come up for breakfast. We said the usual things.

"Send some manuscript down," Jerry said to Philip. "I'm no critic—just curious."

"I will," Philip said.

Manuscript of what? I wondered.

He just shook hands with me and Jen. He looked as if he were anxious to be off, away from us, though he was polite all around. But then there was Fanny to say good-by to.

He frowned a little, held out his hand to her. "Good-by, kid," he said, just as if she were really only Philip's little sister.

But Fanny wouldn't have it that way. She came right up to him, put up her arms, and kissed him on the mouth. I saw him look around from over her head in a desperate fashion, and then he kissed her back, and not gently either.

"You're forward," he said, and tried to laugh.

"I know. Someone has to be," she said. "Good-by, my love!"

"Good-by, brat," he said.

She grinned at him in a mocking way.

Then Mrs. Baker hugged Fanny, said, "Dear child—dear child," with tears running down her face, got in beside Jerry, and they drove off.

It seemed strange with them gone. We all went in and had more coffee.

"Funny—I meant to be so useful," Jen said. She looked tired.

"You were," Philip said.

"No, I only meant to be. It had a bad ending."

"I liked the ending," Philip contradicted her.

"What manuscript?" I said to Philip.

"Oh, I've taken to poetry—can you imagine? I am versatile, am I not? You wouldn't be interested, Mother, so you don't need to pretend to be."

"Of course I'm interested. Only I hope you punctuate, all that. And I hope you don't insult your public by being obscure and throwing in foreign phrases, that kind of thing."

He laughed and said he was clear as crystal. "You ought to read *Finnegans Wake*, Mother," he said. And after a while he went up and got a copy of *Finnegans Wake* and said, "Here you are, Mother. After you read that, nothing will ever seem obscure to you again."

I told before about trying to read that book. It amused me when Philip came one day and asked me for it, said he wanted to look up something. "And I'm sure you aren't reading it," he said.

"No, I've finished it," I told him.

He stared at me and then he gave a big whoop of laughter, which he didn't do very often any more, and he kissed me and said, "Mother, you've surprised me. What did you make of it?"

"Nothing," I said, and he shouted again. But it wasn't quite nothing. Not quite.

One day I saw Philip take a big envelope out to the mailman. I suppose he was sending his poetry to Jerry.

I said to him, "Aren't you ever going to show me any of this poetry of yours?"

"Oh, you wouldn't like it," he said. "It's not your dish at all."

"How do you know what's my dish?" I said.

But he didn't show me his work. That troubled me, because I was afraid he didn't show it because I hadn't been properly interested in his article. And I didn't honestly think that writing poetry was a man's work, either, but I did want Philip to be happy and to have some interest, even if it was poetry.

Then—queer enough I did think it—he got somebody to publish that poetry. When it was actually inside a book, he gave me a copy—very carelessly, though, as if he thought it wasn't much, or anything I'd care about. Before I'd even read it, though, I looked at the flyleaf and saw it said, "For A.A." Amelia Adams. I don't suppose I thought he'd dedicate it to me, but I maybe thought he'd dedicate it to Fanny or Jerry. It was called *Wind from the North.*

The poems weren't as clear as he'd promised they'd be. But there were bits about gardens and woods that I liked, little phrases that I seemed to understand—as comparing a new love to the white curled ghosts of new fern, or there was one called "Hymn to Grosbeaks," which didn't even mention grosbeaks at all, but was about cruelty, bright-colored and alluring, which reminded me of what Jerry had said that day by the window about the beaks of grosbeaks being cruel. And there was one called "Words," which seemed to say we had outworn most words and that we had to learn to talk with the heart, though it didn't say anything so simply as that, really. And there was one that seemed more violent, about love, but which was called "Hangman's Rope."

I know I didn't feel too happy about those poems. I didn't know whether they were good or not, but it did seem there was something running through them all that was angry and even cruel. Perhaps "cruel" is not the word. But he seemed to make light of all the things we think of as decent—love and kindness and all. Or maybe I didn't understand them. Jerry said I didn't.

As I've said, I get the *Saturday Review* for the Double Crostics, and one week there was a poetry section and in it was a review of Philip's book:

These poems by a new writer deserve considerable attention. It is not malapropos to mention that Mr. Boone was a conscientious objector in the late war. Yet there are no poems of the war in this volume, no evidence of bitterness over the holocaust, such as might have been expected. Indeed, there is singularly little bitterness in the poems, but rather a sharp anger against the abuse ordinary human beings put upon language, love, faith, and the like, particularly against lack of perception, the atrophy of the vision. There is a clarity here, not often seen in these days, and which augurs well for this writer. He is no disciple of Eliot, Pound, or Auden; he does not see the world as a waste land, but he does make a sweeping indictment of us as human beings for letting it often seem a waste land. These poems are more simple of form than is common now, but do not be deceived by their simplicity. They are deep.

I was angry about that mention of Philip in the war, terribly angry. It certainly wasn't necessary to mention it. I was puzzled, too, because I didn't see the poems the way the reviewer did. I did see the poems as bitter.

I went up to Philip's room and showed him the review. I didn't want him to know they had mentioned the war, but I thought he'd see it sometime and it might as well be me who gave it to him. I ignored that remark, and I said, "Well, Philip, they seem to think highly of your poetry. That's fine."

He read it slowly; then he smiled at me. "But you bristled at that beginning, didn't you, darling?" he said.

"Well, I can't just see why they had to bring it in. What's it got to do with it?" I said.

"But, you see, they were right—it did have something to do with it. Everything, in fact."

He didn't explain himself. He did say, "But I think my main road will be criticism, Mother. You have to be able to create something yourself before you know what criticism is."

"You do?" I said. "I wouldn't have thought so from some of the criticism I've read. Sounds generally like snarling at those who do create."

Philip laughed. "Oh, but those aren't the real critics!" he said.

"And while we're about it," I said, "do you think it was so smart to dedicate your book to Amelia Adams? Why should you, for heaven's sake? You never even see each other any more."

"But why not? They were for her."

"How do you know she'll ever so much as see them?"

"Perhaps she won't. Still, they are for her. You got a book dedicated to you, didn't you?"

"And there was no sense in that, either," I said.

"Oh, yes, there was. Father was telling you something—just as I have tried to tell Amelia something. I don't think you listened, any more than Amelia will. Odd, isn't it, how we all talk to the wrong person? Fanny told you once, but you didn't believe her, did you? Father loved you; he always loved you, even if he couldn't live with you. He gave you his big gift, but you didn't accept it. Amelia won't accept anything either. It doesn't seem to matter; we go right on loving. Queer, I know."

"I don't know what you're talking about," I said.

"That's just what I've been saying. You don't know what we're talking about, Father and I. Yet we both talk to you, in a way. You're wonderful, Mother, but you don't listen—except to Mrs. Baker; you did hear her, bless you, darling! But we're all like Mrs. Baker, you see, we all have sore spots that need healing—and Father said to you, 'You wouldn't listen when I was with you, but please listen to this. This is what I always wanted to give you, but you wouldn't let me. Here it is.' That's what he was saying, Mother. But he was always lonely without you, always. *The Ginkgo Tree* is one of the most beautiful books of our time, and one straight out of a terrible loneliness. And I suppose all of us are lonely at one time or another and that's why the book says something to so many people. But you see, Mother, it was all for you. 'Out of my loneliness,' he said, 'I made this for you.' I do wish you could feel that, Mother."

"But there was no reason for him to be lonely," I said. "He wanted it that way."

"Oh? He was lonely here too, Mother, and not creating anything at all."

"Look, Philip, he could have created a home if he'd had a

mind to; he needn't have left it all to me to create. That's just
as hard as making a book, and even more useful. But it was
only his special kind of creating he wanted to do. You do
like to make touching situations where none exist!"

"But we all have to create what's in us to create," Philip
said. "Sorry—I'm just upsetting you to no purpose. But I'm
more like Father than you seem to realize. And Fanny's more
like you than you realize, too. I mean she has a will like yours—
she's sensitive, too. But she will get what she wants out of life,
whereas I—well, I doubt if I ever do."

"Well, for goodness' sake, what do you want? Aren't you
doing what you want to do? No one's stopping you from anything, that I can see."

"I want an Amelia who believes in me," he said. "You see,
that is something that is a contradiction in terms. I'll never
get it. I'd even take her not believing in me, God help me, but
that won't be, either. And a very good thing, wouldn't you say?
You know it wouldn't work out— All right, I'll stop."

But I couldn't stop. I said, "Philip, are you lonely here too?"

He turned and looked down at some papers on his table.
"Yes," he said, "lonely enough. But it's home—I don't want
to be anywhere else, Mother."

He picked up a pencil, and I went away. I went into my own
room and shut the door. I picked up Walter's book, looked at
that "For Cornelia." It seemed to me I couldn't stand it, all
this talk of loneliness and not listening and all. Only neurotics
gave in to loneliness, to self-pity. Goodness knows, I could
have given in if anyone could; I'd had reason to pity myself.
But I loathe that kind of self-indulgence. At least Philip called
this home; he loved this place and didn't want to leave it. But
why should he be lonely? He made his loneliness himself, be-

cause he liked that kind of thing, as Walter had. I slapped the book down against the table, and I did feel terribly angry, I remember. They were all making me out a fool, making it seem I just wasn't sensitive enough to understand all their mental gymnastics. And if Walter had wanted to give me something, couldn't he have given me something I wanted, such as weeding the garden from time to time, or seeing that the house got painted? I never asked him for a book. Was it a present to me, when he had taken himself out of my life to write it? No, I can't quite understand that kind of reasoning. But I didn't like it that Philip seemed to think I ought to understand it. I didn't like it that he mooned over Amelia Adams—who was she to scorn Philip? Though I knew she hadn't been able to take the war business, and I have never quite taken it myself. But it was stupid of him to so much as want her.

Then I sat down and read that book for the third time. Talking to me, was he? Well, I tried to listen. I said I would, and I tried. I tried to see it the way Philip did, as if it were a message to me. I tried to see whether this boy was really like Philip, whether Philip's mother was really like me. There was a place where the boy stole something so he could give his mother a present. Well, I could see Philip doing that. And the boy was worldly—he'd had a very worldly upbringing—and he saw everything he did through his mind. Philip is like that some, too. But that mother, with her lovers, her selfishness—she made me shiver. No, if that was the way Walter saw me, this was no present, that's sure. But then there was a scene toward the end where the boy talks with his mother, trying to tell her how he feels, and the mother never understands a word he's saying. I read that scene over twice, because it did ring some sort of bell in my mind. Yes, in a way I did know what that felt like. I'd just gone through a scene something like it. Only surely I understood more than this fool of a woman. I didn't always approve of what people wanted, but I understood more than that. Yet that scene made me feel uncomfortable, and even sad. And at the end of the book, when the boy sees his mother never will understand him—very touching, that is. He knows and he accepts it. He doesn't need his mother any more. He's grown up and independent at long last.

Yet Philip was here, wasn't he? He must still need me, or he wouldn't be here. I couldn't have borne it if I'd thought Philip thought of me as this woman, but I didn't think he did. Philip was loving; no matter what happened, he always loved me. But what if he thought, as he'd said about Amelia, that I was the wrong person to love? Why did he say we always loved the wrong people? And why did he say he was lonely? Was it just dramatics, or was it real? I remembered a time when I was a little girl and Father was going somewhere with Mother, and Mother had been getting me ready to go with them. Father said, "Leave Cornelia with the Carneys, why don't you? She won't add to the occasion." He didn't know I heard him. But I came in and I said, "Do I have to go? I'd rather go down and play with Letty." Father was relieved and said, "Sure, why not?" But I went down the hill and waited till I knew they were gone and then I came back here and went up to my bedroom and just sat there all afternoon by myself. Yes, I guess I was lonely then. But I was too proud to let anyone know it.

Maybe you get into the habit of fighting when you know you're not loved, the way I knew my father and mother didn't really love me. You get prouder and prouder and never show your feelings. And maybe I've always been a little gruff and unsentimental because I didn't want to get hurt as I was when I was a child. Maybe that's what they meant when they said I didn't understand—maybe that's all there was to it. But I certainly don't believe in going around with your heart on your sleeve. Why should you? I can see now how I must have annoyed my folks. Mother was gentle and Father was lazy and evasive, but I was all will and fight and I wanted my own way and tried to get it. I suppose I wasn't very appealing. And I think Mother tried to love me but found it difficult—maybe the same way I felt about Fanny when she was little. We just couldn't get together on anything.

All the same, I have never been as insensitive as that woman in the book, never. It's true I don't love many people, but I've always loved Philip and Jen—and now I love Fanny too. It's stupid to say you ought to love everyone; it's not possible, and people who pretend they do are liars.

It's March now. I've been sitting here all winter, it seems, writing these things down. The snow is falling lazily, but there is a look in the air of spring. I can't seem to think whether or not I am getting anywhere in all this. I feel as if I should admit right now that it isn't only because I want to work out puzzles that I'm writing this. I ought to admit that I am alone in the house, except for Bessie, and that I am sometimes lonely, that I am doing what I have always done, fighting loneliness with work of sorts. I'm not a writer, that's plain enough. I can just put down the truth; I can't make it up. I married a writer; I have a son who's a writer. Funny. I haven't a spark of imagination. The grosbeaks were here today in a big flock. I can't tell about grosbeaks in the abstract, as Philip could. I can't make anyone see the hills in the snow, and the way the buds look faintly red—not so it seems poetic and beautiful. I'm a woman for facts, that's all. I don't put things down the way I wish they were, but the way they really were. I'm going to stop to-morrow, just finish it all up and stop. I'm tired.

24

FINISH IT UP, Cornelia Boone. Make your findings and be through with it. You're alone; that's the first finding-out of all these words.

No, I suppose I have to tell how they left me. Things have happened since the time Philip's poems came out, yet they seem almost unnecessary to put down—they're all things that were bound to happen, I suppose. Philip didn't make any money to speak of out of his poems, for who buys poetry these days? But he's gone on writing, essays and so on, and now he has a regular job as a music critic on a New York paper.

I must admit I never thought he'd go away from this house. I thought it was more true than he'd meant, even, that he'd never do anything with his life. Partly I was always angry that this was so; partly I was relieved to have him doing nothing, just staying here with me. I suppose I thought the world would be cruel to him after his war record.

Fanny finished college and got a job teaching in a school about fifteen miles from here. She bought a little English car and drove back and forth every day. I remember how I felt when she told me about this job.

"*Teach school?*" I said. "Fanny, that's impossible. That's dreadful. I couldn't wish anything worse for you!"

It did seem dreadful, a girl with all those looks and brains, teaching school like her stick of an aunt.

"I don't know what you mean," she said. "I haven't any special talents otherwise—but I want to be a teacher. I do want that very much, and I think I'll be a good teacher. What's wrong with that?"

"It's the dullest life on earth, and thankless," I said. "You weren't made for dullness, Fanny. You were made for a gay and exciting life."

"But I don't find teaching dull," Fanny said. "I like it."

"Nonsense! No one could *like* it!" I said.

"You'd have made a good teacher, Mother," Fanny said. "A really first-class one, I think."

"Heaven forbid!" I said. Yet the truth is that when I was young and planned to go to college, wanted so much to go, I'd thought I would be a teacher. It was the last of my desires that day I was talking with Fanny, however; I had no regrets on that score.

"Anyway, I've signed a contract," Fanny said. "And I've bought a car. I'll pay you board—if you'll let me stay on here, that is."

Fanny has a will, all right. I didn't get anywhere at all trying to persuade her to get some other kind of job. Philip seemed to find it amusing. Of course there was one good thing about it—Fanny was still here in this house. It infuriated me, though, whenever I thought of the waste. No one has a greater ability to wear clothes, to walk with an air. She could have been a model if she'd desired. Not that that's any life, either, but I'd have liked it better than teaching. Any office would have been pleased to take her in.

"Of course," Fanny said, "what I really want is to marry Jerry and look after him. In that sense, teaching is second choice."

"Well, you can put that out of your mind," I told her.

"Oh? Mother, you mustn't tell me what I can put out of my mind. You just don't know. I don't tell you what to think, do I?"

I laughed and said she'd better not try.

By this time Amelia Adams had finished school too and had a job in some sort of research foundation—chemistry, I think. She came home now and then, but I seldom so much as had a glimpse of her.

It was quite pleasant here during that time—the children here, Jen running in and out, a kind of permanence in things. I suppose life was exactly as I liked and wanted it. Of course there were little worries about this and that, but in general things seemed to have settled down. Sometimes Philip and Fanny went to town to a concert or a show. I went with them occasionally, but not often. Philip fussed along with his writing, but I couldn't talk with him about that, somehow.

Then one day—in the next spring, it was—Jerry called Philip. I heard Philip talking to him somewhat excitedly; then I heard him ask him to come up that week end.

Philip came in and said, "What do you know! You'd never guess what's happened!"

Fanny was sitting there, looking over some school papers. She didn't look up. She said, "I know. Jerry's married." Her voice was flat.

"Married? Jerry? Heavens, no. His mother is! She married

her lawyer. Jerry was upset, but I think it's wonderful. He's coming Friday. Mind?"

Fanny put her papers down, got up, and went out to the garden.

"He's coming—I don't suppose it matters whether I mind or not," I said. "But you've upset Fanny. She minds, you know."

"I know. Wouldn't it be wonderful, though, Mother, if things did come out right for them? For someone?"

"I wouldn't call what you call 'coming out right for them' wonderful at all. It would be the worst thing possible for them both. They're not alike; they wouldn't get on. And besides, Jerry doesn't want her."

"Oh, Mother, you're smarter than that!" Philip said. Then he fished in his pocket, took out seven dollars and a half, and dropped it in my lap. "A poem, partner," he said.

"Thank you," I said. I glanced up at him, and he was suddenly older to me, not a boy playing at writing, sculpturing, all that. The word "partner" always touched me. It had a boyish ring. But this time it didn't sound boyish at all. Then he said, "That makes ninety-seven dollars and a half so far this year, doesn't it? It hardly pays my way, does it?"

"It doesn't matter," I said.

"Oh, it matters. I know that. It ought to be more by now, and I'd hoped it would be. I wonder what I'd thought I'd use for money if Amelia married me? Luckily, she didn't."

"Yes, luckily," I said. "Not because of money. I daresay we'd have made out moneywise if we'd had to—but you're too unlike, son. It wouldn't have worked."

"I suppose not. But the odd thing is, Mother, in the beginning we were alike. We do change, don't we? Amelia has some sort of complex about honesty and it gets stronger all the time. Well, you know, I have one too. You won't believe that, I know, but it's true. I was a slow developer, wasn't I? But still, I haven't changed in that way. Even when I seemed the most unconscionable liar, I still had this feeling about honesty. Hard to explain, but it's so. You see, I never lied to myself."

Then he laughed and said, "It doesn't matter now, does it?"

Of course it did matter. I knew that. I sat and thought about what he had said. All those lies he had told when he was a boy—weren't they real lies? Of course they were. But I was confused. He said he'd never lied to himself—but what difference did that make, when he'd certainly lied to me and others? I remembered how Jerry had told me once that Philip had been afraid I'd send him away from me, as I'd sent Fanny. That had angered me so. But maybe it was all part of the same thing—maybe he'd felt he had to lie. Only *why*? And whatever did he mean by saying he'd never lied to himself?

I thought of the boy in the book, who had seen himself so clearly, even when he was behaving badly, and I began to see Philip as really like that boy. The war—how did that business fit in? Had he really believed he shouldn't go, inside him? Or had he told himself that his attitude was false? Even when he wouldn't admit it to me or anyone else? And that time in Princeton? What did that mean in his terms? I didn't want to think of that time, ever, but I thought about it that day, sitting there with the seven dollars and a half in my lap. What had really made him that desperate? If he never lied to himself, it must be that he truly saw his case as desperate. No one would do an act like that for a lie to outsiders. No one. Was it that he couldn't do any more lying, that he had to find some way out? But out of what? He'd read the book; that was one thing I knew. He'd seen the boy in it as himself. He wasn't strong enough to stand it. Yet, I thought, sitting there, remembering in a kind of sickness, Philip was not weak now. Odd—he wasn't weak any more. I don't see just what had happened to make me think that, for things weren't any different from what they'd ever been. Philip lived with me—on me, you might say. He'd been afraid of war. He'd never married. Why did I think right then that Philip was strong? I can't see, myself. It was true, though. And I saw that he'd been strong for quite a long time, for years—maybe ever since that time in Princeton. He stayed here, but it was true that he didn't need me as much as I'd thought he did. Maybe he stayed here for Fanny's sake; he'd always wanted to protect her. Not that she needed any protection from me, heaven knew. Fanny went her own way and always would.

It's odd, the relationship Fanny and I have always had. You would think an independent girl like Fanny would resent me, would have resented terribly coming to live with me when she did. She's never seemed resentful. But it's true that we've never been close in the way Philip and I have, which is probably natural enough. She's been polite to me, friendly enough —on the outside, at least. Only I never move her against her will, which is just as strong as it was when she was a little girl.

Queer, children are. You would have thought, wouldn't you, that Fanny and I would have been more sympathetic toward each other, being more alike? It hasn't been true. Yet we respect each other, I think. Love doesn't seem to go by rules, by likenesses. Yet I do love Fanny too. Probably, the way things were, she couldn't ever feel for me what she felt for Walter.

I'm getting away from what I was thinking about Philip, and yet it's all one thing, I suppose.

Jerry came. I said to him right away, "Well, we were quite excited about your mother's news, Jerry."

"Yes," he said.

"It's wonderful," Philip said.

"Is it?" Jerry said. "I hope so."

"Of course it is."

Jerry gave his mocking grin. He didn't seem to want to talk about his mother.

Then Fanny drove in. "Here comes our schoolmarm," I said.

Jerry stood up, though he was apt to be impolite in that way, and Fanny came in, dropped books on the table, said, "Hi, Jerry!" and went off to the kitchen.

Jerry just stood there for a long time before he sat down again. When Fanny came back, Philip said, "Jerry's brought you a present. Your second."

"It's not for Fanny. It's for you," Jerry said.

"Well, I'll let her hear it—mind?" And he got out this record of what he called "Requiem for a Child Killed by a Bomb." I believe it was issued later under the title "Requiem for Percy Hawkins," but I always think of it by that first dreadful name. It was that thing like a lullaby that they'd worked on that time together. Philip played it all through.

Fanny sat there in her gray suit and very white blouse, just listening. When it had finished she said, "Very loving. Very kind."

No one said anything, and she went on, "Odd, coming out of someone so unkind, so unloving, isn't it?"

She got up and walked out of the room.

"One for you," Philip said.

Jerry said, "But it really was for you, not Fanny."

He stood up. He's so tall and dark. He seemed even taller and darker than usual that day. I'd always found him sinister, and I found him so that day, towering there above us. Yes, some people have a darkness in them, a frightening darkness, and Jerry had it. Yet when he spoke the feeling went away somehow.

"All right," he said. "*All right.* It's all wrong, you know. It's completely wrong."

He stalked away, and I thought of his arm, and all the hopes he'd had. He went out the door and down the drive. He was gone a long time. Philip sat there, fiddling with a flower he'd taken out of a bowl on the table. He pulled petals off one by one. Once he gave me a quick smile, pitying me somehow.

Then they came in. Well, I hadn't wanted it to happen. Of course not. But I must say I never saw a girl look more beautiful than Fanny did when she came in with Jerry that day from the garden—just the way a young girl ought to look when she's loved, not strong and purely lovely the way she always looked, but soft and tender and so radiant it made you want to cry to look at her. No one knew better than I that things could happen to love, but as I looked at them standing there it did seem for a minute that nothing could ever happen to their love. And Jerry too—all the tenseness and anger was gone from his dark face.

"Bless you, children," Philip said before they'd spoken at all.

"We're blessed already," Fanny said.

Why did she want a temperamental man like that? She's orderly, disciplined, competent. She wouldn't have an orderly life with a musician, would she? Of course not. No, there's no reason in love. She didn't ask for our blessing—she had Jerry and she didn't care whether anyone approved or not. Yes, as Philip said, she got what she wanted.

"Do you mind very much?" Jerry said to me.

"It wouldn't matter, would it, whether I did or not?" I said.

"No," Jerry said. "Not an iota. Still, it would be pleasant to have you like it. I don't suppose you ever will."

"It looks as if I'd have to," I said.

Fanny laughed—not mean laughter, but what she said was mean enough.

"No, don't try, Mother," she said. "It doesn't matter at all. In a million years you wouldn't want me to go, to marry anyone—but I grew up free, you know. I grew up *free!*"

"You're not exactly in a prison now, are you?" I said. I was angry, and hurt too.

It was Jerry who said, "Don't, Fanny. *Don't.*" And Fanny looked up at him, then came over and kissed me and said, "Lovely prison, but I'm getting out."

I liked it that she kissed me, but I drew away from her. I stood up and looked around at the three of them. I remember exactly how I felt, like a stone, a heavy stone that had the power of speech.

"I've had enough of this," I said. "You'd think I put chains about you. I never have. You're quite welcome to go whenever you like—nor have I ever by so much as a word said you weren't. To hear you talk you'd think I were a monster of some sort who held you here against your will. I won't have any more of it. I've never done anything, ever, but keep this place going as a home. Your father brought you here, Fanny; I didn't ask you to come or beg you to stay here. So don't talk to me about prisons or freedom. You've gone to college as you wished; you're doing the job you want to do. Philip also. You three seem to be in a conspiracy to make me out cruel and possessive when I'm neither. You'd think I weren't a human being, with feelings the same as your own. I'm tired of it. You're a lovely child, Fanny, but you're willful. You will marry whomever you wish—but I shall have my own opinions as to the wisdom of your choice. I know what willfulness is too, because I am possessed of it. I chose your father and would have him, whether or not. I was wrong. You all think I put him out of my life, but I did not. He put himself out. You know that but refuse to believe it. You are all young and romantic, and you like melodrama. Well, I will not be the villain of your piece any more. Go on—marry anyone you like. No one is stopping you. I wish you happiness, but that doesn't mean you'll have it. Now run along, the lot of you. I'm tired of you all."

Fanny put her hand on my arm, said, "I'm sorry, Mother. I'm sorry." Then she took Jerry's arm and went away. Philip sat still on the sofa.

"You too," I said. "Go somewhere else, will you?"

Philip still held the ragged flower in his hand. "No, I prefer to stay here," he said. He was almost cold.

"Just so you prefer it and don't blame me for your sitting there," I said.

"Sit down," he told me.

I wanted to walk away from him, up to my room, but I sat down.

"I am staying here because I want to," he said clearly. "I like it here. I like being with you. And I daresay I am to blame for Fanny's remarks. I wouldn't want her to come to a reasonable contentment by any such road as mine, you see. When I was young I was foolish enough to want you different. I see now that people don't change as easily as all that."

"What do you mean—different?" I said.

"Oh, I wanted you to know what I *meant*—but you never did, and I don't suppose you ever will, Mother. That doesn't mean I don't love you, so don't look so stricken. But it does mean I can see why Father went away; he was a man who had to get to the meaning of things, and you simply wouldn't let him. He thought Fanny's silence, her stubbornness were a sign she was just like him. Well, she wasn't like him at all, except that she's got a good brain. Oh, she loved him, she truly loved him, and she's made herself into something fine, hasn't she? But I'm the one like Father, you see. I suppose really that's why you've always liked me best. I think Father tried terribly hard to make you proud of him, but he thought, you see, that perception was something for pride. I thought just the same —I wrote you my poems, I brought you flowers, I showed you my secrets in the woods, I made you valentines, and you never really saw them at all. Oh, you were pleased enough that I remembered you, but the gift itself you never saw. So I know how Father felt, always having his gifts spurned—even his last big one. You never knew what he *meant*, and so— Well, I still care about perceptivity, Mother; I care very much indeed. But if you don't have it, you don't. I don't break my heart about it any more. And you needn't even pretend to have an interest in my writing. I won't stop doing it. I hope you'll make it easy for Jerry and Fanny to marry, but if you don't, they'll marry anyway."

"Well, what are you here for?" I said. I was angry; I was hurt. "Why do you stay here if you think I can't see beyond my nose, if you think I don't have any feelings? No one's making you stay here! Why don't you get out where you can be as sensitive as you like?"

He put the flower down beside him on the sofa. He put out a hand—oh, he has beautiful hands, Philip—and touched my arm.

"Because I'm so fond of you, Mother," he said.

I got up. I said, "I don't understand you! I just don't understand you!" and I went upstairs to my room.

I sat down at the desk and I put my head down, and I must confess I cried. Everything went round in circles in my head, and I cried and cried. I know I thought about how strong Philip was. He was fond of me, in spite of hating everything about me. It was all so queer. He was like Walter, he said. That was queer—that was ironic, wasn't it, that Walter should have taken the wrong one? Only maybe that was the way it always worked out—you *wanted* the wrong one. Just as Fanny wanted Jerry and Philip wanted Amelia—people they couldn't be happy with.

But what had Philip meant about Walter's always trying to give me things? What had he ever given me? The book—I'd count that if they thought it so important—but what else? Then I remembered him sitting by the hearth, reading to the children; I remembered him talking with Mother so interestedly; I remembered him noticing a new dress of mine, saying it was the color of delphiniums; and— No, those weren't gifts, were they? But somehow it had made a great sadness go through me, Philip's saying that. And I ought to have said more to Walter about the book; only then, of course, I couldn't. It was too late. Maybe if I'd had the education I'd wanted, I'd have understood it better. No—no, that's just not true, is it? Because Philip understood, even when he was little, what it was he wanted me to understand. Maybe it was true, I was just born without understanding.

But I'm proud. I've said that before, but I say it again. I'm proud as Lucifer. I washed my face. My eyes were red, but I put powder on and I changed my dress and brushed my hair and went down to dinner. I told Bessie we'd use the best dishes because it was a celebration—Fanny and Jerry were engaged. I went out and got fresh flowers for the table, got down the tall goblets. I could hear the record-player going upstairs and I was glad not to have to face them all right now. But at last dinner was ready and I called them down.

I was lighting the candles when they came in.

"How elegant!" Fanny said.

"Well, it's a celebration, isn't it?" I said.

We sat down, and Philip began at once with gay nonsense, putting a piece of shadblow in his buttonhole and telling Jerry that Fanny was very pernickety about housekeeping and he'd have to forbid her touching his scores and so on.

"You can clutter the whole house with them," Fanny said.

"And will," Jerry said. "*What* house? Three rooms, maybe, to begin with."

"Look out; it will be a house," Philip said.

"Oh, I can slap Fanny down," Jerry said.

"You do that. She needs it occasionally. As Mother says, she's willful."

"I'm well aware of that. But so am I," Jerry said.

Still, they looked so happy. They laughed a good deal, and the dinner was good, and the room looked lovely, though I suppose any room full of handsome young people always looks lovely. I remember wishing I'd asked Jen for dinner—and then I thought, Is it true, is it really *true*, that I can't enjoy anything without showing it off to someone? Even my own children? It was kind of a shock, thinking that.

"Well, when we do get a house," Fanny said, "you must come and stay with us, months at a time. We'll put a sign, 'Genius at Work,' on your door, and no one will whisper near it."

"No one whispers here," Philip said. "Oh, I'll come see you, but I'll write my poetry in my own room, thank you."

"Or maybe you'll be married too," Fanny said.

"I doubt it. Don't work at it."

Then I said, "No, you let Philip work out his own destiny, Fanny. He'll manage. He's been working at being a poet a long time, really—ever since he was a little boy. I remember his first poem:

> *Bird, bird, flying over the hill,*
> *Singing 'Kuroo—kuroo,'*
> *Where are you going, bird?*
> *Let me come too!*

That was his first one. Now he writes about hangmen's ropes, but he got started long ago, and he'll manage."

They were all staring at me in a queer way. But it was Philip I saw. He put up a hand and pushed his hair back as I've seen him do many times, but he kept looking at me as if he couldn't believe his ears. Then he gave me a smile, straight out of his boyhood—that sweet, open, loving smile that turned your heart over.

"Yes, hands off. I'll manage," he said, and that was all.

Weddings are so short. Fanny's is somewhat of a blur in my memory. It was June, and the garden was beautiful. There were huge white clouds in a very blue sky. "What is so rare as a day in June?" was proved true that day. The yellow roses were in bloom—red ones, too—and the delphinium made a blue border. Joe had the grass looking like velvet. The headmistress from Fanny's school was there, and Mr. Abingdon and a teacher from Philadelphia, a few young people, Jen, and Jerry's mother and her new husband. We didn't have champagne—I didn't know whether it would be safe or not.

Mrs. Baker—I still call her that—looked very pretty, and she was sober and quiet. She didn't go chirping on as she had once, and I thought her husband must be very good for her. I've never known how the marriage has gone, but it's still going, at least.

I remember Mr. Abingdon's saying, "I didn't even know you had a daughter, Mrs. Boone." I remember Fanny, standing there by Jerry in her dress of cream brocade, with the veil like one of the clouds in the sky outside and her gray eyes so soft and beautiful—and even Jerry looked handsome and distinguished. And then it was over.

Then Philip and I were alone here, and it was almost as if Fanny had never been with us at all. But there was a small difference. One night Philip came in and sat down by me. He had some papers in his hand. "How does this sound?" he said, and he read me a piece of an article he'd written. I didn't make any to-do about his coming. I said what I thought, and he said, "Thanks," and went away. And after that he came quite often with a poem or a page or two of something and asked what I thought of it. I don't suppose he respected my judgment much, but he came, and it touched me. Yes, it was important that he came, I know that.

And weeks, and even months, went by, and I felt close to

happy. Then one day Jen was here and she said, "Amelia Adams is home. I saw her this morning. It always seems such a pity; Philip certainly did love her, and I suspect he still does. But there's something so perverse about the young. She's an extraordinarily interesting-looking girl."

"Nefertiti," I said.

Jen looked surprised. "Exactly," she said.

"I'm quoting the boys," I told her.

"They're right. An *ancient* kind of beauty, that's what it is. Yet she's as modern as the atom bomb, you might say."

"And as destructive," I said.

"Oh, I wouldn't say that. I wish we could do something about them, but you can't interfere, can you? It just doesn't work—and you might make things worse instead of better. They don't listen to us."

"Not much," I admitted.

"Probably that's to the good in the long run. Because we've worked out our lives doesn't mean we can work out theirs. Every life's different. You know, Cornelia—well, it may make you mad, but I'm going to say it. I used to like Fanny better than Philip. I did. I felt terribly sorry for her, and I suppose I resented it that you let her go away. I still don't understand it —no, don't try to explain anything—but what I want to say is that I have come to love Philip. Oh, I still love Fanny, you know—no one could be lovelier—but Philip has come to seem very special, very lovable. He's sad, though. I don't pity him, but he's sad. And I do wish Amelia would love him—or some-one. I thought when he was little that he was all charm and nothing else, I'm afraid. I was wrong. There's a good deal more—I don't know whether to give you the credit or not. Anyway, you can be very proud of him."

"I am proud of him," I said.

It was true. I was proud of him, and in a new way. I didn't quite understand it myself. I didn't even understand Philip, his strange life, his poems, his war record, anything about him. But all of a sudden I knew I was proud of Philip. Everyone had always depended on me, but that day I realized that I could depend on Philip. Queer, isn't it, when he was so undependable as a boy?

I looked at Philip that night at the table. He was cheerful enough, but I saw it was true. He was sad. Deep inside he was melancholy. But he was strong enough not to show it on the outside any more.

"It seems strange without Fanny," I said.

"But we'll get along," he said.

The next day Philip asked if I needed the car. He wanted to spend the day in town at the library. So he went off. I remember going into his room. There were papers on his desk, but I didn't read any of them. There was a copy of his poetry book on the bookshelf, and I took it into my hands, looked at that "A.A." for a long minute. He was always busy, Philip; he didn't seem to be discontented; and yet I remembered that day when he had talked to me so seriously, the things he had said to me. I realized he had got to this place by suffering and will, and that he would always be lonely in this house. Yet somehow it did not make me so sad as it once would have done. He loved me, I knew that, even if he didn't like the way my mind worked, even if he thought I'd been cruel to Walter —he still loved me. I stood there, holding that thin little book, and I knew right then what he'd meant about gifts and why he'd looked at me as he had when I quoted that childish poem.

"I'm sorry, Walter," I said. Now why did I say that? I wonder. But I did. I said it two or three times. "I'm sorry, Walter." But Walter couldn't hear me.

I went downstairs and to the phone, still with the book in my hands. I phoned the Adams house and asked for Amelia. Her voice was very crisp and cool when it came.

"Mrs. Boone, Amelia," I said. "Could you come over for a few minutes? Philip is away, and I would like to have a talk with you."

"What about?" Amelia said.

"Does it matter? Just come," I said.

"Thank you, I'd rather not," she said.

"Very well. I'll come there," I told her.

"Oh, I'll be down," she said crossly, and hung up.

I just sat down and waited. It was autumn, and the leaves were falling. It looked all gold everywhere past the window.

Amelia rapped at the door, and I called, "Come in!" I didn't rise to greet her. She came in, stood there with her head up, reluctance all through her. She had on a short blue jacket lined with red, and a blue skirt. I still swear she has no looks, but perhaps she is interesting. Her face is too narrow and she looks haughty, though she wasn't that when she was young and ducked her head so shyly.

"Come in, Amelia. Sit down," I said.

She came and sat down in the chair with the carved back. "What did you want to see me about?" she said.

I handed her the book, and I said, "Have you seen this?"

"No," she said.

"Why not? Were you afraid to?"

She just looked down at the book, not opening it. "Certainly not," she said.

"I thought you were hipped on honesty," I said. "That's a lie, Amelia."

She looked up at me then, and now I know what they mean when they say eyes are blazing. She was furious with me.

"I have never been afraid of anything or anyone," she said.

"Oh? Not even life?" I said.

"What is it you want, Mrs. Boone?" she asked.

"I just want to ask you one question, and then you may go."

"Well, what is it?"

"Do you love Philip?"

She hesitated. Then she stood up. "I used to," she said.

"That wasn't my question," I told her.

"You haven't any right to question me at all, have you? But no, I don't love Philip."

"Lie Number Two," I said. "For one so dedicated to the truth, you are doing badly, Amelia. All right, that's all I wanted to ask you, but now I am going to tell you something. Sit down."

She still stood there. *"Sit down!"* I ordered her, and she did sit down, but stiffly.

"I don't know what your quarrel with Philip is; he doesn't confide the affairs of his heart. I don't even know why he cares for you. It doesn't seem to me you are the sort he would care for. That's neither here nor there, is it? But I do know you think him a liar, a coward, not dependable. I know that much. But what are you, child? You've lied to me twice in a few minutes. You're too much of a coward even to look at the gift Philip made you, for fear you'd soften against your will. You're not dependable, either, whatever you may seem to be, with your test tubes and such. You love, you take your love away. Now I'm not speaking without knowledge. I've had gifts given

me that I haven't looked at either. That's something I'm going
to have to think of till I'm old and done for. I've had a book
dedicated to me too, and I hardly said thank you for it. But
you young are supposed to be so perceptive, aren't you? I want
you to take that book home and read it. It's for you, as you
will see on the flyleaf. I want you to read it, and then I want
you to come down here and tell Philip what you think of it,
even if it isn't anything favorable. Even if you don't love him,
there is no reason to scorn a gift, is there? If you don't, I shall
certainly be convinced that you are a coward. Philip isn't going to pursue you against your will; you ought to know that by
now. But you don't let a man give you all he has to give and
then ignore him. Or if you do, you're a fool. I never thought
you that. I'm not begging you to admit you love him. I've
never even liked you, and I've not wanted you for him. But
you can't do what you are doing to a man's pride and not be
punished for it. That's all. Run along now."

She sat still for as much as a minute; then she got up and
went away with the book, not saying another word. She held
her head up, but I thought she looked in a state of shock.

That was a queer thing for me to do, wasn't it? Out of character.

Philip came back near suppertime. I didn't mention Amelia,
nor was there any word from her. I felt a little frightened at
what I had done. And the evening went by, and nothing happened.

I didn't sleep much that night. I kept thinking of other
things I might have said—maybe more important things—
about the way Philip had grown up and put away childish
things, of how proud I was of him, all that. But I'd said nothing of that at all, just about the gift of the poems. And maybe

the young don't think that important—I don't suppose they do. It took me a good many years to find out it was important, and why should I expect them to learn anything younger than I did? She must have read that book at once—it wouldn't have been natural not to—and yet she hadn't come. I felt I'd maybe been stupid, interfered in a way I shouldn't have, and that Philip wouldn't like it.

In the morning I felt tired. I didn't enjoy my coffee. I went out and began to rake leaves, though Joe was coming to do it later. But I had to be busy and I didn't want to talk with Philip.

It was about ten when I saw her coming down the road on her bicycle. She turned in at the drive, swung off her bike, and put it down on the grass.

"Is Philip here?" she asked.

"He's in his room—up the stairs, second door to the left," I said, and went on raking. There wasn't a spark of feeling in either of our voices. Sometimes I get an odd feeling that Amelia and I are a little alike—not putting what we feel into our voices. I wanted, more than I have wanted many things, to hear what Amelia said to Philip, but I didn't hear. I just went on raking till Joe came and said, "I said as I'd take care of the leaves, Mrs. Boone!"

She was up there a long time, over an hour. When she came down, Philip wasn't with her. She stood there, looking at me angrily. "Well, I've thanked him. Are you satisfied?" she said.

"If you are," I said.

She put her hands out in front of her suddenly, just looked at them, I don't know why; then she let her arms drop limply.

"I did lie," she said in that same stiff voice. "I do love him, of course. I called it just decent pride, but that was a lie. Good-by, Mrs. Boone."

So I saw it hadn't come out right. Maybe she'd just been too slow about it and it didn't mean anything to Philip any more. I went upstairs and stopped at Philip's door, which was shut. I wanted to go in and comfort him, but after a time I went into my own room without knocking. It was half an hour afterward that Philip came out and started toward the stairs. Then he saw me sitting there and paused.

"What are you trying to do?" he said, not coming in.

"I detest fools," I said.

"Oh?"

He just stood there in the doorway. He looked white, exhausted.

"The girl loves you, heaven knows why. Didn't she tell you so?"

"Hardly," he said.

"Well, I daresay you didn't make it easy for her. You don't make it easy for anyone," I said.

"Is there any reason I should make it easy for her?"

"Not much. Except that she did have the gumption to come see you."

"Yes. It's too late," he said.

"Why? You haven't got one foot in the grave yet, have you —either of you? You might have sent her your book, you know. You didn't even bother. Well, if I were you I'd get my bike out and go after her and stop all this nonsense. She loves you. What more do you want? She said so."

"She said so—to you?" Philip said slowly.

"Yes, to me."

"To you?" Philip said again.

I heard him going down the stairs. I got up and went into the guest room—Fanny's room, I still call it—and I looked out the window. I could see Joe down there, raking. He is quite crippled with arthritis now, but he keeps on at his chores. His back looked very bent. Then I saw Philip come swiftly out of the drive on his bicycle and go off up the road. He had on a tan jacket, and his hair swept back in the wind. I thought of the bird. It seemed as if he were the bird, going away and away forever.

They married. Of course they married. As Jen had prophesied, Philip went away from me, and I suppose I pushed him into it myself, which is funny. I didn't look far enough ahead, or I thought I could manage what was ahead according to my own desires. Yes, I saw Philip and Amelia living in this house. It didn't seem unreasonable, did it? It wasn't as if Philip worked in an office—he worked here and could go on working here. I'd accepted the marriage, and I suppose I would have accepted Amelia as part of this family, as I accepted Jerry. But they went away. Philip came to my room after some remark I'd made about changes I planned in the rooms up here.

"This is going to upset you, Mother," he said. "I've taken a job in New York—music critic. I've *taken* it, so there's no argument necessary. It'll be something of a wrench for us both —not just for you. But you know it wouldn't work, living here. Of course you know. I'll miss you—I'll miss the house and the hills and Bessie and Jen—but I'm going. Give me your blessing, Mother. I'll go without it, but I want it."

It was just pride, not love, that made me say, "Bless you,

Philip, bless you both! Don't give me a thought. I'm not upset!"

I had to do it just to show him I was bigger and more generous than he thought. He gave me that wonderful sweet smile
of his; he kissed me; his eyes filled with tears.

I went down and outside, walked to the wood road and
through the woods by myself, not even tempted to go to Jen.
It was like that time I stopped taking money from Walter—a
feeling of taking a big step alone and wondering if I could
manage it. Only then I had Philip to help me, and now I had
only myself. I said to myself, "Suppose something should happen to Jen?" I sat down on a log that had fallen across the
path, and I looked at dead leaves on the ground. I did feel
queer that day, but determined no one should ever know it.
No one ever has.

They went. The last thirty-four years might never have been.
Any day someone will come and get the rest of Philip's possessions, and there will be not so much as a picture or a book to
tell me he has lived all these years in this house. It's funny—I
wanted this house and I have this house. That's what I have,
this house. No, of course I have Jen, and we sit and talk together, sometimes of old days, of things we have shared,
though I try to jerk her out of the past and into thought of
what's ahead. I make my jams and jellies, I plant new bulbs, I
write to the children. I'm proud, and I don't tell them I ever
get lonely.

I meant to sum it all up, but what is there to sum up? A list
of my mistakes? There's no advantage in that. Mother said
once, "Don't say that, Cornelia! To mean well and not do well

is no excuse I will accept. You might as well say straight out that you are a fool." So I cannot claim ignorance for an excuse. Yet I suppose I have been ignorant, and that angers me. Philip says we change, but we don't, not enough to say so. That's about what this acrostic says, that we don't change. I wanted Philip with me, that's true, and I had him for a good many years. I wanted to run my own life and I've run it. I've loved my son, no matter how many disagree with the fact. There have been some uneasy moments, remembering Walter, but all that is over and done. Only sometimes I think about that moment in the woods when I looked down at the dead leaves and felt no one would ever know me, no one. I hate self-pity, and I shove the thought away. It may be true, for all I know, that everyone in the world feels like that sometimes.